1983

A Year in the Life of Jenna Rae

By Jason Ayres

Contents

December 2022

"Come on, open up, I know you're in there."

The man's voice was harsh and determined, accompanied by a fist pounding against the flimsy caravan door. Inside, Jenna lay curled on her sagging mattress, wrapped tightly in a thick duvet, desperately trying to retain the sparse warmth within. So frugal had her life become that heating was now an unaffordable luxury. On bitterly cold days like this she stayed in bed, cloaked in layers, sheltering from the chill.

At fifty-nine, with no savings, no pension and no realistic hope of finding work in Pencarven, her once-prosperous Cornish village, Jenna's existence was now stripped to the bare bones, with a future that had never looked bleaker. And now, the man outside had come to evict her from her caravan, her final refuge in a world scarcely recognisable from the one in which she had grown up.

His hammering refused to let up, and neither did the freezing December rain that had been pounding on the metal roof all morning, creating a merciless racket she could do nothing to block out. She couldn't even switch on the radio or television to drown out the noise – her electricity had been cut off three days ago, thanks to the man outside. Even her phone, her last link to civilisation, had finally succumbed to its fading battery despite her attempts to eke it out.

It was no use; she was going to have to face him. She knew exactly who he was and why he'd come, which made this all the more painful. How had her life ended up in this state? Her parents, her grandparents – and generations more of her family who had lived and died here in Pencarven – would have been horrified to see her reduced to this.

With the village almost completely stripped of its heritage, she was the final original resident left, "the last woman standing" as she often called herself with grim pride. But today, it seemed, her long, defiant fight against changes she was powerless to prevent was drawing to its inevitable conclusion.

"Hurry up!" barked her visitor, impatience verging towards anger as his fist struck the door ever louder.

Jenna was hit by the chill as she dragged herself out of bed, her aching body protesting with every reluctant movement. Cold and undernourished, she barely had any food left other than a few tins, and with the power out, no means of cooking even the little she had.

She didn't dare glance at the mirror, knowing her grey hair would be a tangled mess, her clothes a mismatched collection from the charity shops of Camelford. Sporting an old fleece advertising a long-defunct surf shop in Newquay, she was about as far from the carefree, sunlit days of her youth as it was possible to be.

Shuffling to the door, she noticed a new tear in one of her socks, her big toe now poking through. It was just another mark of poverty; one her spiteful visitor who revelled in her suffering would doubtless find gratifying.

"Alright, I'm coming!" she called, raising her voice, at which point his hammering finally stopped. She braced herself for the inevitable conflict to come, then unlocked the door and pulled it open. An icy gust and a spray of rain burst inside, splashing her already cold cheeks, as she came face to face with her tormentor – a man she had come to despise, despite the blood they shared.

Elliot Cadwallader, owner of the caravan park and an opulent mansion up on the cliffs, looked every inch the entitled heir. He stood, unbothered by the downpour, beneath a sleek blue-and-green umbrella emblazoned with the words 'The Cadwallader Country Club and Spa'+ – one of many local enterprises that belonged to him. He didn't technically own the whole of Pencarven, but given his wealth and influence, he might as well have.

His dark hair was immaculately styled, his face clean-shaven and his whole appearance meticulously groomed, as always. He wore a tailored blue Italian suit, custom-made, with a silk tie in the club colours that perfectly matched his umbrella. The overall effect was of a successful, charming businessman, but it did not impress Jenna. His fine appearance meant nothing given the utter contempt he reserved for her on the increasingly rare occasions when they encountered each other.

Oddly, these meetings often left her with a fleeting sense of satisfaction. Elliot was a man who expected to get his way, using his wealth and power to bend people to his will. She remembered him, years ago at his father's funeral, proudly boasting that he could now "buy whatever, and whoever" he wanted. The memory fuelled her resolve to resist him – he might have bought up most of Pencarven, but he couldn't buy her, and she knew that infuriated him.

Her resistance, though admirable, wasn't doing her any favours. The prime reason she was enduring such hardship was her refusal to play along with his plans. It was a stubbornness that had cost her greatly, but she felt she owed it to her family, to her roots, and all those who had come before her, to make a stand against him, however futile it might ultimately be.

"What the hell are you still doing here?" he said, his voice sharp with disdain as he peered inside. "You were supposed to be gone by today."

"Won't you come in?" she said, injecting a playful note into her voice. She might as well wind him up a bit, in what little time she had left. "I'd offer you a cup of tea, but some vindictive tosser seems to have cut off my electricity."

He glanced around her modest living space, making no effort to disguise his disgust.

"I'm not sure if I should," he replied, with a condescending look. "I might catch something. But since it's teeming down out here, I suppose I'll have to risk it."

His remarks were unjustified because although the caravan and its furnishings were old, she kept things as clean and tidy as she could. She stood back and gestured for him to enter.

"Would you like to sit down?" she asked cheerily, determined not to let him see the desperation of her situation.

"I'll stand, thanks," he said, stepping inside gingerly in his polished Gucci loafers, as though he might tread in something unpleasant.

"So, what's this about?" she asked, adopting an air of innocence as if his visit was unexpected.

"You know full well what it's about," he replied. "I handed you the eviction notice myself, six days ago."

"Yes, on Christmas Day," she said, her voice laden with fake cheeriness. "And there was I, thinking you'd come bearing gifts for your big sister."

"Half-sister," he corrected her coolly. "And anyone looking at us wouldn't even think we were that, thank goodness. You're an embarrassment. Let's face it – we may have been born from the same woman, but we both know which side the best genes came from. I was sired by a superior stallion, shall we say?"

"Is that so?" she countered, her tone sharpening. "If pedigree were based on wealth alone, maybe you'd have a point. But your father wasn't half the man mine was. Yours was a privileged, entitled narcissist – rather like you, funnily enough. Ever heard the saying 'the apple doesn't fall far from the tree'? My father was a decent, hard-working man who cared for his family in a way you'll never understand."

"Your father was a weak-willed drunk who cared for you so much, he took his own life when things got a bit tough," replied Elliot, with his trademark sneer that she had seen hundreds of times before. "Our mother was lucky to escape when she did. She did much better the second time around – and I'm living proof of that."

"Proof of what? How to be the vilest human being to ever walk the earth? And that's saying something, considering your father's track record."

"You can insult my character all you like, but let's be honest – I'm the one who has everything, and you're the one with nothing. So, who's really winning here?"

"It's not a competition," replied Jenna, hating how his words struck home. She wasn't motivated by money or possessions but that didn't take away the sheer injustice of it all.

"Life is totally a competition," he replied smugly. "It's one huge game. Winners and losers. Think of it like Monopoly, and I'm just better at it than you."

"Oh, are you?" she replied, keen to clarify a thing or two. "Is it a fair game if you start the game with hotels on Mayfair and Park Lane and all the money in the bank? You didn't earn any of that. It all came from being the son of the famous, or rather infamous, Blake Cadwallader."

"You can't blame me for that," he replied. "If you'd been a little nicer to my father after he married our mother, maybe he wouldn't have cut you out of the will."

"Cut me out? I wouldn't have taken a penny from him if he'd offered it. Not after the things he did when he first came to Pencarven. Care to hazard a guess at what his idea of me being nice to him was when I was twenty and he was forty? You don't know the half of it. If I'd been stronger then, I would've exposed him for the man he really was. Then perhaps he wouldn't have destroyed my family, my village, and my way of life."

"It's my village too, you know. I grew up here and I rather prefer it the way it is, now all the peasants have been cleared out."

"You were hardly ever here! Blake packed you off to boarding school when you were seven, then it was straight to Cambridge. You don't even have a Cornish accent!"

"Whatever," said Elliot, dismissing her words with yet another sneer. "And you can say what you like about my father. I've heard it all before and it's all lies."

"Oh, so you've heard the rumours, then?" replied Jenna, with the delicious feeling that she was starting to get under his skin.

"Hearsay and jealousy," he replied defensively. "Every successful man comes up against it. Whatever you're referring to, there's no proof anything happened."

Jenna laughed triumphantly. "You see, your choice of words betrays you. You deny the evidence, not the facts. That's what the guilty always do."

"You can't prove anything and none of it matters now, anyway. He's been dead for five years, and now I own everything that was his – including this caravan park, what's left of it. You're the only one left here now, you know that?"

"Only because you bought all the others off," said Jenna, a touch of resentment returning to her voice as she thought about her last few friends who had lived in the caravan park. They'd each sworn to stand by her – her allies, her community, they'd said – but in the end, the allure of Elliot's cash had proven too much. One by one, they had deserted her, deciding to take their chances elsewhere, leaving her alone to hold her ground.

"You were offered the same deal as them," he said. "It's only your stubbornness and pride that's kept you here, and look where it's got you. You don't even own this caravan, you only rent it. You could have walked away from here months ago with twenty grand in your pocket. Most of the others settled for even less. Now, your time's up, and you've got to leave anyway – and I don't have to give you a penny."

"I'll be alright," said Jenna, trying to sound resilient though she was consumed with despair about what the future might hold. 'Alright' was a far stretch from reality.

"Oh, really?" replied Elliot, his tone dripping with scorn. "And where exactly will you go? You've got no money, no home, no job. Face it – you're finished, Jenna. I had to pretend to be nice to you while our mother was still alive, but you can rot in hell now, for all I care."

"I've still got my pride," she replied, grasping for some shred of dignity, even though she could feel how hollow the words sounded. Pride wouldn't shelter her from the elements or put food on the table. Pretty soon, she wouldn't even have a table. But pride was all she had left – the one part of herself that Elliot hadn't been able to strip away from her, in the way he had from everybody else.

"Well, I hope it keeps you warm at night," he replied, echoing her thoughts. "Now, I suggest you gather up your meagre belongings and get out before this dismal sardine tin gets towed off to the scrapyard. The sooner I get it out of the way the better. The bulldozers

8

move in on Tuesday to start demolishing the old clubhouse. After that, we'll begin the golf course development in earnest."

"Another essential component of your millionaires' playground," she replied, thinking of the caravan park in happier times when it had been owned by her uncle and packed with holidaymakers in the summer. She had even worked here for a while, as a children's entertainer.

"Oh, it's not just a vanity project. This is going to be one of the most immaculately manicured links courses in the world. We've already got the DP World Tour interested in holding an event here, and who knows, maybe we could even host The Open. Donald Trump may think he got his hand on one the crown jewels of British golf when he bought Turnberry, but he'll be seething with envy when he sees this place."

"Maybe," she said, "but you haven't built it yet. And my lease doesn't run out until midnight, so as far as the law's concerned, you can't kick me out until then."

"If it hadn't been for you, we could have started work here weeks ago," he replied. "This caravan is in the exact spot where the bar's going to be in the new clubhouse."

"Well, I'm sorry I've been such a thorn in your side," she replied. It almost felt worth putting herself in this mess, just for the satisfaction of knowing she had held up his plans.

"Yes, well if I were you I would leave now, while it's still daylight. At least then you'd have time to find a bed for the night. Perhaps one of your pauper friends in the village will take pity on you."

"You know very well they've all gone," said Jenna. "You said as much earlier. I'm the only original resident left. You, and your father before you, have driven us all out. I hope you're proud of yourself."

"It's called progress, Jenna," he replied with a patronising look. "If your sort were in charge, we'd all still be living in mud huts and riding horses. It's not my fault that people like you can't afford to live here anymore."

"Oh, it's your fault, alright," she retorted, her voice rising as she thought of the years spent watching the traditional way of life in her village be ruthlessly swept away. "But nothing can change the legal fact that you can't kick me out of here before midnight. So, despite all your wealth and influence, right now I'm still the one in charge. So get out of my caravan."

She drew strength from the anger that he had sparked inside her, and without even thinking about it, moved toward him, pushing him towards the door. His surprise at this was evident; he hadn't expected this amount of resistance.

"Go on, get out," she said, her voice full of fire, as he raised his arms to shield himself. "Or are you going to use your physical strength against me? The puny, defenceless woman – powerless to resist? That was your dad's style, after all. He got a kick out of it."

He stumbled backwards, caught off guard by her boldness, and she reached behind him to yank open the caravan door, propelling him outside with one last shove.

"You're only delaying the inevitable!" he shouted as she slammed the door in his face, his voice muffled by the pounding rain. "You're finished, Jenna – finished! Do you hear me?"

She didn't answer but swiftly locked the door, her hands shaking as she turned the key. Outside, the rain continued to batter down, hammering on the thin metal roof. A few seconds later, there was another knock – softer this time.

"Jenna, I think I left my umbrella in there," he called, his tone almost pleading. "Can I have it?"

She glanced at the discarded umbrella he'd put by the door.

"You can collect it tomorrow, along with the caravan," she shouted with great satisfaction.

"Stupid cow!" he shouted back as he stomped away. She watched through the narrow window as he made a dash through the rain toward his luxury Mercedes, parked about thirty yards away by the derelict clubhouse. His gentle stride soon turned into a sprint, as he rushed to escape the rain drenching his perfectly coiffed hair and designer suit.

She couldn't help but break into laughter as he suddenly slipped, landing hard on the muddy ground. When he rose, she was delighted to see the huge brown stains now marring his right sleeve and the seat of his trousers. That would serve the bastard right.

This moment of amusement was sweet but brief, as thoughts of the uncertainty that lay ahead returned while she watched him drive away. By tonight, she'd have to leave the caravan – and possibly the village too, where she had lived her entire life.

Had it all been worth it, standing her ground against Blake, and now his son, all these years? She liked to think so, but in truth it had brought her little but hardship. She sank back on the bed, wrapping the quilt around her as she pondered what she was going to do. She couldn't stay in Pencarven, that much was clear.

Homelessness – the word itself sent a shiver down her spine – was a very real and terrifying prospect, no longer something that just happened to other people. Now, it was happening to her.

Maybe she could go into Camelford, beg for help from the council, and throw herself on the mercy of the system. But it was Saturday, and with Monday a bank holiday, would there even be anyone available to help her before Tuesday?

That left the grim prospect of at least two nights sleeping rough – a terrifying thought at the best of times, but in the bitter cold of winter, it was almost unthinkable.

She drifted into a shallow sleep for an hour or two, waking to find that the rain had ceased and the sun was tentatively breaking through the clouds. Her stomach was rumbling, and she rummaged through the cupboards until she unearthed half a forgotten tub of Pringles several weeks beyond their best-before date. It wasn't much of a meal, and they tasted stale, but it would have to do. Her only alternative was eating cold baked beans out of a tin, and she couldn't face that.

Feeling claustrophobic in the cold, lonely caravan, Jenna decided she needed some fresh air. She wrapped her raincoat tightly over the top of her fleece and stepped out into the now sunny afternoon. If this was to be her last day in Pencarven, then she wanted to take a final look around, to reminisce about happier times and remind herself of what she, and everyone else who used to live here, had lost.

The caravan park, once alive with laughter, music, and the scent of barbecues on long summer nights, was now a bleak sprawl of overgrown grass and abandoned pitches. Her caravan was the last, a lone survivor stubbornly defying the relentless advance of change. Soon it too would be gone, swept aside to make way for Elliot's grandiose plans.

She began her descent along the narrow, winding road that led from the park toward the seafront. The road itself was unchanged, its curves and dips familiar under her feet, just as they had always been. The familiar scent of sea salt assailed her nostrils, allowing her to believe, for a moment, that nothing had changed. But as she grew closer to the village, she knew that her illusions would soon be shattered.

As she approached the beach, Jenna paused at a bend in the road which was a great vantage point from which to observe the bay. The coastline remained as breathtaking as ever: the cliffs at either end framed the crescent-shaped beach before the endless stretch of the Atlantic met the sky at the horizon. It was a stunning view that delighted all who saw it, many claiming it was one of the most beautiful sights in England. But that view now came at a cost, one which only the wealthy could afford to pay.

She moved on, descending towards sea level. Her footsteps carried her past the beach, where she remembered families with deckchairs and windbreaks, while children shrieked as they splashed in the waves.

Many of the families had stayed at the caravan park when this was a thriving resort, alive with the vibrant spirit of the school summer holidays. She thought about her sweetheart, Alfie, and the surf shack he had talked about building, a construction that never came to fruition after fate had taken him from the world at a tragically young age.

Further along, she arrived at the weathered stone wall separating the beach from the harbour, and approached the site of what had once been Shelly's Café. Gone were the red-checked tablecloths and the chatter and gossip of locals catching up over endless cups of tea. In its place stood a sleek coffee house boasting exotic brews and exorbitant prices. A blackboard out front advertised a raspberry mocha latte for seven pounds. It was a far cry from the 10p cups of tea Jenna remembered as a child.

Next she passed the former chip shop, now transformed into a trendy tapas bar with minimalist decor and a name she could barely read in its flowery, italic font, let alone pronounce. She thought of the days of generous portions of thick chips and battered cod wrapped in paper, enjoyed by pensioners and children on the seafront, under the gaze of watching seagulls ready to pounce on the unwary. It seemed unbelievable that there was no longer anywhere you could get takeaway fish and chips in Pencarven.

The amusement arcade, once a haven for teenagers and a shelter on rainy days for all, had vanished entirely. In its place stood an art gallery, its pristine windows displaying abstract paintings that looked like random splatters to her untrained eye. She remembered the rattle

14

of coins when the fruit machines paid out, the flashing lights of the pinball machines, and the young men competing for the highest score on the video games. She had also enjoyed playing them, particularly a game called *Asteroids* at which she had frequently beaten Alfie.

She continued along the seafront road, looking up at the spire of St Piran's Church, built higher up in the village, which was set on several levels due to the steep nature of the slopes behind the seafront. Although Jenna was not religious, she could still feel keenly a sense of loss at what had become of the old building.

The eleventh-century construction, once the heart of the community, was now an exclusive restaurant with a Michelin-starred chef, promising an immersive dining experience. The stained-glass windows remained, but instead of casting colourful light onto pews and parishioners, they illuminated elegantly set tables and diners completely disconnected from the village's history. The bell tower had long been silent; no longer did it toll to mark the hours or call the faithful to gather.

Turning away, she headed toward the harbour. The old fishing boats had vanished, replaced by sleek yachts bobbing gently in the water behind a robust sea wall that hadn't existed in her youth, leaving the village vulnerable to flooding. It was here, dead centre of the harbour area, where her family's pub, and her home for the first twenty years of her life, stood.

To her disgust, it was now called The Gilded Mermaid with a pretentious, arty sign promoting the new name. To her, it would never be anything other than The Fisherman's Arms. The building's structure was the same, but its soul had been sacrificed on the altar of progress, like everywhere else in this over-gentrified place.

She couldn't even bring herself to go in anymore but still paused outside the entrance. She could hear that it was busy inside, which was understandable in the afternoon on New Year's Eve, but it wouldn't be full of the sort of people she had any desire to mix with. And in any case, she didn't have any money.

The pub's former name was apt, as it truly was busy with fishermen back then, with their thick chunky jumpers and straggly beards, downing pints of cider and real ale in front of the fireplace. They were long gone but hadn't been replaced by mermaids.

Now it was filled with the wealthy – the filthy rich, as she thought of them. Some stayed in overpriced Airbnbs, others were the new residents who had bought their way into Pencarven at obscene prices. Then there was the second-home brigade, who popped in for the holiday season before buggering off back to London until Easter. They contributed very little to the local community, if it could even still be called a community.

The pub – or wine bar, as it now styled itself – also had a board outside, advertising cocktails with ludicrously fanciful names, at ten pounds a pop. How much the pub charged for a pint these days, Jenna had no idea, but if the coffee was seven pounds at the café, she couldn't imagine getting much change from a tenner. Not that a ten-pound note would be of any use, as there was a sign outside stating that they no longer accepted cash.

She continued to the far end of the harbour, where some faded graffiti marked the wall. Years ago, someone had scrawled 'Emmets Go Home' in yellow paint, an appeal that had fallen on deaf ears. Beyond here was the main road in and out of Pencarven, winding steeply as it descended into the village. Jenna paused by the harbour wall, looking up to where the South West Coast Path stretched along the cliffs, connecting Pencarven to the other villages scattered along this rugged coastline.

It was a windy day, and the tide was high. Out beyond the shelter of the harbour, waves were crashing with great force against the rocks at the far end of the bay. The wind whipped at Jenna's hair, carrying flecks of salty spray that peppered her face too. Turning her gaze back to the village, she thought of her parents, of Alfie, and all those who had once lived here. Her only comfort was that most of them had been spared having to see this.

Jenna closed her eyes, letting the salty air fill her lungs as the question, *what am I going to do?* echoed in her mind, empty and unanswered. For a brief, hopeless moment, she considered throwing herself into the sea. From where she stood, she saw no future, no way forward. But she didn't want to give Elliot the satisfaction. No, whatever it took, she would survive – somehow.

When she opened her eyes again, she was surprised by the presence of a woman standing in front of her. And not just any woman, but one Jenna instantly recognised. She was staring into the face of Wendy Wood, one of the most famous British pop stars of the last four decades.

"Hello, Jenna," said Wendy, her voice friendly and unassuming, as though speaking to an old friend.

Jenna's shock wasn't because of seeing someone famous in Pencarven. They flitted in and out all the time. Over the Christmas season alone, she'd spotted a former Spice Girl, one-half of a popular comedy duo, and a presenter from *Dragons' Den*. But those people always kept themselves in their elite bubble, barely acknowledging the existence of ordinary folk like her. So for one of them to go out of their way to speak to her now was unprecedented.

"How…how do you know my name?" stammered Jenna. What possible business could the legendary Wendy Wood have with her?

"I'm here to help," replied Wendy, her iconic spiky blonde hair and battered leather jacket giving her a timeless rock-star look. Despite her forty years in the music business, she still looked every inch the rebel Jenna had idolised as a teenager. The feeling of awe was unmistakable, but Jenna's negative perception of the rich and famous who came to Pencarven tempered this with caution and suspicion.

"Help? Why would someone like you want to help someone like me?" replied Jenna. "Are you here to join in the New Year's celebrations with your rich friends?"

"I'm not here with anyone, and I've no more desire to mix with the sort of people I've seen down here, than you have," said Wendy, trying to reassure her. "I came here specifically to see you. I travelled down last night to make sure I had plenty of time to find you today."

"Well, I don't need anyone's help. If I wanted help, I'd have given in to my half-brother when he tried to buy me off a few months ago. But I'd rather die than take anything from him."

"And how's that working out for you?" asked Wendy, casting her eyes over Jenna's raggedy attire.

"Look, I don't know what you think you want with me, or even why you've come here, but whatever it is, you've had a wasted journey."

"Come on, Jenna, hear me out. It's bloody freezing out here. Let me buy you a coffee, and we'll discuss it."

"I'm not a charity case," insisted Jenna, though she had to admit, the thought of a lovely, warming hot drink after three days without a kettle was appealing. Even if it meant setting foot in one of the new businesses she had boycotted, in protest at the changes.

"And I'm not a charity," said Wendy. "Believe me, what I've got to offer you is better than anything money can buy. I'm living proof of it. So come on, let's go and get in the warm and talk about it."

Realising she had nothing to lose, and curious as to why Wendy had gone to all this trouble to find her, Jenna swallowed her pride and complied. Together, they walked back along the harbour towards the pretentious coffee shop she had passed earlier. She was relieved to see it wasn't too busy inside, and as they took a table, she worried she might have been rude before. Wendy seemed genuine enough, so perhaps she should try to make amends.

"Listen, I'm sorry if I was a little brusque earlier," said Jenna. "It's just that I was a bit taken aback when

19

you approached me. I mean, people like you don't usually talk to people like me."

"If by that you mean the sort of people who come to Pencarven, then please don't tar me with the same brush as them. I'm more than aware of what goes on down here. There's a guy I follow on YouTube who's done a stack of videos about the reality of life in Cornwall. He goes around different places, interviewing the locals about how things have changed."

"What locals?" asked Jenna, as she sipped gratefully at her large cappuccino. "I'm the only one left."

"That explains why he couldn't find anyone to talk to when he came here a couple of months ago," said Wendy.

"It wasn't always like this," said Jenna. "When I was growing up, back in the seventies and eighties, Pencarven was a wonderful place to live. Then it all changed. I can almost pinpoint the exact moment."

"It wasn't by any chance in 1983, was it?"

"As a matter of fact, it was," said Jenna, wondering how Wendy seemed to know so much about her. "Now how could you possibly have known that?"

"It would probably be easier if I showed you, rather than explain," replied Wendy. "Hold out your left arm."

"Why?" asked Jenna. "What are you going to do?"

"Nothing bad. Trust me," said Wendy, looking her straight in the eye. Mesmerised by the gaze, Jenna complied. There was something very convincing about Wendy that was persuading her that this was the right thing to do.

Wendy held out her arm, and as Jenna watched, an ornately carved golden bracelet appeared. Then, seemingly alive, it detached itself from her and slithered across her hand towards Jenna, whose fingertips were lightly brushing the end of Wendy's. The bracelet was transferring itself to her, and disconcerting as this ought to have been, Jenna felt no fear.

Within a couple of seconds, the bracelet had coiled itself around her own wrist and sealed itself into place with a soft click. She opened her mouth to speak, but before she could, a serene warmth began to flow into her mind and radiate through her body, enveloping her in a soothing mental embrace.

"There," said Wendy, withdrawing her arm and lifting her latte to her lips. "How do you feel?"

"I'm not sure," said Jenna, still trying to process the supernatural event she had just participated in. "What just happened?"

"What just happened is that I've changed your life. Or rather, given you the chance to change it. Just like I did with mine. If it wasn't for that bracelet, you would never have heard of me."

"Why not?"

"Because a year ago, I was nobody – a failed singer confined to a mobility scooter, thinking about the life I could have led."

"That's not true," said Jenna. "You've been famous for decades."

"I have now, but I wasn't then, if that makes any sense," said Wendy.

"None whatsoever," said Jenna.

"That's because the timeline – and everyone's perception of it, including yours, has been altered. And it was me who changed it, with the bracelet I've just given you. It sent me back to the beginning of 1982, the year I had a shot at fame and blew it. The second time around, knowing what I knew and with the bracelet to guide me, everything was different. And now you've got the chance to do the same."

"In 1982?" asked Jenna. "I can't recall much of significance happening in that year."

"No, 1983. It moves on a year with each new recipient. You said yourself that was an important year in your life."

"It was an awful year. The boy I was sweet on was killed at sea, the village was devastated by a flood, my father killed himself, and that monster Blake Cadwallader came to Pencarven and started the process that turned it into what you see today."

"There you go then, sounds like you've plenty to get your teeth into. No wonder the bracelet chose you."

"It wasn't you, then?"

"No, the bracelet led me to come here. It gets inside your head and helps to guide you – when it feels like it."

"When it feels like it? So it's alive?"

"I'm not sure. It's a bit difficult to explain, and I think it works differently for each person. I hardly used it at all in the latter part of the year, which is how long you'll be there. How old are you?"

"Fifty-nine," replied Jenna.

"You'll be nineteen when you go back, in your old body. Then, like I say, you'll have the complete calendar year ahead of you to turn things around, with the help of the bracelet. Then you'll come back, hopefully to a life that is much improved. Mine certainly was."

"This is a lot to take in," said Jenna, her mind racing with the possibilities.

"I'm sure it is, but you'll have plenty of time to get the hang of it," said Wendy. "You're not exactly happy about what's happened to Pencarven, are you?"

"That's the understatement of the year!" exclaimed Jenna.

"Then go back and stop it from happening. And save the ones you love. It's all in your hands."

"I will," said Jenna, with conviction. Not once did she question the fantastical tale Wendy had shared because the bracelet's comforting warmth made it all seem completely plausible.

They talked for a while longer, and Wendy explained a little more about the mechanics of how the bracelet worked, how it was invisible to all but the wearer. By the time they had finished, Jenna had enjoyed three coffees, and a welcome slice of a fancy Italian cake, the name of which she couldn't remember. Much as she might want to malign the coffee shop that had usurped the former café, she had to admit it was delicious.

"And now I must go," said Wendy, two hours after they arrived. "I want to be back in Oxford by tonight. And you need to prepare. Find out as much as you can about 1983 before you go back at midnight; it could prove useful."

"I'm not sure how," said Jenna. "My phone battery is dead, and my electricity's been cut off. By tonight, I have to vacate my caravan or I'll be forcibly removed."

"No problem," said Wendy. "I booked my accommodation for two nights. It was the minimum they would allow. But I've no desire to hang around here with all these pretentious bastards. I'm seeing in the New Year back home with Emily and Benny. So you can stay there instead."

She raised her voice with the words 'pretentious bastards' just loud enough for a smartly dressed couple at a nearby table to hear. They had been casting disparaging looks at Jenna's appearance the whole time they had been there, which hadn't gone unnoticed by Wendy, who had no time for people adopting a superior attitude. She'd had enough of that in the early days in her band.

"Are you sure?" said Jenna, her reluctance to accept help still stubbornly in place. But then she glanced at the bracelet, which was pulsing a soft green light back at her from a central jewel in its design. Instinctively, she knew it was telling her that this was all going to be okay.

"I can't use it and it's already paid for," said Wendy. "And you sound like you need it. Just relax, charge your phone, find out as much as you can about 1983, and then go back and change your life."

"Thank you," said Jenna gratefully, already feeling a spark of excitement for what lay ahead.

Wendy's accommodation turned out to be one of the old fishermen's cottages just off the harbour front, and not just any cottage. It was the one where Alfie had lived with his father Ned back in the early 1980s.

Back then, she remembered it being a rather ramshackle affair, but it was unrecognisable now, having been completely modernised. A leather sofa, plush soft furnishings, and a large 4k television, made for an extremely welcoming living room.

"It's luxurious," remarked Jenna. "So different to the last time I was in here, nearly forty years ago."

"So it bloody should be, at three hundred quid a night," said Wendy. "No wonder indigenous folk can't afford to live here. Anyway, it's all yours. Don't thank me, thank the bracelet. And now, I must get going."

The two women bade each other farewell, leaving Jenna alone in the cottage. It was only then that she discovered a well-stocked fridge and a bottle of chilled white wine. Wendy must have known, somehow, that she was going to end up here and had provided for her accordingly. She wished her benefactor could have stayed; she liked Wendy and would have enjoyed the company. Perhaps she could look her up when she got back.

She realised then that she didn't have her phone charger – it was back at the caravan. So, despite the welcome comfort of the cottage, she needed to make one last trek up the hill in the cold. As she stepped inside the desolate caravan, she was reminded of all the hardships she had endured. Looking around at what she had been reduced to, she vowed that she would do exactly what Wendy had told her. There was no way she was going to let herself, or any of the others in the village who had struggled like she had, go through any of that again.

As she closed the caravan door for the last time, a wicked impulse flickered in her mind. She could torch it, and watch the flames consume the place that had been her final refuge. Then, when Elliot came the next morning, he'd have the shock of thinking his half-sister had perished in the fire.

But would he even care? Probably not – but that wasn't the only reason why it wasn't worth bothering. Because if Jenna achieved what she was already planning to do, then Elliot Cadwallader would not be coming to tow away the caravan the next morning.

Because Elliot Cadwallader would no longer exist.

January 1983

"Happy New Year!"

Jenna had tried to imagine what her arrival in 1983 might be like, and to her delight, it turned out to be exactly as she had envisaged. As Wendy had suggested, she had arrived at the very stroke of midnight, finding herself in the middle of The Fisherman's Arms, amidst an eruption of cheers, laughter, and the clinking of glasses.

Until that moment, she had doubted whether all this was going to happen, despite the presence of the bracelet. But now here she was, surrounded by familiar faces beaming with booze-filled joy at the anticipation of another new year ahead of them.

If only they knew, she thought, as she saw David, her father, glass raised behind the bar, and the man she had once hoped to marry, Alfie, among the joyful crowd. Neither had lived to see the end of another year.

Alfie was leaning casually against the bar, and she instantly remembered why she had been so smitten with him, admiring his sun-bleached tousled hair, which framed his face with its natural curls. Seeing him alive and vibrant filled her with hope that his fate might yet be avoided.

She felt hands grab her from both sides as the pub's regulars linked arms and fell into a rendition of 'Auld Lang Syne'. She couldn't help but feel awash with emotion as she saw her mother, Morwenna, join her father behind the bar and plant a big kiss on his cheek. She remembered there being tension between them at this time, brought on by financial worries and David's excessive drinking, but all appeared well tonight.

Morwenna was forty-four years old, with dark, wavy shoulder-length hair, streaked with the first signs of grey. Tonight, she wore a simple floral dress beneath a knitted cardigan, practical and reflective of her rural upbringing.

David, who was a few years older, was a strong, solid man, who used to play rugby as a prop forward for Bude. His light sandy hair was thinning slightly on top, which he made up for with a thick, bushy beard. He had a thing about always looking smart behind the bar, so was clad in a crisp white shirt, waistcoat and a bow tie, which always came out on special occasions.

They looked so happy right now, that she had to wonder how many more moments like this they had left. It couldn't be many. She wanted to rush over and hug them but held back because she didn't want to do anything out of character that might look odd. To them, she was still nineteen-year-old Jenna, but that was no longer true. She was now effectively a fifty-nine-year-old actress playing the part of her younger self in a re-creation of her life, and she wanted to keep that to herself for now.

"Give us a kiss, love," called out the man who had been standing to her left, holding her right hand as the song came to an end. He grabbed her playfully by the waist and pulled her towards him, attempting to lock lips with her.

This was all rather overfamiliar, but not unusual. On these tipsy New Year's celebrations, she recalled it wasn't uncommon for the menfolk to circulate around the pub, offering handshakes to the other men and kisses

28

to the ladies. No wonder there were always so many coughs and colds going around the community in early January.

This man was William Polkinghorne, known to all as Willy. And for most of the time Jenna had been growing up, he had been Chilly Willy, his ice cream man name, which was plastered all over his van.

He was about forty at this time, with 'hairy' being the best word she could come up with to describe him. He had long, brown curly hair, descending well beneath his shoulders, and a large moustache. While he didn't sport a beard, she recalled that he didn't shave very often and was stubbly as a result – particularly in the winter when there was no ice cream to be sold and he drank the previous year's profits in the pub.

Despite this rather lecherous, and perhaps some would say inappropriate, approach, she allowed him his kiss but turned her face so it planted on her cheek rather than her lips. She could recall Willy being rather a pain in the arse at times, particularly after a skinful. But right now, all she felt at seeing him was happiness, just as she did every other familiar face in the pub. They were alive again with her right now, and it was a moment to savour.

She looked around, spotting more faces long gone. Chatting away by the fire was Shelly from the café and gift shop, who'd taught her a tongue-twisting rhyme about the seashells she collected on the beach as a child.

She had already clocked Alfie, who was at the bar with his father, local fisherman Ned Trelawney, a rotund gentleman who always drank from an old-fashioned metal tankard. Her Uncle Morgan was also there. He was Morwenna's brother, who ran the caravan park where

Jenna had been living forty years from now. Others included her school friend, Janet, who she remembered worked in a supermarket in Camelford, Trevor from the amusement arcade, and PC Matt Stevens, the local bobby.

It was a lot to take in, and she felt dazed as she stood in the centre of the room, watching everyone, and reacquainting herself with the pub as it had looked so long ago. The timber beams that criss-crossed the ceiling were dark with age, stained by years of smoke from both tobacco and the fire, while the walls were adorned with framed black-and-white photographs of the village – snapshots of men hauling in nets from dozens of boats. These scenes of the harbour bustling with activity from decades past were a proud reminder of the village's fishing industry which had sustained it for generations.

Between the pictures, ship wheels and anchors hung continuing this nautical theme, while old rope nets were draped in one corner, their purpose now purely decorative. Although fishing continued in Pencarven, it was a fraction of what it once was.

The fishermen that remained all drank here, and were all present tonight, among the rest of the locals who were now returning their attention to the bar, as the fire crackled in the hearth. The pub being open this late was a rarity in 1983, due to the strict licensing laws. New Year was one of the few occasions when an extended licence would be granted.

Even so, she knew they wouldn't be open much longer because the extension would be for an hour at most, so the clamour for more drinks was now verging on a stampede for those desperate for more.

"Hey, Jenna, where are those glasses?" called out David from behind the bar. "You were meant to be collecting them! I've almost run out here!"

"That's not a problem for me," said Ned, handing over his tankard, taking advantage of the situation to jump the queue. "Just fill that up again."

"I'll be right over, Dad," said Jenna, hurriedly looking around for the empties and starting to gather them up as her parents dealt with the onslaught. She had been so overwhelmed by the excitement of her arrival that it hadn't crossed her mind that she was probably working tonight. This had been her main place of employment during the winter months after turning eighteen.

In the summer she had done seasonal work, mostly at her uncle's caravan park. This was quite usual given the nature of most of the businesses in Pencarven, where generations of local families both lived and worked together. Morgan's children were too young for work at this time but would join her in working at the park by the late 1980s.

The next half-hour or so was a whirlwind of collecting glasses, pulling pints, and reacquainting herself with one old face after another. It was quite a challenge to adjust and try to live in the moment, so it was a relief when David finally rang the bell to call time an hour after midnight.

It was only then, after everyone had gone, that she could finally wind down and take stock. It also gave her a chance to wish her parents a proper happy New Year.

"Let's make it a good one, as John Lennon might say if he was still with us," said David as they relaxed in front of the dying embers of the fire with a couple of brandies. Her father was fond of his nightcaps, and they often did this after closing time, though to her concern, Jenna noticed that he had filled his glass almost right to the top.

"Oh, I intend to," she replied, having done an efficient job of hiding her unbridled joy at seeing her parents again. Her only concession had been to give them both huge hugs, which she felt was justifiable given the celebratory nature of the occasion.

"You did a great job tonight, Jenna," said David. "It's always a lot on a night like this for just the three of us, but you know I like to give the other staff a night off for New Year."

"Anytime, Dad," she replied, having cherished the opportunity to get behind the bar again. It didn't escape her notice that he hadn't given the same thanks to his wife, even though, from what Jenna had seen, she had worked just as hard as he had.

"Well, it's time we were getting to bed," said Morwenna, eyeing David's almost empty glass. Jenna suspected she wanted to get him upstairs before he filled it up again.

"Are you coming up, too?" she added.

"I'll be up in a minute," said Jenna, who wanted to linger in front of the last of the fire for a while longer.

Finally, when they were gone, she could relax. This had gone rather well, she thought, but her father's words about making the year a good one echoed in her head.

There was so much she needed to do, and right now, she didn't have a clue how she was going to do it. She looked down at the bracelet on her wrist to see the jewel pulsing softly, a light green colour. Was that to reassure her? Wendy had said it would guide her. She would doubtless find out how when the time came.

Climbing the stairs to her old bedroom, Jenna felt a mix of exhaustion and exhilaration. Her room was just as she remembered it – posters of The Jam, Blondie, and Velvet Temptation on the walls, a stack of 7-inch singles next to her record player, and a large toy seal from a teenage visit to the Cornish Seal Sanctuary on her bed.

The room was small but cosy, with floorboards that creaked, and sloping ceilings that followed the contours of the old building's roof. The wallpaper was a soft pastel yellow, faded slightly with age, and the ageing wooden floorboards creaked gently underfoot. An antique oak dresser stood against one wall, every inch of its surface covered with colourful seashells, not bought from Shelly's shop, but collected by Jenna at low tide throughout her childhood.

For the first time, she caught a view of herself in the mirror and marvelled at her appearance. Her skin, so soft and unblemished, her hair, tousled and blonde, and her clear green eyes looking back at her. The image was a far cry from the ageing Jenna she had left behind.

She changed into a blue and white pair of pyjamas featuring The Smurfs, noting how easy it was in this supple young body, devoid of aches and pains. Slipping beneath her duvet, which she recalled her mother always referred to as a continental quilt, she wondered how she was ever going to get any sleep tonight, given the swirling thoughts about the day's strange events and what lay ahead.

But sleep did come swiftly, and several hours later she awoke in daylight to the cries of seagulls and the distant rumble of waves. These were sounds that would remain constant over the next forty years, while Pencarven itself would change. That was, of course, unless she could intervene.

It was cold in the room. The pub was old and hadn't been modernised, relying on open fires and electric plug-in heaters. It was long overdue for the installation of central heating. All of this would happen eventually when the pub changed hands, but although her family managed to make a living from the pub, it was one of three in a village with a population of only around five hundred in the winter. This meant times were lean during the colder months, as they were for any business that relied on tourism to survive, leaving them with little to invest.

She dressed quickly, opting for a pair of jeans, a Blondie T-shirt, and a thick woollen jumper of the style favoured by the many fishermen in the village. It wasn't particularly ladylike, but rather like her mother, she favoured clothes that were practical and essential in the conditions. As she descended the wooden stairs, which were even creakier than the floor in her room, the aroma of frying bacon reached her, and she recalled that her mother always cooked a big fry-up at the weekend and on bank holidays.

By the time she came into the kitchen, Morwenna was already dishing up. Like Jenna, her mother had lived in Cornwall all her life. Rae was not a Cornish name but her married name, taken from David who was not locally born and bred. Originally, she had been a Rowe.

David had come here as an evacuee during the war as a child, in 1939, and had been housed by a local couple. By the time hostilities ceased, with his parents dead, he had grown up and forged a life in Pencarven so decided to stay. There was nothing left for him in Birmingham, though you could still occasionally pick up twinges of the accent in his voice.

There was quite an age gap between him and Morwenna. They had fallen in love in the mid-1950s, when he was twenty-four, and she was seventeen, marrying soon after. Jenna was their second child; she had a brother, Jacob, five years her senior, but he had left Pencarven a few years ago, citing the lack of prospects. He had no desire to go into fishing or tourism, instead ending up running a small electronics business in Bristol. He still came down occasionally, for special occasions, but Jenna had always felt a little betrayed by him turning his back on his roots.

Morwenna and her brother Morgan were the children of Arthur and Dorothy Rowe, both now passed on. Arthur had been from the last generation of tin miners in this part of Cornwall, and once that industry had gone, he had recognised the tourism potential earlier than most, opening Rowe's caravan park in 1935.

After he retired, Arthur passed the business on to Morgan, and it continued to thrive. Jenna would have dearly loved to have seen both her grandparents again, but she had arrived a little too late. Arthur had outlived Dorothy by a couple of years, before dying in 1981.

The kitchen was warm, also containing an open fireplace, which was roaring away as her mother busied herself with the old-fashioned range that had been in use for decades. She turned as Jenna entered, greeting her with a cheery look.

"Morning, love," she said. "Sleep well?"

"Like one of those logs," replied Jenna, gesturing towards the woodpile next to the fireplace and instinctively taking her seat. It was as if the last forty years had never happened and she was looking forward to the generous portions her mother always served up. There would be homemade bread, either fried or toasted, to go with it too. Shop-bought bread from a supermarket was something her mother wouldn't entertain having in the house.

Not that there was much in the way of supermarkets in Pencarven, other than a small Mace which was mostly used by holidaymakers. There were butchers, greengrocers and a small independent grocer to cover most needs.

"Where's Dad?" asked Jenna.

"He's out the back," she replied, just as he came back in. "Speak of the devil."

The pub, being only a few feet above sea level at high tide, didn't have a cellar due to the flood risk, so all the beer was stored in a cool room at the back of the pub.

"I had to change a couple of barrels," he said. "The IPA ran out just as we were finishing last night, as did the lager. I'm going to have to get on to St Austell and see if I can get them to come earlier this week as we've been cleaned out of almost everything over Christmas."

"That's good, though, right?" asked Jenna, recalling the pub's financial struggles, as Morwenna plonked a toast rack down on the table, full of thick, crusty slices. Jenna took one and scooped up some butter from what she remembered referring to as a child as the moo cow dish.

"It is, but it's such a battle getting through the winter," said David. "The fishermen don't spend as much as they used to, and there aren't as many of them."

"Ned seemed to be knocking it back last night," said Jenna.

"He's a dying breed," said Morwenna, placing a plate in front of her which was heaped with bacon, sausages, grilled tomatoes, and eggs from the chickens that they kept out the back.

Jenna thought for a moment, and then an idea struck her as she dipped a thickly buttered slice of toast into her egg yolk. Nothing could beat her mother's cooking, which gave her inspiration.

"I've got an idea – why don't you start doing food?" she suggested. "You're an amazing cook, Mum, and think of the money we'd make in the summer."

"We can't do that," said David. "We'd be betraying Michael."

"Michael?" asked Jenna, trying to place the name before it snapped into place. "From the chip shop?"

"Yes, we've had an agreement for years. He's got no seating, so he recommends to his customers that they sit outside the front of the pub here to eat their fish and chips, provided they buy a drink. In return, I don't do food. It works for both of us."

"Fair enough," said Jenna, remembering that once Blake had got his hands on the pub, that agreement had gone out of the window. "What about doing bed and breakfast, then? Plenty of money in that. Look at Jacob's room, lying empty. We could be making money out of that."

"We could if we had the money to do this place up," said Morwenna, reflecting Jenna's thoughts from earlier about the lack of modern facilities. "But we haven't. It's not up to the standard required for paying guests."

"We'll just have to make this place as successful as we can, with what we've got then," said Jenna. "I've got a feeling that there is a hot summer on the way. That will help."

"I hope so because we haven't had a decent one since 1976," said David. "Wow, we shifted some beer that summer, and the one before. That was when lager began to take off. Willy knocks it back like there's no tomorrow though I can't stand the stuff, personally. I'm pleased you're taking an interest in the business, though. It's more than Jacob ever has."

Jenna's predictions about the summer were based on historical fact. She had remembered this being a good year, and following Wendy's advice, had looked it up. To her surprise, she discovered that July 1983 had officially been the hottest month of the twentieth century. It was odd that years after, that was all but forgotten. All people ever talked about was 1976.

Right now it was cold and wet outside, but at least she had the summer to look forward to. Despite the weather, she couldn't wait to get out there and see if the real Pencarven of 1983 lived up to the idyllic one that she pictured in her memories. Was it nostalgia or was it real? It was time to find out.

When she got outside, it was cold but sunny. The pub was the only one on the seafront, with the other two behind it in the maze of small streets and cobbled lanes that sloped up away from the shore. The area was typically quiet for the time of year, though there was some activity around the few fishing boats that remained in the harbour. There, Jenna could see Ned in conversation with another fisherman, who had just come in and was landing his catch. She walked closer, hoping to pick up on their conversation.

"How did you do this morning, George?" asked Ned, who was tinkering around with the ropes by the side of his boat.

"Dreadful," said George, who was a few years older than Ned, perhaps in his mid-sixties. "There's less mackerel out there every year. It's just like what happened with the pilchards in my grandfather's time. Overfishing is what causes it."

"Yes, but there's fewer of us going out than there used to be," said Ned. "There ought to be more fish to go around."

"Not as many of us, maybe, but what about all these big trawlers? And I don't know what we're going to do when this new EEC Common Fisheries Policy comes into effect later this month."

"What's that, then?" said Ned, stopping and lighting up one of his favoured Woodbine cigarettes.

"Honestly, Ned, do you not take any notice of what's going on in our industry? This new law's going to introduce all sorts of quotas and give the Europeans more rights to fish in our waters."

"Won't affect us, though, will it? We're nowhere near any other countries. It's not like we're on the North Sea, or like when we had the Cod Wars with Iceland. Who's going to come around this coast and steal our mackerel? The Welsh?"

"You don't know what's going to happen. All I know is that every year, there are fewer fish in that water, and the margins we make on them get squeezed more and more."

"He's right," said Jack, a younger fisherman who had wandered up to join the conversation. "It's time we got out."

"That's all very well for you to say," said Ned. "How old are you, Jack, thirty-five? You've got time to start again. I'm nearly sixty, and this is all I've ever known. I don't know how to do anything else."

"Tourism," said Jack. "That's the future."

"What sort of tourism?" asked George, who seemed genuinely interested.

"Boat trips. Fishing trips. And cruises to see the seals. Kids love that sort of thing. And the caves you can't get to on land. That's what I'm planning to do."

Jenna listened, fascinated at what Jack was proposing. This sounded like absolutely the right thing to do. She felt a sensation on her wrist and pulled up her sleeve to see the bracelet glowing bright green. Then, she felt a strong urge to get involved, so she walked over from where she had been hovering, a few yards away, and joined in the conversation.

"That's a brilliant idea, Jack," she said. "They're already doing that in St Ives and other places. Tourists love it."

"And what would a young lass like you know about it?" grumbled Ned. "Tourists are a bloody nuisance in my opinion, clogging up the place in the summer, making a mess and causing long queues everywhere. There were some nights last year I had to wait nearly half an hour for my tea from the chippy."

"You could learn to cook," suggested Jack.

"I haven't cooked since my Mary died," said Ned. "And I'm not having tourists trampling all over my boat. My pride and joy, she is."

"A pile of rotting planks is what she is," said Jack, casting his eye over Ned's boat, *The Buccaneer*.

"Nothing wrong with her a lick of paint won't cure," said Ned.

"Why don't you do it, then?" asked George.

"I just haven't got round to it yet," said Ned. "It's all in hand. I'll get the boy to give me a hand."

Jenna might have found this funny, had it not been for the knowledge that his ramshackle, poorly maintained boat was going to lead to the death of his son shortly unless she stopped him.

"I don't think you should be going out on that boat at all," she said. "It's not seaworthy."

"And I don't think a teenage girl who knows nothing about the world should have the audacity to try and tell a fisherman of over forty years' experience how to run his business."

41

There wasn't a lot she could say to that. Ned might have come across as an ill-informed, misogynistic oaf, but this wasn't a battle she would be able to win today. She would back down for now, and regroup.

"If you say so," she replied, turning back to the others. "Jack, I think you're onto something there. You should give it a go."

"I will," he said confidently. "You've inspired me. I've got a bit of money saved up, so I'll pack in the fishing, spend the rest of the winter doing the boat up, and in the spring, Jack's Boat Tours will be open for business!"

"You're a bloody idiot," said Ned, looking to George for support, but he didn't get any.

"You know, I might do that too," said George, thoughtfully. "Times are changing, Ned. Perhaps we need to change with them."

"You're an idiot too," said Ned, as Jenna walked away, leaving them arguing behind her.

She had enjoyed that. Had she made a difference already? There was no way to know, but she couldn't remember Jack ever running any boat trips from the harbour in the previous timeline. And anything that kept working- and middle-class holidaymakers coming, as opposed to the rich elite, had to be good for Pencarven.

She walked along the mostly deserted seafront, where nothing was open. It seemed rather desolate, but Jenna knew that was only because of the season. From Easter onwards, the area would be buzzing. Today was exceptionally quiet, though, because the café and the handful of shops which opened all year round, were closed for New Year.

It gave her a feeling of being at a loose end. Here she was, having been given this amazing opportunity, but there was nothing to do yet. Perhaps she was being impatient and should just enjoy the moment, though she could not help but feel she should be getting on with things.

She thought about going to see Alfie but wasn't sure how to approach him. At the beginning of 1983, they had been close friends and inching towards becoming more, but had never crossed that line. She had been sweet on him but had been waiting for him to make the first move. It had always seemed inevitable that they would get together. However, just as they were making the first tentative steps in that direction, his life had been cut short. Perhaps this time, she needed to move things along a bit.

After three hours walking around Pencarven, exploring every inch of the place, she felt suitably refreshed as to the layout of the village in 1983 and concluded it wasn't nostalgia – it truly was how she remembered it.

Then she returned home where, relieved not to be working, she decided to watch television and soak up a little 1980s culture, but she was disappointed with the choice of programmes. The big highlight of the BBC's evening – a New Year festive special with Val Doonican – wasn't her cup of tea at all.

The following evening was her next shift at the pub, which opened at 7pm on a Sunday. She hadn't seen Alfie since a brief hello on her arrival, so was pleased to see

43

that he was one of the locals crowding into the pub as soon as she opened the door. They all looked rather desperate, but given the nature of the licensing laws, allowing pubs to serve for limited hours on a Sunday, perhaps it was understandable. By ten past seven, she had already served twelve customers, which wasn't bad business for a seaside pub in the depths of winter.

Both Alfie and his father were in, as were Willy and PC Matt Stevens, who was off duty and often socialised with the regulars. Matt was in his mid-thirties, tall and lean, with a neat crop of blond hair and a friendly demeanour. He wasn't an authoritarian copper but was firm when he needed to be, and a proven dependable figure in the community. He lived in the police house near the top of the village, which still had an old blue police lamp outside, reminding Jenna of *Dixon of Dock Green*.

By the time she'd finished serving the first lot of drinks, Willy had already downed his first pint of lager and was angling for another, leaning his glass at forty-five degrees towards her and tapping it impatiently on the counter. This was something that irritated Jenna almost as much as people waving pound notes in her face.

"Fill her up again, Jenna. I'm wasting valuable drinking time here."

"Steady on, Willy, you've got all evening," admonished Matt alongside him.

"I didn't realise you were policing my alcohol intake now, Matt," replied Willy. "I'm not driving anywhere tonight, so you've no need to worry."

"I'm pleased to hear it," said Matt.

"Nope, the van's safely put away until the spring," said Willy. "And I'm still drinking last year's profits."

"You can't make that much out of ice cream, surely?" asked Alfie.

"Oh, you'd be surprised, lad! The mark-up on ice cream is amazing. It costs me about 5p for the raw ingredients and a cone, and I knock them out at 30p a time. 40p if I stick a Flake in them and they're cheap when you buy them in boxes. On hot days in the summer, I can shift hundreds. You do the maths. Some of the folk around here knock tourism, but I'm not complaining."

"That's very impressive, Willy," said Matt. "I am sure the tax man must be very happy with you. It must be nearly time to file your annual return, mustn't it?"

"Um, yes," said Willy, looking momentarily worried at the mention of tax, before regaining his composure.

"Well, if it keeps you in beer all year round, you must be doing well," said Alfie.

"Ah, but he doesn't drink all year round, do you, Willy?" said Matt.

"Erm, no," said Willy. "I don't drink during the summer."

"And why is that?" asked Alfie.

"Because I told him if I suspected he was taking that van onto the beach under the influence, where kiddies are running about, I'd breathalyse him, didn't I, Willy?"

"That's right. So it's a year of two halves for me," said Willy. "Work through the summer, drink through the winter."

"That's all very well," said Ned, who was puffing away on a Woodbine. "But you lot are becoming obsessed with tourism. Relying on a few months a year, dependent on some decent weather, doesn't sound like a sensible business model to me."

"Yeah, well, at least I don't come in here stinking of fish," said Willy, creating titters of laughter from the regulars, much to Ned's annoyance.

"He's got a point, Dad," said Alfie.

"No, he has not! I do not smell of fish!"

"I don't mean that. I'm talking about catering to tourists."

"Oh, not this again. We're fishermen, son, and always have been. When I die, you'll take over *The Buccaneer*, just like I did from my father."

"What if I might have other things to do?"

"You mean like last summer when you buggered off to Newquay on a jolly for three months leaving me to manage on my own?"

"I was not on a jolly. I was working as a surf instructor."

"That's not a real job."

"Nonetheless, it's what I want to do. And this summer, I want to open a surf shack on the beach and set up here. I've done my sums and it's a solid business proposition."

"I think that's an excellent idea," said Jenna, chipping in for the first time. She knew he had wanted to do that before his untimely death, and he deserved to get a second shot at it.

46

"Trust you to stick your oar in again!" said Ned to Jenna before turning back to the others. "She was down the harbour yesterday, encouraging the other fishermen to pack it in and start doing boat trips. I don't know what this village is coming to. Why do you keep coming out with all this stuff?"

"Because she's right," said Alfie, catching Jenna's eye and giving her a smile that made her feel all warm inside. She was as attracted to him as she ever was, and could see he was appreciative of her support. That could only help.

She had hoped to get a moment alone with him to talk privately, but that proved impossible in the busy pub. By the time the bar closed at half past ten, he had already gone.

It was a few days before she caught up with him properly, spotting him down towards the far end of the beach, close to where the road began to ascend towards the caravan park. It was late afternoon on a cold and clear day, about half an hour before sunset, and the sun was sinking towards the western horizon, away across the calm and shimmering water. As she approached, she noticed he was taking measurements and making marks in the sand.

"Hi," she said, causing him to look up. "What are you up to?"

She already knew, because with a sense of déjà vu she recalled that they'd had a similar conversation in the past, in that other timeline.

"This is the perfect spot to build my surf shack," he said. "It's the highest point on the beach, and the tide rarely, if ever, reaches this point, even in the winter."

"But if it does? We've had floods before."

"I'm not planning to keep stuff here permanently. Just a wooden structure with boards, wetsuits, and so on that can all be moved in an emergency. I can borrow Dad's van when I need it. Most of the gear would only be here in the summer anyway, it rarely floods then."

"I'm worried about the rest of the time and the rest of the village. Do you know we're the only settlement on this stretch of the coast that hasn't got a proper sea wall? Why do you think that is?"

"I'm not sure," he said. "Have you asked any of the parish councillors?"

"I'm going to go to one of their meetings, but I'm not sure if they would have the funding or the power. These things are probably decided at a higher level."

"Perhaps you would be better off getting Gordon to put it to the district council."

"I wouldn't trust him as far as I could throw him," replied Jenna. "Something needs to be done, though, because the way things are now, we're courting disaster."

"It's certainly worth investigating. Let me know if you need my help with it, and by the way, thanks for sticking up for me with my dad the other day."

"You're welcome. I hope he's not too pissed off with me."

"He's pissed off with most people most of the time, to be honest. He just doesn't like the way the world is changing and can't accept that I don't want to go out with him on the boat anymore."

"But you still go?"

"Yeah, out of loyalty, I guess."

"Well, perhaps you shouldn't," suggested Jenna. "*The Buccaneer* isn't exactly in mint condition. I worry something might happen to you."

"You worry about me?" he asked, looking into her eyes.

"More than you could know," she said, an audacious thought coming into her mind. It was bold, far more so than anything she would have done the first time around. But that was one of the benefits of being back here with all that life experience she had acquired. She wasn't the timid girl she had been before.

Steeling herself, in the hope he wouldn't reject her, she walked towards him, never breaking eye contact, until she was close enough to kiss him.

He met her halfway, as their lips touched for the first time. As they did, she felt a warmth spread through her, banishing the chill of the cold January air.

"I wasn't expecting that," he said quietly, when they reluctantly pulled apart, neither of them wanting to end the moment.

"Neither was I," she replied. "But the time just seemed right."

They stood together, watching as the sun dipped lower, casting hues of red and orange across the sky.

"Jenna," he began, "there's something different about you the last few days."

"In a good way?" she asked, with a tinge of concern. She had been trying to play her old self as closely as possible since her return, determined to keep her altered identity a secret.

"I think so," he said. "I've noticed it when you've been working behind the bar. You seem more confident, more self-assured."

"Perhaps I'm just growing up," she replied. "I'm going to be twenty in a couple of months. I was thinking about life at New Year, you know when people make resolutions and stuff.

"Yeah, like Dad last year. He decided to give up smoking, but only lasted until lunchtime on New Year's Day."

"No offence, but I'd like to think I've got a lot more willpower than your dad and there is so much I want to do. For myself, for the family, and the whole village."

"Like what?" he asked.

"I understand why your father doesn't want change, but it's inevitable whether we desire it or not. What we need to do is ensure those changes are for the benefit of all of us who live in Pencarven so we can preserve the community and prosper. Because if we don't, others will come here and everything we've always held dear will be lost forever. That means embracing tourism, for a start, which is why I think your surf shack and Jack's boat trips are great ideas."

"You'll get no argument from me on that front."

"No, but I'm not sure everyone here has our best interests at heart. We must get these sea defences sorted out, and if Gordon won't help us, we'll find someone who will."

She already suspected that Gordon was a wrong 'un, because of how easily Blake had put him in his back pocket after his arrival later in 1983. Something would have to be done about that when the time came, and she would need to plan for it. It was one of so many things she needed to do and it was high time she wrote it all down and made some concrete plans.

"I'm with you all the way," said Alfie, and they kissed again, before walking hand in hand back towards the harbour.

Back in her room, she felt thrilled and excited by their encounter. They hadn't really talked about what this meant for their relationship ongoing, or if they were even in one, but the kisses were further than they had got before. Had they even needed to say anything? If he had felt the same as her, then the unspoken bond they had formed was surely more than enough.

With Alfie's help, she felt more confident she could achieve the things she wanted to do, and looked to the bracelet for confirmation. It glowed green back at her, which was all she needed to know.

Now, it was time to plan. She opened a stylish A5 notebook, decorated with pictures of shells, that must have come from Shelly's gift shop, a small annexe on the side of the café. Perhaps it had been a Christmas present because it was brand new. Then she began to write, listing key dates, tasks, ideas for how to tackle them, and people she needed to get on her side.

As she wrote, she noticed that sometimes the bracelet turned red, suggesting that perhaps that particular idea wasn't a good one. When she crossed it out, it turned green again. That was very handy. If it was going to help her like this, she was less likely to go down the wrong path.

There was so much to look forward to, but also much to be wary of. None of this was going to be easy, even with the bracelet's help.

By late evening, after a break for dinner, she returned to her notebook, and by bedtime she had written a solid twelve pages of notes, containing every possible scrap of information she could think of.

As sleep overwhelmed her, she felt full of confidence. Her destiny, and that of all of those around her, was now in her hands. It was an opportunity she was determined not to waste.

February 1983

Jenna couldn't believe how quickly her first few weeks in 1983 had flown by, and as she flipped her calendar over to February, couldn't help feeling a little underwhelmed by her experience so far.

Sure, she had relished reliving her time in the past, slipping effortlessly back into the old village way of life. But she couldn't shake the feeling that she ought to be doing more. Wendy had suggested that the bracelet would guide her, but it had done precious little during January, other than tackle what she considered to be relatively minor problems – like the night she had dreamt that a fox would get in and kill Morwenna's chickens, due to the rickety state of their coop.

Armed with this foreknowledge, she had insisted that her mother help her make repairs, which they spent the following afternoon doing, hammering in fresh nails, and securing the chicken wire tightly in places where it had become loose. Thus the hens were able to cluck away contentedly inside as the sun set, oblivious to the danger they had been in.

That was all very well for the chickens, but it was hardly a world-changing event. She knew all the serious stuff was still to come, so concluded that perhaps these small-stakes tasks were to prepare her for later. But it was frustrating that she was no further forward than when she had started. Should she be more proactive, or was it up to the bracelet to tell her? She wasn't sure, and it wasn't giving her much in the way of clues. Maybe she just needed to be patient.

In the meantime, she had been enjoying immersing herself in the popular culture of the time. Music had always been a great love of hers, and she listened to Radio One a lot, which she thought was so much better back in this era when it wasn't trying to be cool. She could listen to cosy old presenters like Simon Bates and Steve Wright all day. They were like long-lost friends, with their cheesy jingles and cheery chat that so summed up the era.

It was fascinating hearing songs come into the charts that were new to everyone else, yet old classics to her. During those first few weeks, she had enjoyed watching new entries from Joe Jackson, Fleetwood Mac, and Kajagoogoo climbing the charts, as well as the massive hit 'Down Under' by Australian band Men at Work, which she was confidently able to predict would soon make it to the top.

She would often sit in her room when she was free in the afternoons, her small transistor radio perched on the windowsill with its aerial angled to catch the optimum signal, which wasn't great on the medium wave frequency in her area. She often found herself fiddling with it, swapping between 275m and 285m in a bid to find the best sound.

Listening to the radio was nostalgic, but television was a treasure trove of old memories. The tunes she was hearing on the radio, she could listen to any time in the modern era if she wanted to, but much of what appeared on TV was lost forever in the mists of time. She wasn't sure if a lot of it still existed in the archives because some of the things that came on, she hadn't seen since their original broadcasts.

One afternoon, she had flicked the television on for an hour between shifts in the pub and had been delighted when Gus Honeybun appeared. Gus was a puppet rabbit she had grown up watching almost every afternoon. He was the mascot of TSW, formerly Westward, the local ITV station broadcasting in her region. Every day, this rabbit would appear alongside a presenter who would read out birthday wishes to delighted children while Gus clowned about, misbehaving and doing his trademark hops, one for each year of the child's life.

Gus was one of those peculiarly local phenomena created by the old ITV franchise system. Known by almost everyone in Devon and Cornwall, he was almost completely unknown elsewhere in the country and, in later years virtually forgotten, other than a small exhibit dedicated to him at the theme park Flambards. Whatever had happened to Gus? Jenna wondered. She guessed when all the ITV stations had merged, he had become surplus to requirements.

Early 1983 was a time of broadcasting innovation in Cornwall, as in January the county got its very own local BBC station, which had caused arguments at breakfast time. Her father insisted on having this new station on the radio, while Jenna wanted to listen to Radio One's breakfast show presented by Mike Read. And both shows soon found themselves competing with another medium, as Jenna discovered when she came down to breakfast on the first day of February.

It was sometime after nine, and she could already smell bread baking in the oven. Her mother was an early riser and liked to bake and prepare all the family meals early in the day. Usually, this took place against the backdrop of one of the two competing radio stations, but today, as soon as Jenna came in, she noticed an addition to the kitchen surfaces. Sandwiched between the bread bin and the toaster was her parents' portable television, which Morwenna had brought down from her bedroom.

"What's this doing here?" she asked, as she came into the kitchen, making a beeline for the kettle.

"Breakfast television!" her mother announced excitedly. "It's brand new and started today!"

"I thought it started a couple of weeks ago," said Jenna, momentarily confused, recalling a similar conversation recently, when her mother had been watching television in the living room early one morning.

"That was the boring BBC version with Frank Bough," explained Morwenna. "This is ITV's. I like it much better! Look at who they've got on!"

It was to be expected that Morwenna preferred ITV's offering. Jenna's home had always been more of an ITV household than a BBC one during her formative years. She didn't know why; it was just the way it was.

She peered at the 14-inch screen and had to admit it was a star-studded line-up. Rather like *Breakfast Time* on the BBC, the hosts were all sitting on the sofa, and among the household names she could see were David Frost, Michael Parkinson, Angela Rippon, and Anna Ford. But it didn't exactly look dynamic, an opinion she wasn't shy about voicing.

"It looks just as dull as the other one to me," she said. "Do you think it will catch on?"

"Yes, this is the future!" said Morwenna eagerly.

Jenna already knew that it was here to stay, and this was another step on the route to 24-hour television, which would become the norm by the end of the century. But she also remembered that these early ITV breakfast shows, under the banner of TV-AM, hadn't been a ratings success. They had in fact been a notorious failure, which she remembered the media ridiculing at the time.

"You're not going to have this on every morning now, are you?" she asked.

"It's better than that Radio Cornwall your dad likes," she replied.

"Where is he, by the way?" asked Jenna. He was normally around at this time.

"In bed with a hangover," she replied. "He had a lock-in with a few of the regulars last night."

"Do you ever worry he drinks too much?" asked Jenna tentatively, not knowing how Morwenna would react. But she didn't defend her husband, instead agreeing with her daughter.

"All the time," she said. "You know how much we're struggling to keep this place afloat, but he'd rather bury his head in a barrel of booze than do anything about it."

"Like that conversation we had about the food a few weeks ago?"

"Yes, all over some misplaced loyalty to Michael from the chippy. And what's Michael ever done for us? He doesn't even drink here, he's a regular up at The Anchor!"

57

"Then you need to make him see sense. This is a business, after all. I can't honestly see that doing a bit of food here in the summer for tourists is going to make that much difference to Michael's trade. Not everyone wants fish and chips."

Morwenna paused, thinking about what Jenna had said, before replying, "I'll speak to him about it again when he gets up. Now, what are you up to today? It's your day off, isn't it?"

"Alfie and I are going into Wadebridge this afternoon to see that new film, *Tootsie*."

"That's the one with Dustin Hoffman in it, isn't it?" replied Morwenna, almost licking her lips at the thought. "Ooh, I do like him."

"Mum!" protested Jenna, who didn't like seeing her mother expressing interest in someone else, and with good reason. "You're married."

"He's only a film star, love. It's just fantasy, not real life. He's hardly likely to come here, is he?"

"Right," said Jenna, her mother's comments triggering painful memories of exactly what would happen when an actual film star did show up here later this year – the man who would seduce Morwenna and bring the monstrous Elliot into the world, amongst his other sins. That was something she was desperate to prevent at all costs.

She glanced across at the TV, where the new breakfast programme was ending, cutting to a closing shot of a large egg cup with 1983 emblazoned across it. This prompted her to choose what she was having for breakfast.

"Have the hens laid many this morning?" she asked.

"Way more than I need – help yourself."

"Good job we kept those foxes out, huh?" said Jenna.

"Shelly at the café wasn't so lucky," said Morwenna, flicking off the television. There would be nothing on now, other than schools' programmes, until lunchtime. "She lost all hers a couple of nights ago."

After breakfast, Jenna spent an hour or so cleaning the pub and bottling up, by which time her father had finally emerged from his pit. Then at lunchtime she headed off around to Alfie's cottage, now back in its spit-and-sawdust décor, a far cry from the swanky Airbnb she had stayed in, courtesy of Wendy.

She and Alfie had been taking it easy and going steady with their burgeoning relationship. Much as she desired him, she wasn't ready to take things further physically, given all she had to do here. So, in the weeks following that first kiss, they had spent time together going for walks, holding hands, and passing some evenings watching television.

Today's trip to the pictures was to be their first proper date, for which they had planned to take the bus into Wadebridge, but Ned was about to throw a spanner into those plans.

"You two don't need to be wasting money on buses. I've got to go into Wadebridge this afternoon. I'll give you a lift in my van."

Jenna wasn't keen on this idea. Ned's battered old Transit van was in nearly as bad a state as his boat. Plus, if he had been one of the drinkers at the lock-in last night,

59

he would almost certainly be over the limit, though she couldn't smell any alcohol on his breath. But it wasn't the smell of booze she was most bothered about, more his van, which always stank of fish, as he used it to transport his catch.

"Thanks, but we'd prefer to get the bus, wouldn't we, Alfie?"

"Yes, I…" began Alfie, but Ned cut him short.

"Nonsense, boy, I won't hear of it. Plenty of room up front for all three of us."

As she had become accustomed to doing in these circumstances, Jenna glanced at the bracelet and was surprised to see it glowing green. It seemed to want her to go in the van.

"Very well," she said. "But we need to be in Wadebridge by two if we're not to miss the start."

The Transit was a dull red colour, weather-beaten by years of sea air, with rusty patches all over it. As Ned had indicated, it had three seats up front, and she clambered in before realising her mistake. Getting in first meant she would be in the middle, next to Ned. She should have let Alfie get in before her, but it was too late to make an issue of it now.

She looked around at the interior, which was predictably unappealing, cluttered with old newspapers, empty Woodbine packets, and an overflowing ashtray that she could smell, even over the stench of fish.

As Ned turned the key in the ignition to a rather lukewarm response from the engine, Jenna noticed that he hadn't put his seatbelt on.

"Buckle up, Ned," she said. "It's the law now, remember? It came in a day or two ago."

"Pah! What rubbish!" said Ned dismissively, turning the key a second time to little effect. "Come on, you bugger! Start! What's the matter with you? It's not even that cold today."

"Try pulling the choke out," suggested Alfie.

"Do you think I haven't thought of that?" said Ned, trying again and sighing thankfully as the engine spluttered into life. "There you go! Third time lucky!"

"Ned, if you don't put your seatbelt on, I'm not going, and that's that!" insisted Jenna.

"Bossy little madam, isn't she, boy?" said Ned. "And you're happy stepping out with her? It doesn't bode well for the future. I hope you're not thinking of doing anything silly, like marrying her."

"Excuse me, I am here," protested Jenna.

"Look, just put the belt on, Dad," said Alfie. "They made it law for a reason."

"Bloody stupid reason, probably," said Ned, reluctantly complying. "I reckon these things kill more folk than they save. What if we crashed and the van caught fire and we were strapped in and couldn't get them off?"

Jenna looked at the bracelet, which again was green.

"I'm confident that won't happen if you drive safely," she said. "I assume this thing has passed its MOT?"

"Dave at the garage in Camelford always puts it through for me if I bung him a case of mackerel."

61

"That doesn't exactly fill me with confidence, but I'll risk it this once," said Jenna, as Ned drove down the narrow lane that led to the harbour, before ascending the hill that led away from the village towards the junction with the B3263. But as they crested the rise at the top of the hill, they were in for a surprise.

The familiar figure of their village constable was there, next to his recently upgraded police car, a Mark III Escort. As they approached, he waved at them to pull over, and after they had stopped, asked Ned to wind down his window.

"What is it, Matt?" asked Ned impatiently. "We're running late as it is."

"Just checking that you are wearing your seatbelts, which I'm pleased to see you all are. As of yesterday, it's now a legal requirement, and an offence not to wear one."

"So I've been told," said Ned.

"I'm glad," said Matt. "Because I'm sure I overheard you mouthing off about your objections to wearing them in the pub the other day."

"No, that wasn't me, that was Willy. You want to keep an eye on him. He thinks he's Nelson Piquet in that bloody ice cream van of his."

"Very well," said Matt, stepping back and casting a critical eye over the van. "And while you're in Wadebridge, check your tyre pressures. Your rear offside tyre looks a little underinflated to me."

"Right you are," said Ned, winding the window back up as Matt stepped away to let him know they were free to go. But as soon as they were out of earshot, he made his feelings known.

"Who does he bloody think he is, sneaking around checking up on people like that?"

"He's just doing his job," said Jenna.

"Well, he clearly hasn't got enough to do. I don't know why we need a policeman in Pencarven anyway. It's hardly the crime capital of Cornwall, is it?"

"Good job I told you to put your belt on then, wasn't it?" she replied.

Ned's complaining went on until they arrived in Wadebridge, when much to Jenna's relief they were able to get out and escape from it.

They arrived at the single-screen cinema in time to see the low-budget local ads, which always amused her, introduced with the nostalgic kick of the Pearl & Dean music. There was even a cartoon before the main feature, something that never happened in modern cinemas anymore.

She enjoyed *Tootsie* but had to pretend she was watching it for the first time. In truth, she couldn't remember half the plot anyway, but it was curiously relevant to her own situation – dealing as it did with the lead character pretending to be someone they were not.

During the film, Alfie put his arm around her and she leaned into him, enjoying the moment. Afterwards, they went for tea at a local café, before catching the last bus of the day home. It was a lovely, uncomplicated day out, sharing jokes and just making the most of the simple pleasure of being together.

Jenna had experienced very little of this in her adult life. She'd had boyfriends and relationships but had never felt comfortable, given what had happened to Alfie, and then what Blake had put her through when he had first come to Pencarven. The Blake business was something that she had scarcely allowed herself to think about since it had happened. All of it had soured her on relationships for life, but things felt different now. Maybe Alfie really was the soulmate she should have been with all those years.

A few days after their trip to Wadebridge, Jenna's quest to bolster the village's sea defences began in earnest, though it didn't get off to a great start. Having never taken the remotest interest in it before, she decided it was time to seek support from Pencarven Parish Council.

They met on the first Monday of every month, and so it was that she went along hoping to state her case. Quite how she was going to do this, she still wasn't sure. She couldn't just come out and state that there was going to be a catastrophic flood in December that would devastate homes and businesses. No one could know that in advance. So, this was more a fact-finding exercise – to gauge support and get a handle on what needed to be done.

She was to be sorely downhearted at what turned out to be one of the most dispiriting and pointless experiences of her life. The council met at the church hall next to St Piran's, a crumbling stone building with rotting wooden window frames and a damp, musty smell inside. Although she had ascertained that any parishioner could attend these meetings, she soon discovered that her contribution would be limited, if allowed at all.

There were seven members on the council, but only five turned up, including the chairman. He was James Pascoe, the landlord of The Anchor, and easily the youngest member, though even he was in his sixties. He explained to Jenna that although the public was allowed to attend these meetings, they were not permitted to speak, except at the chairman's discretion. After much pleading and explaining her cause, he finally agreed to allow her to state her case as part of any other business at the end.

She was the only observer, and James seemed surprised that she had turned up at all. She soon discovered why. What followed was two hours of the most interminably dull conversation she had ever heard in her life, about such trivial matters that she soon realised it was unlikely she was going to get any help here.

The meeting began with apologies for absence, which included a lady called Gladys, who allegedly had a bad hip and couldn't make it. Jenna wasn't surprised as she remembered Gladys when she had been a dinner lady at her primary school, and she had been pretty ancient then. She certainly hadn't seen her since coming back to 1983. Later, when she got hold of some back minutes from earlier meetings, she discovered Gladys hadn't attended for months.

The other absentee was in hospital and apparently on his last legs, for which there was a brief expression of sympathy. Jenna wondered if this might lead to an opening on the council but the bracelet disagreed, with a red pulse. Once the remaining five members, all men, got into the meat of the agenda, she realised why.

Topics included repainting a faded and rusting slide in a children's playground – an admirable enough cause, but they spent twenty minutes arguing over what colour it should be. One councillor insisted on keeping it red, while another championed blue, claiming it would match the sea. Jenna suspected this was more about their relative political affiliations than any aesthetic reason.

There was also a lengthy discussion about putting some more benches on the seafront, and another about installing a new litter bin near the chip shop. Each of these, and the many other similarly trivial items, required funding. It soon became clear that very little was available and they could afford to do only one of the half a dozen items proposed.

Finally, almost two hours after she arrived, James allowed her to speak, at which point she stood up and made what she thought was a well-articulated case for the sea defences, even though by that stage, given all she had heard, she wasn't expecting much in response.

"That's all very well," said James once she had finished her spirited speech, "but there's nothing we can do about it. We don't have the funding for anything like that. This is a matter for the district council or possibly the county council, but I'm not sure which. Perhaps you should take it up with Gordon Pentreath."

"Don't worry, I will," she said, annoyed that he had made her sit for two hours listening to all that rubbish. Why couldn't he have just told her it was a waste of time when she had told him what she had come for before the meeting?

66

"Why isn't Gordon here?" she added. "Doesn't he take an interest in issues that affect our village?"

"You obviously don't know how local politics works," said James, giving her a withering look that screamed 'Go home, little girl, you don't know what you're talking about'. "Gordon is a district councillor. It's not the done thing for him to come to our meetings."

"Don't you even talk to each other?" she asked in frustration. "And can't you see how serious this situation is? All it's going to take is one bad storm and the low-lying buildings on the seafront will be inundated."

"I can see why that might concern you, Jenna, what with your father's pub being right in the firing line, but it's not an issue for me. The Anchor is sixty feet above sea level, so barring a tsunami, I've nothing to worry about."

She looked to the other members for support, but they just stared at her blankly – well, three of them did, anyway. The other one, an elderly retired fisherman, had fallen asleep and was now snoring gently, his head nodding forward. What a farce this had been. She took her leave and went home, disillusioned at the lacklustre state of local politics.

She would have no choice but to take it up with Gordon, but he proved to be a difficult man to track down. Although there was a small council office in Pencarven, which doubled as a tourist information centre in the summer, it was closed most of the time during the colder months. A sign on the door suggested that Gordon was there one day a week for a few hours on Friday mornings.

That meant a delay of another few days in a month that was already ticking by. And when Friday came, she wasted another two hours waiting outside the deserted building. Gordon didn't show up until after eleven and then seemed just as surprised to see her as the parish councillors had been. It appeared he didn't get many visitors. Didn't anyone care about what went on around here?

Jenna was no fan of Gordon, because as far as she was concerned he was an extremely dodgy character, even though she had no proof of the things she suspected him of doing. But the circumstantial evidence alone was enough to condemn him in her eyes.

In the old timeline, Gordon had never been exactly poor. He was always smartly dressed, drove a decent car, and had an accountancy business based in Camelford. It was enough to live a comfortable lifestyle, but certainly not the extravagant one he later acquired. After Blake came to Pencarven and liked what he saw, it seemed he got everything he wanted, including planning permission for his mansion in an area of outstanding natural beauty, for starters.

If Blake wanted something, the council was only too happy to oblige, and Jenna was convinced that there were more than just a couple of brown envelopes containing a few tenners passing Gordon's way. Within a few years, he was driving expensive cars and had a second home in Spain, plus a substantial seafront property in one of the neighbouring villages that fell within his district.

It was blatantly obvious he was in the back pocket not only of Blake but of his other rich friends who had come to the area, and as far as Jenna was concerned, Gordon was as much to blame as any of them for what had happened to Pencarven over the years.

For now, all that lay in the future, but for all she knew he had been up to no good long before Blake arrived. That included the lack of funding to protect the village, and she didn't mess about, airing her concerns as soon as she accosted him on his arrival.

"Can you tell me, Councillor Pentreath, why Pencarven is the only settlement on this stretch of coast with no proper sea defences?"

He looked back at her, putting on his polished charm, but to her it came across more like smarm.

"It's all very complex, and based on budgets set on an annual basis. We have to spend the money where we feel it is best allocated but you can rest assured I have Pencarven's best interests at heart."

"Oh really," said Jenna, who had been doing her homework. "Because I've been going through the minutes of the council meetings from last year, and it's come to my attention that you did in fact vote against defences for Pencarven, a motion that was lost by a single vote. How do you explain that?"

She could tell he wasn't prepared for this unexpected challenge when the charm dropped for just a second. Was that a hint of anger she had detected in his eyes? It was only fleeting before his smooth persona reasserted itself and he resumed his politician-style patter.

"I can assure you that we have had expert surveys and analyses carried out, and the conclusion was that the flood risk in Pencarven was low and that the money could be better spent elsewhere."

"Really?" she asked. "How do you explain then that the low-lying properties here have had minor flood damage three times in the past decade, whereas no other settlement ten miles along the coast, in either direction, has had a single incident?"

"Young lady, I don't know where you are getting your information from, but I'm sure that isn't true."

"It's coming straight from the horse's mouth because I live in one of the properties that's under threat. Which you would know if you bothered to spend any time in the village. We all know each other here, but you don't know me, do you?"

He looked at her, trying to place her, given the information she had given him about living on the seafront before the penny dropped.

"You're David's girl, aren't you? From the pub."

"Well done," remarked Jenna sarcastically. "And those numbers I gave you are fact. It was all recorded in the *Cornish & Devon Post*. I looked it up on microfiche at the library."

"Yes, well, you're clearly a very resourceful young woman," said Gordon. "But I'm sure your skills could be better employed elsewhere. In a few weeks, the ladies of the village will be making plans for the spring fair. Why don't you get involved with helping them out?"

"Stay out of things that women don't understand – is that what you're saying?"

"Your words, not mine," said Gordon.

"That's not good enough. This village is wide open and defenceless to the sea, and you won't do anything about it. Not only that, but you also voted against it. That smells fishier than Ned Trelawney's van to me."

Gordon's polished façade was now well and truly gone as he leaned forward threateningly.

"I would be very careful what you go around saying if I were you," he said. "There is such a thing as slander."

"If you've done nothing wrong, you've got nothing to hide," she retorted. "And if you have, then I'm going to find out what it is and expose you."

"Good luck with that!" he snorted. "You're way out of your depth. Now, it's nearly lunchtime. I suggest you go home and watch *Rainbow*. Leave the politics to the grown-ups, okay?"

She couldn't be bothered to argue anymore, so just issued a standard "Whatever," and went on her way. What a scumbag he was, far worse than she remembered.

Outside, she looked down at her bracelet and spoke to it, something she was getting in the habit of doing. It couldn't talk but it could give her yes and no answers.

"He's dodgy, right?"

The bracelet glowed green.

"And we're gonna nail him?"

Green again. That was all she needed to know for now.

On the way back, she passed the café and saw Morwenna inside, gossiping away with Shelly. On a whim she went in, just fancying a cup of tea and a scone. Despite Gordon's threats, she was keen to try to get support from her friends and family, and this seemed as good a time as any to start.

Jenna liked Shelly. She and her mother had grown up together, and Shelly had run the café for as long as Jenna could remember. Shelly wasn't her real name; that was a nickname based on the colourful shells she collected and sold in her shop. She had been born Fiona Penrose, but no one had called her by her given name for years.

Any hope she had of talking about the problems facing the village soon faded, as the two of them were deep in conversation about *Coronation Street*.

"So do you think Deidre will leave Ken?" asked Shelly.

"Oh, I hope so," said Morwenna. "Ken's so boring, isn't he? Who wouldn't go for a man like Mike Baldwin? He's exciting and has got so much more going for him."

Once again, Jenna felt uncomfortable at her mother expressing interest in men other than her father, and leapt to Ken's defence.

"Ken's steady and dependable. He took on Deidre's daughter when her real father left. Not many men would have done that."

"Well, I still think she's going to leave him," said Morwenna confidently.

"Me too," said Shelly. "They've been leading up to this for weeks."

"I confidently predict that you are both wrong," said Jenna, with authority. "She'll stay with Ken, you'll see."

"And what makes you such an expert?" asked Shelly. "Do you have inside information from people at Granada?"

"No," said Jenna, sensing an opportunity here. She had to get the villagers to take her seriously about the flood threat. If she could convince them that she had some sort of sixth sense and could predict the future, perhaps they would start to listen. It was worth a try.

"You're just guessing, then," said Shelly.

"No, I'm just very good at predicting the future," replied Jenna. "Oh, and Len Fairclough's going to be killed off soon too."

She wasn't so confident of her timing on that one but knew it had to be some time soon, as she remembered there was some scandal involving the actor who played him, which had led to him getting the sack. She had a good grasp of what was going on in all the soaps because as an ITV viewer, her mother watched them all. Now Jenna was watching them a second time around.

"If you say so," said Shelly. "Now, Morwenna, there's something else I've been itching to tell you. This man came in here yesterday, who I've never seen before. I got talking with him, and he said he was working for a big film studio, and they were down here scouting for locations for a blockbuster movie."

"About what?" asked Morwenna.

"Pirates, or something. Anyway, I was chatting to my cousin in Polzeath the other night, and it's the talk of the town down there. Rumours are, Sean Connery's going to be in it."

"Wrong!" declared Jenna.

"Oh, I suppose you know all about that too, do you?" asked Shelly.

"As a matter of fact, I do. It's not Sean Connery, it's Blake Cadwallader."

"Ooh, I like him!" gushed Morwenna. "He makes me go all gooey!"

Her choice of phrase, even if it hadn't had any intentional sexual innuendo attached, almost made Jenna throw up, given what was later to transpire. She couldn't bear to hear any more.

"Listen, I've got to dash," she said. "I just remembered I promised to help Dad with the lunchtime session."

That hadn't gone well, and she needed a few minutes in the fresh air to compose herself. She wasn't meant to be working at the pub but decided to head there anyway. Perhaps she could drum up some support among the locals.

Those hopes were soon dashed when she heard what they were talking about at the bar. A major story had just broken in the news that Shergar, the 1981 Derby winner, had been kidnapped. Now the regulars were speculating about who might be responsible.

"Well, I reckon it's some foreign betting syndicate that's stolen him for breeding," said Ned. "Stands to reason, doesn't it? Disguise him as a different horse, then mate him with lots of mares, and he'll produce loads of sure-fire winners they can bet on. But because they don't know that Shergar's their dad, they'll be long odds and they can clean up."

"A ridiculously convoluted scenario," replied Matt. "And if that were the case, why would they ask for a ransom?"

"All right, clever clogs, since you're the detective, why don't you give us your theory?" asked Ned.

"Constable, actually, but I'll take your promotion as a compliment," said Matt. "I think it's more likely that it's the IRA. The horse was at stud in Ireland, after all. They are the obvious candidates."

"I think you've hit the nail on the head there," said Jenna, sensing another opportunity for a prediction, though she wasn't sure how long it would be before the truth came out that it had indeed been the IRA who were responsible. If memory served, this story had dragged on for some time.

"What about the mafia?" suggested Willy. "They have branches everywhere. Trust me, I know."

"Why, are they trying to muscle in on your ice cream business?" asked David from behind the bar. "And how do you know? From something you saw on the telly?"

"All right, there's no need to take the piss, and how do you know they haven't got their fingers in the ice cream trade? It's big business in Italy, you know. Haven't you seen the Cornetto ads on TV?"

"There, see, I told you he got it from the telly," said David.

"Well, I'm sure he'll turn up eventually," said Ned. "Maybe he'll come galloping into Pencarven with Lord Lucan aboard. Now that would be something, wouldn't it?"

It was clear that Jenna was going to get even less sense out of this lot than she'd got from Morwenna and Shelly in the café. Leaving the men in the bar to their ill-conceived theories, she took herself off upstairs for a long soak in the bath.

Naked in the water, except for the ever-present bracelet on her wrist, Jenna reflected on the progress of recent days – or rather the lack of it.

"Tell me what to do," she urged the bracelet, seeking some sort of sign. But none was forthcoming, not a pulse of any colour. She sank deeper into the bubbles, trying to clear her mind as she sought desperately for answers. What was she going to do?

March 1983

The 29th of March 1983. The date had been indelibly engraved on Jenna's mind for almost forty years, for it was the day that Alfie and Ned had perished at sea.

No one knew exactly what had happened on the fateful afternoon when the boat did not return. By the following morning, the coastguard was called out but there was no sign of *The Buccaneer* – at least not at first. It was only when the charred remains of planks from the boat began washing up on shore later that day that the awful truth began to dawn. Ned's boat hadn't simply gone down – it had suffered a catastrophic event, serious enough that there had been no time for Alfie and Ned to raise the alarm or escape.

Jenna remembered exactly where she was when she heard the news. On the day *The Buccaneer* was lost, her Uncle Morgan's caravan park had opened for the year, earlier than ever before. It was the first day of the school Easter holidays, and keen to extend the season, Morgan had invested a considerable sum on building a whole new clubhouse over the winter.

This contained an extended bar, a small arcade with indoor rides and video games for the children, and a decent-sized entertainment room with a stage. There was now also a small indoor swimming pool, perfect for this time of year when it was still too cold for days on the beach.

The previous summer, Jenna had filled the role of children's entertainer and had agreed to take on the job for the entire extended season in 1983, as well as helping with the rest of the entertainment outside of the school holidays – this largely meant bingo and various other activities for the senior citizens who liked to visit during the spring and autumn. Morgan intended to keep the park open through to the October half-term if he could get enough bookings.

It was on the afternoon of her second day in the original timeline when Morwenna arrived unexpectedly to see her, just as she was winding down the kids' club for the day. Jenna had been running a painting session at the time and was tidying up a rather messy table where toddlers and primary-school-aged children had splattered paint and water everywhere, despite her best attempts to minimise the spillages by putting down copious amounts of newspaper.

Morwenna had waited for the last child to be collected, then sat Jenna down to tell her the tragic news, which left her devastated. Although her relationship hadn't developed far with Alfie, it had always seemed an inevitability that they would get together. It was only on receipt of this shocking news that she realised just how much she had loved him. But she had never told him, and now it was too late.

Or so it had seemed. But those events were no longer set in stone. She had the chance to change them, but how? The mystery of what had happened to Ned's boat had never been satisfactorily resolved, though there had been much speculation, particularly in the pub. There, the drinkers had advanced various theories, from the plausible to the ridiculous, with Jenna recalling Willy suspecting the IRA, who by that time had been implicated in the kidnap of Shergar. Quite why they would want to bomb a small fishing boat in a remote part of Cornwall, he wasn't able to explain.

Other than those few burnt planks, the rest of the boat was never recovered, presumably ending up at the bottom of the sea. Any faint hopes that Alfie might somehow have survived were dashed a week or two later when his body was discovered, washed up on rocks near Polzeath. Ned's body was never found. The exact cause, therefore, was never determined, but the fact that Alfie's corpse was covered in severe burns along with the flotsam that had washed up made fire a certainty. What no one knew was how it had started.

Now, finally, the truth of what had happened that day was about to be revealed to Jenna, coming to her as it did during sleep. When she woke up on the first Sunday in March, which also happened to be her twentieth birthday, she was in a feverish state, having just experienced the most vivid dream of her life. The bracelet was heightening this traumatic moment, flashing red far more strongly than it ever had before.

In her dream, she had just seen exactly what had happened to *The Buccaneer* that day. Ned and Alfie had gone out as usual, without noticing a severe electrical fault with the engine. The wires below were fizzing and sparking and at some point shorted out, causing a fire to break out right below the engine. To exacerbate matters, diesel had been leaking down there for some time, and with various rubbish such as old chip papers, oily rags, and other clutter in the vicinity, it was a disaster waiting to happen. Within seconds, the whole area was ablaze.

Any hopes of putting it out or getting help were swiftly quashed, as Alfie discovered that neither the fire extinguisher nor the radio, with which they could have sent out a Mayday, worked. They had both been broken for a long time, but slapdash as he was, Ned hadn't got round to fixing either.

Realising they were going to have to abandon ship, they prepared to leap overboard, but before they could do so, a massive explosion ripped through the craft, incinerating it and the occupants aboard. Alfie was thrown clear but badly burned. He perished quickly, while Ned went down with the ship.

It was so real and so horrific that Jenna burst into tears on awakening. What a devastating and tragic waste of life, all brought on by Ned's negligence.

She lay back in bed for a moment, recovering. It had been the worst nightmare she had ever experienced, yet she knew this was no dream. She had been witnessing the exact events that had transpired that day, forty years ago, yet were still three weeks in the future here. The bracelet knew what had happened and had transmitted the details directly into her mind. So, surely, all she had to do now was just persuade Ned and Alfie not to go out that day, didn't she?

The bracelet disagreed, pulsing red at her. Perhaps it wasn't going to be as easy as she thought. But at least she had some time, so the first thing she planned to do was go and check out the boat.

Putting a brave face on things, she headed downstairs, where Morwenna had prepared her a bumper breakfast for her birthday. As she sat down with her mother and David, she was momentarily distracted by a story on Radio Cornwall about the launch of a brand-new music format.

The compact disc had arrived in the shops, and the radio's reporters had been out at a record store in Truro testing them out and asking shoppers what they thought. The general reception was positive, though there were complaints that they were too expensive. It was funny hearing people talk this way about things that, by her time, were old hat and cheap as chips, being sold for pennies in charity shops.

After breakfast, she made her way down to the harbour to try to get a decent look at *The Buccaneer*. It was Sunday, so none of the fishermen were about, and she was tempted to climb on board, given that the tide was out and the boat was sitting on the sand. The bracelet wasn't keen on this idea, and when she thought about it, she realised why. If she was seen tinkering about on the boat a few weeks before its potential demise, that could be seen as suspicious, if she was ultimately unable to prevent its destruction.

Instead, she walked all around the outside, inspecting it in detail. What she saw hardly inspired confidence. Every part of the exterior was in a poor state of repair, from the fraying ropes to the rusty metalwork and fading paintwork over planks that she suspected might be starting to rot, beneath the seaweed and barnacles clinging to the side.

Even without the electrical faults, diesel spills, and defunct safety equipment, the boat was an accident waiting to happen, with any number of things that could consign it to a watery grave.

Her family were planning a special Sunday dinner for her birthday, which Morwenna had scheduled for five o'clock, neatly sandwiched between the lunchtime and evening sessions in the pub. It felt odd to be turning twenty again. Back in her old world, she had been dreading reaching sixty, especially considering her circumstances. At that age, with what little she had, it had been difficult to imagine starting again. But here all things were possible, and being twenty now, rather than still a teenager, might give her a little more credibility when dealing with the likes of Gordon.

She wasn't the only one thinking about a fresh start. As she made her way up from the harbour, she spotted Jack attaching a large board to the railings close to where he moored his boat. She had seen him repainting and overhauling it in recent weeks, and it looked all sparkly and new. Ned could have taken a leaf out of his book.

"What do you think of this, Jenna?" said Jack excitedly as she approached.

She cast her eye over the colourful sign, featuring a picture of the boat, some seals, and some caves, reading the words out loud.

"Jack's Boat Tours. 10am, 1pm, and 4pm daily. Come and see the seals, and explore the secret smugglers' caves. £2.50 per adult, £1.50 for children under 12, and concessions."

"Looks good, huh?" said Jack.

"It looks wonderful!" she said. "I'm so excited for you!"

"And I have you to thank," he replied. "You encouraged me that day when Ned was rubbishing the idea. As soon as I'm up and running, you can have a free trip on me."

"When are you planning to start?"

"Good Friday, to catch the Easter trade. Morgan says he's opening up the caravan park early this year."

"That's right," she said. "I'm going to be working there." She was genuinely pleased for Jack, seeing his new endeavour as one that could only benefit Pencarven.

Since she didn't need to be back home until the afternoon, she decided to visit Alfie. He had specifically asked her to come around that morning, and when she got there, she was delighted when he presented her with a bunch of flowers and a box of Terry's All Gold for her birthday. She was chuffed that he had remembered her saying a few weeks ago that she loved dark chocolate.

She wondered if she ought to say something about the boat but wasn't sure how to go about it. The bracelet didn't seem to think it was a good idea, but when Ned came into the room and the topic came up, she decided to mention it anyway.

"Flowers and chocolates, eh? You're setting a precedent there, boy. She'll expect them every year now, you know."

"And I'll be happy to give them to her," said Alfie, which should have sent a warm feeling through her, but instead gave her a chill as she thought about all the years Alfie hadn't been destined to see.

"I'm obviously paying you too much," said Ned. "If you can afford to splash your cash around like that."

"You pay me hardly anything," said Alfie. "There's no money in mackerel anymore. That's why I want to start up my surf shack."

"Mackerel's done me proud over the years," said Ned. "Even if the waters aren't as rich as they used to be, I've still managed to tuck a fair bit away for my old age."

"Why don't you spend some of it doing up that boat of yours, then?" suggested Jenna. "The thing's a death-trap. When did you last do any sort of maintenance on it?"

"Have you heard this, boy?" said Ned incredulously. "It seems that she's now an expert on boat upkeep, along with all the other things she keeps telling us we need to do. You've got a right one on your hands here!"

"She's got a point, Dad. The boat's in a right state."

"That boat's my livelihood, and I know her like the back of my hand. She's got a good few years left in her yet."

"Well, not with me you haven't," insisted Alfie. "Spring's nearly here, and I'm determined to build this surf shack. Tourism is the future, whether you like it or not, so I'm not coming out on the boat this summer."

"Oh, aren't you?" asked Ned. "So tell me, who's going to finance this little venture of yours?"

"Well, I've got a few people interested," said Alfie unconvincingly. Jenna knew that he hadn't. "And I'm going into Camelford tomorrow to see about getting a loan."

"Against what?" asked Ned. "You've got no collateral. Have you even written a business plan?"

"I'm working on it. Jenna's going to help me."

"No doubt she's got a degree in business studies to go with all her other talents," said Ned sarcastically.

"Look, Dad," said Alfie, hating having to go cap in hand. "I was wondering if you might lend me the money."

"What, finance your new venture so you can leave me to go out on the boat on my own? You know it's much easier with two, and I'm not getting any younger."

"That's why you should switch to tourism, like Jack. No more heavy work."

"I'm not running boat trips for tourists," insisted Ned. "I told you before, I don't want them here."

"I doubt anyone would be brave enough to get on board that thing even if you did," said Jenna.

"All right, boy, I'll tell you what I'll do," said Ned, ignoring Jenna's remark. "I'll give you the money for your surf shack, provided you promise to come out with me two days a week during the summer."

"But that will be my busiest time!" protested Alfie.

"Not if you've no shack to begin with, it won't be," said Ned.

"Very well," said Alfie. He couldn't fault his father's logic. "Perhaps I can get someone else to cover for me while I'm not there."

Jenna bit her tongue and said nothing. There was nothing else she could do right now, and at least this way, Alfie was getting the finance he needed for the shack. She would just have to figure out a way to disable the boat later.

Before that, she had another problem to deal with. A few nights after her birthday, she had another vivid dream, this time about a flood. Not a disastrous one like she was expecting in December, but one of the more regular ones, where the sea came up so high it escaped from the harbour, reaching the street where the pub and several other low-lying buildings were at risk.

This was a fairly common event, occurring once every three or four years, and in her dream, Jenna foresaw it happening the following evening at high tide and realised she needed to issue warnings.

The pub and the other buildings along the front were prepared for the eventuality of minor floods. They were equipped with sandbags that were able to cope with several inches of water. Usually, she recalled that the folk along the front had a good handle on the local tides and weather conditions and were able to predict what was coming. They had the sandbags out long before the waves broke onto the road. But this time they seemed unprepared, even her father, who dismissed her claims.

"Look, it's a new moon tonight and a spring tide," she insisted. "And the wind's whipping in off the sea. It's the perfect set-up for a flood."

"That's not going to happen," said David. "I listened in on Radio Cornwall earlier and they were predicting a calm day, with only a slight breeze. Look out there now – the sea is as flat as a pancake."

She looked out the window, where she could see the ocean glimmering in the spring sunshine.

"Well, it won't be later," she said defiantly. "We need to get the sandbags out."

"Not according to the forecast. I'm sorry but I don't see the point."

"Forecasts can be wrong. I'll do it myself if I need to, and get Alfie to help me."

Before she did that, she went and knocked on the doors of everyone else along the harbour front, insisting that a flood was on the way. Some listened, some didn't. But when the wind suddenly picked up around dusk, those that didn't had cause to regret it as high tide approached.

Great waves were now crashing forcefully, higher and higher up the beach, creating a tremendous crescendo and plumes of spray. It was a spectacular display for those watching, including Jenna, from the safety of the pub windows, and despite the more sheltered nature of the harbour, it didn't take long for the water to surge in. Soon it was flowing across the road towards the front doors of the most vulnerable buildings. Some of them had heeded Jenna's warnings; others hadn't, and paid the price as water surged into their shops and homes.

It was a short-lived flood, as the waters were up to the road for less than half an hour before the tide began to recede. Those who had acted on Jenna's advice had every reason to be thankful towards her. In the eyes of them and everyone else, she had just gone up in stature. Other than a few curmudgeonly types like Ned, who still considered her far too clever for her own good, this could only help her gain support within the community.

Bolstered by her success, she again sought out Gordon at the council office, but he remained dismissive of her.

"So, you predicted one small flood," he said. "Big deal. And you managed it quite adequately with sandbags. So where's the problem?"

"A small flood, yes," she said. "But what happens when the big one comes?"

"If it comes," he said. "It's only you that seems to think so."

"Oh, it will come," she confidently stated.

"Quite the little Nostradamus, aren't we?" he said. "Unfortunately, we don't base our financial decisions at the council on the fanciful predictions of teenage girls."

"I'm twenty, actually," she said, looking up at a poster on the wall advertising the forthcoming district council elections on the 5th of May. "You know, you ought to be careful. There's an election coming up soon. If you don't act in Pencarven's best interests, you could find yourself booted out on your ear."

"Hardly," said Gordon. "I've held this seat since 1973. No one even bothered to oppose me at the last two elections."

"Well, perhaps it's time that changed," she said, flouncing out of the room, with the bracelet giving her the green seal of approval. What a cracking idea had just come to her. She was going to run for the council.

Having no idea what that entailed, she had to go and do her homework, but within a week, she had her nomination forms ready to go. They had been signed by Matt and Shelly, who had been one of those who had listened to Jenna's warning, put her sandbags out, and was now only too grateful to help.

88

She made no secret of her plans and sought support everywhere she went, including while working behind the bar. But on the day she submitted her forms, the regulars were not in a supportive mood.

"Pint of Carling Black Label, please," said Willy, who was first to the bar, as always, on Friday teatime.

"That'll be 64p, please," said Jenna as she poured, fearing the inevitable backlash. She and David had spent the afternoon repricing all the drinks on the plastic board behind the bar using small white letters and numbers that were pegged to the black background.

"What!" said Willy, outraged. "It's gone up again?"

"It was the budget," explained Jenna. "Geoffrey Howe's put beer up by a penny."

"Yes, but it was 59p before. That's, what, a ten per cent increase?"

"8.4 per cent actually," said David, emerging from the door that led from behind the bar to the private part of the building. "Which, when you factor in inflation and other rising costs, isn't unreasonable, considering it's the first price rise in twelve months."

"I notice you always put it up just before the tourist season," said Willy. "You must be coining it in."

"In this economic climate?" asked David. "We're barely breaking even as it is. There are a lot more overheads to running a pub than there are to selling a few ice creams, you know."

"It's just as well the drinking season's nearly over for me then, isn't it?" said Willy. "It'll soon be time to dust off the old van and get back out there."

"And how much will you be selling your ice creams for this summer?" asked David.

"35p, I reckon," said Willy.

"And how much were they last year?"

He paused before replying, "30p."

"I rest my case," said David.

Willy wasn't the only one to complain about the price rises, but it was the way the world was going. To Jenna, even after three months of living back in 1983, everything still seemed remarkably cheap, and she still hadn't become used to people handing over pound notes and giving them their change in the heavier and larger silver coins that were still in circulation at this time.

As the month drew towards its close, Jenna finally felt as if she was starting to achieve things. Predicting the earlier flood and deciding to stand for council represented good progress, but with less than a week to go, she was getting increasingly nervous about the impending boat disaster. Putting her even more on edge was the bracelet's illogical approach to the matter.

For a start, it didn't want her to warn Ned or Alfie of what was going to happen, or even inform them about the electrical issues and suspected fuel leakage on the boat. Every time she considered it the red light came on. At one point, she began to wonder if she was going to be able to save them at all. From what Wendy had told her, she was here to correct the timeline or keep it on track where required. What if it wanted Ned and Alfie to die?

She wasn't going to allow that to happen, whatever the bracelet had in mind. She would warn them, close to the time if necessary, and highlight the problems. Surely

Alfie wouldn't allow the boat to go out in that condition if he knew about it. Clearly he didn't, so Ned must have been deliberately concealing it from him.

A few nights before it was due to happen, she fell asleep thinking about just that, slipping into a dream which shed more light on the situation.

In this dream, she did exactly as she had considered, showing a horrified Alfie the shoddy state Ned had let the boat get into, insisting on immediate repairs. How Jenna knew about it was not questioned, but with the boat repairs complete, and *The Buccaneer* apparently seaworthy again, it sailed out to resume fishing activities in early April.

And then, tragedy struck again. The hull was in very poor condition, and out at sea began taking on water. The details were sketchy, but the outcome was the same. The boat sank, and they both went down with it.

Her dream didn't end there, presenting further alternatives depending on Jenna's actions, but whatever she did, the outcome was always the same. The message was crystal clear – if *The Buccaneer* continued to go out, tragedy would always strike eventually.

What then was she to do? The temptation to say something was overwhelming, and as Ned and Alfie went out just four days before the fateful day, she was distraught with worry, even though she knew that nothing would happen on that day. She spent the whole afternoon glued to her bedroom window, gazing out over the harbour, waiting for the boat to return. From what Alfie had told her this was the final time he would be going out before the 29th.

Finally, that night, she got the answers she sought. The bracelet laid out in detail what she needed to do, and she made sure she got an early night the following evening, setting an alarm for an hour before dawn, remembering to account for this being the night when the clocks went forward.

Dressing quickly and quietly, she crept ever so lightly down the stairs, doing her best to minimise the sound of the creaky floorboards by keeping her steps to the outside where they were less worn. Outside, she made her way to the harbour, looking carefully around to ensure she wasn't seen by anyone, but it was Sunday and the village was still and silent, the only sound coming from the distant waves lapping at the shore. Even the gulls were quiet this morning.

All the while, she was grappling with the gravity of what she was about to do. There were no two ways about it, she was on the verge of committing a serious criminal act, even if it was with the best intentions. She was merely bringing forward an event that was going to happen anyway, but in a scenario that would cause no harm to anyone. But as she kept telling herself, try making that stand up in a court of law.

It explained why the bracelet had wanted her to keep quiet all these weeks. If she had kept banging on about this, then she would have marked herself out as a prime suspect in what was about to happen. This way the finger of blame, if it was to fall, would not be pointing in her direction, and preferably not in anyone's at all. If the whole thing could be written off as an accident, it would be best for all concerned.

She boarded *The Buccaneer*, which was easily accessible due to the low tide. The sky to the east was beginning to glow red, signalling that dawn was on its way, and there was just enough light for her to see what she was doing, and to awaken the gulls, who now began their morning squawking.

Checking the device on her wrist, she could see it was glowing green, so she knew she was on the right track. Guided by the torch she had brought with her, she made her way to the engine bay, where the faulty wiring was located. The wires were old and frayed, some of them showing blackened scorch marks from previous overheating. There was rubbish all around, including empty, greasy chip wrappings which were undoubtedly a fire hazard. She also noticed a strong smell of diesel, which she suspected might have been leaking for some time.

Why hadn't Alfie noticed this and questioned Ned? Or perhaps it was normal for diesel engines to smell a bit. She didn't know but it didn't matter now, anyway.

Her task was to manipulate the wires to create a short circuit that would spark the fault the next time the boat's electrics were switched on. She didn't have a clue what she was doing but followed the instructions the bracelet seemed to be transmitting to her, using a couple of small hand tools it had suggested she bring along.

First, she located the power isolation switch and turned it off, ensuring her safety. Then, with shaking hands, she repositioned the wires, placing a particularly corroded one in contact with an exposed metal surface. Finally, she turned the power back on and stepped back.

The crackling and fizzing began immediately. The acrid smell of burning plastic mingled with the diesel, and she knew it was time to leave. Her heart was pounding, with adrenaline rushing through her as she raced back onto the deck and off the boat, making sure she didn't leave behind any evidence of her presence. Not that it would probably matter anyway, because if this all went according to plan, there would be very little left of the boat to sift through.

It was lighter now as sunrise approached, but there was still no one around, and she made it back to the sanctuary of the pub unscathed. Then she snuck back up to her room, looked out of the window, and waited.

For a while, nothing happened, leading her to doubt the effectiveness of her actions. But then, after about ten minutes, she saw small, dark puffs of smoke beginning to emerge, and the flicker of flames. It was almost full daylight by now and there was still nobody about, which was good. The last thing she needed was some well-intentioned villager raising the alarm and extinguishing the fire too early.

It was a good job too, because anyone near the boat would have surely been hurt given what happened next. Jenna had been expecting an explosion like the one she had seen in her dream, but the ferocity of it still surprised her given that the boat was powered on diesel, which was far less flammable than petrol.

Somehow a build-up of vapours in the enclosed space, the earlier spillages, plus the litter, had created the right conditions for a massive explosion to rip through the boat, sending up a sizeable fireball and scattering debris in all directions across the harbour, some even reaching as far as the road.

That woke the villagers up for sure, and within seconds people were emerging from their homes and running towards the burning wreck, concerned that someone might be hurt.

"It's *The Buccaneer*!" she heard Jack shout.

"Was Ned on board?" asked Shelly, as more and more villagers came out to see what had happened.

It was quickly established that Ned was still safely tucked up in bed, sleeping off his Saturday night boozing, when the locals went round to hammer on his door. There Alfie, who had heard the explosion, was already up and able to confirm they were both safe.

Jenna, watching the chaos below with everyone running about, was still wrestling with the ethical implications of what she had done. Later in the day, when it became clear that no one had been hurt and there had been no damage to any other boat or property despite the explosion, she felt better. The bracelet had known what it was doing, and now two lives, including one extremely special to her, had been saved.

Whether she succeeded or not in all the battles that she knew still lay ahead in 1983, it had been worth coming back here for this moment alone.

Alfie was alive, and with him by her side she was going to be so much stronger than she had been before.

April 1983

Early April was cool and damp, but that did not deter the first hardy souls of the year from making their way down to Cornwall for the Easter break.

Jenna's uncle had invested considerably in the caravan park over the winter, something she knew would pay off handsomely over the next few years. The site offered a mix of static caravans, spaces for visitors to bring their own, and a field for tents, although Morgan was keen to expand the number of statics, having added twelve more since the previous season. He had figured out that the revenue from them, being booked in advance, was more reliable than hoping people would just turn up ad hoc to rent a pitch.

The most impressive addition was the new clubhouse, now boasting far more facilities than previously, though evening entertainment remained modest. Jenna recalled that this would expand over the next few years, as would her role. By the late 1980s, she had been employed full-time at the thriving park, though the changes already sweeping through Pencarven soon led to a decline. During the new century the park's fortunes waned, closing entirely as a holiday destination by 2017, leaving just a few long-term residents behind.

One person not so encouraged by the development was David. The past couple of years had been lean at the pub, with the country in recession and poor summers not helping. When he learned of Morgan's improved clubhouse facilities, he understandably worried about their impact on The Fisherman's Arms. His reasoning was simple: if holidaymakers had everything they needed on-site, why would they venture into the village in the evening?

This concern led to tension between the two men, not helped by Jenna working at the park during the day to run the children's activities. David saw this as a betrayal. Jenna did her best to assuage his fears, arguing that more visitors to the caravan park would benefit the village as a whole.

Since Morgan was not offering much in the way of food yet, this was proving to be the case. Although the park was only about a third full this early in the season, many visitors were already making their way into the village in search of sustenance during that first week of the Easter holidays.

Shelly's Café served Cornish pasties and cream teas, all baked on-site to the appreciation of the early-season holidaymakers. Meanwhile, the chip shop's evening trade picked up, with dads driving down to collect family suppers to take back to the caravans, often slipping into the pub for a quick pint before heading back. This was something Jenna highlighted to her father, as she got chatting with the new arrivals when she was working behind the bar.

The number of tourists was small compared to the summer, but they were one of many signs of spring all around her, like the wilting daffodils around the war memorial which were coming to the end of their season and being superseded by bright-red tulips.

Jenna always loved this time of year, when Pencarven shook itself out of its winter slumber. The days grew longer, the gulls got louder, and the cobbled streets started to hum with life again. This was the Pencarven she cherished.

During that first week of the school holidays, Jenna ran her first kids' clubs of the year. With the weather remaining cold, most of this was confined to indoor activities which she split into two sessions: under tens in the morning and the older ones in the afternoon.

For the little ones, she focused mainly on arts and crafts, setting out paints, coloured paper, board games and puzzles. They arrived bundled in woolly jumpers and anoraks, having trudged through the rain from their caravans, yet they remained cheerful and enthusiastic, their bright eyes full of holiday excitement despite the modest entertainment on offer.

The older ones were harder to please, but simple table tennis or pool competitions, with a small prize at the end, went down well. It was all rather basic, but that simplicity was refreshing. It was heartening to see kids enjoying some simple fun in an era before so many had become glued to their phone screens and other distractions.

To placate her father she still worked at the pub in the evenings, leaving Morgan to handle what little night-time entertainment there was at the park.

Since Ned's boat had gone up in smoke, speculation about the cause of the accident had been the talk of the town. This continued into the following week when Ned came into the pub early one evening looking uncharacteristically cheerful. Making a beeline for Alfie, who was keeping Jenna company at the bar, he couldn't wait to tell of his good fortune.

"It's good news, boy! I heard from the insurance company this afternoon. They're going to pay out."

"You've successfully conned them, then," said Willy, who was occupying his usual bar stool.

"What do you mean by that?" demanded Ned, who knew very well what Willy was getting at. It wasn't the first time he had faced such accusations, having already had a grilling from Matt who had been extremely suspicious about the whole incident. Fortunately for Jenna, none of his enquiries had come in her direction.

"Everyone knows you torched that boat yourself," said Willy. "It's obvious."

"And how did I do that, then?" asked Ned. "If you recall, I was safely tucked up in bed when it happened and there are witnesses to prove it. They woke me up when they came banging on the door to see if I was alright."

"It's true," said Alfie, leaping to his dad's defence. "He slept through the whole thing."

"Maybe you used some sort of remote device to blow it up, then," suggested Willy.

"You'll be accusing me of being in the IRA next," said Ned. "It was an accident, pure and simple. The electrics were screwed, that's what the firemen said."

"And whose fault was that? I can't believe you're copping for the insurance. It can't have been worth bugger all."

"Twenty grand they're paying me," said Ned. "Enough for a replacement and loss of earnings."

"Bloody hell, mate, how did you convince them it was worth that much?" asked Willy. "You should run for council. You're even more crooked than Gordon."

"How do you mean?" asked Jenna, who was eager to hear about any aspersions being cast on Gordon, even if it was only from Willy whose opinions were dubious at the best of times.

"Everyone knows he's bent," he replied, but didn't elaborate further.

"Well, if he is, I'm going to get some evidence," said Jenna. "Now that I'm running against him in the election."

"Yeah, in which you've got no chance," said Willy dismissively.

Jenna knew that sadly, under current circumstances he was right. The truth was people like Willy were never going to take her seriously because she was both young and a woman. It was just indicative of the attitudes of the time. Things were going to have to change dramatically over the next few weeks if she was going to turn things around, otherwise Gordon would cruise to a comfortable victory.

"What are you doing in here, anyway?" said Ned to Willy. "Hasn't the ice cream season started?"

"No point yet," said Willy. "I know it was sunny today but it's too cold still. It's hardly worth me bothering for a handful of kids up at the caravan park, so I might as well enjoy a few more beers while I still can."

At this point, he hopped off his stool and headed for the gents, giving Alfie a chance to talk to his father.

"So what are you going to do now, Dad?"

"Get another boat, of course. Those mackerel won't catch themselves."

"But, Dad, you said yourself how tough it's getting to make a living doing that. Jack has packed it in and George was saying in here the other night that he's retiring in the summer. If you've got the money to buy and kit out a new boat, this is the perfect time to do what we talked about."

"I've told you before, I've no interest in running fishing trips for tourists. I don't like them."

"It's a huge opportunity!" added Jenna. "I saw Jack going out earlier and there must have been a good dozen or more people on his boat. And the tourist season has barely started yet."

As if on cue, Jack strolled confidently into the pub beaming from ear to ear, promptly pulling out a large wad of pound notes from his pocket.

"What's everyone having?" he asked, just as Willy returned from the toilets.

There were about eight or nine people in the pub, including a pair of holidaymakers who had just come in. They were wrapped up in thick coats and were warming themselves up by the fire. Jack generously extended his offer not only to the regulars but to this couple too.

"Pint of Carling Black Label for me," said Willy, always first in line if any free drinks were going.

"What's with all the splashing the cash?" asked Ned.

"I've had a super day," said Jack. "I've done three boat trips, and taken over seventy quid. Just for sailing around for an hour or two each time. And that's in April. What's it going to be like in the summer?"

Ned's eyes lit up, finally cottoning on to the possibilities, as one of the tourists who had been out on Jack's boat piped up.

"We had a great time!" said the young woman. "I've always wanted to see the seals."

"Do you like fishing?" asked Ned, turning to her partner.

"I love it," said the man keenly. "Do you know anyone who runs any fishing trips from here?"

"Not yet, but I soon will," said Ned, turning back to Alfie. "Alright, boy, I'm convinced. Surf shack it is for you, fishing trips for me."

"Nice one, Dad," said Alfie, who was used to his father's sudden changes of heart whenever he sniffed there was some money to be had. "I knew you'd come round eventually."

Alfie was already pressing ahead with his surf shack plans. He had secured permission from the district council months ago, submitting a simple sketch and filling out a short form, after which they granted him the right to put up a small temporary structure. It would be about the size of a single-car garage, mostly wood on raised stakes driven into the sand, designed so it could be removed if ever required.

No permanent foundations were needed, just a sturdy, well-anchored frame that would keep the boards and wetsuits dry and safe. In a few weeks, he'd have a proper place to hire out gear to holidaymakers. He was also keen on offering surfing lessons but wasn't sure how he'd manage both teaching and running the hire shop. But he had plenty of time to figure that out. Jenna, keen to encourage him, offered to assist on that front when she could find time.

While he was working on his project, Jenna turned her attention back to the looming election, for which the odds still seemed stacked against her. She could talk about the need for sea defences all she wanted, but that alone wasn't going to be enough to alter the dyed-in-the-wool voting habits of the constituents. She needed to seriously undermine Gordon's position in some way. This wasn't intended to be malicious or underhand. If he had been up to no good, as Willy had suggested, then his misdeeds needed to be uncovered.

At first, she believed exposing his suspected financial dealings might be enough. But soon, she would discover that what lay beneath Gordon's smooth and sophisticated businesslike exterior was far darker than just dirty money.

She had been hoping the bracelet might give her some pointers, but it hadn't done much during the first half of April. With the election just three weeks away, she was beginning to question where all this was going. One area she did feel far more confident in was her relationship with Alfie. Now that his life was no longer in danger, she allowed herself to grow closer to him, and as spring blossomed, so did their romance.

It culminated in a special moment for them on the first genuinely warm evening of the year. Alfie had been working from dawn until dusk on his new shack every day for a fortnight, and now that it was finished, he wanted to show it off to her. They wandered down to the beach at dusk, enjoying the vibrant hues of orange and red stretching across the sky.

It was around eight in the evening and still pleasantly warm – enough for them both to be wearing light summer clothing for the first time that year. Alfie had made it a small occasion, bringing along a bottle of white wine and two glasses in a picnic basket, so they could toast the official completion of the new shack.

Despite the fine weather, the beach was deserted, leaving them to enjoy some time alone. They settled by the shack's doorway, sipping wine and relishing the quiet intimacy of this private time together. Jenna savoured every second, remembering how these moments had never been destined to happen in the other timeline. And as they kissed, slowly and tenderly, she felt it was time to take things further.

"You know what we should do?" she asked, looking directly into his eyes. "We should christen this place properly."

He needed no further encouragement. There, on the shack's wooden floor, Jenna gave herself to Alfie for the first time. Although she had experienced sex many times in her former life, those encounters had never been completely satisfying, and as for losing her virginity? In the other timeline, the sordid circumstances of it had haunted her for life.

Now, all of that was washed away with the receding tide, as if it had never happened. Tonight, within the simple wooden structure, with the sound of waves breaking on the shore, everything was perfect.

Afterwards they lay close together, wrapped in each other's arms as the night deepened, but it wasn't pitch dark in the shack, as the half-moon was casting light through the open doorway. With the clear night, the temperature had begun to drop, and Jenna pulled Alfie nearer, wondering if they should stay there until dawn or return home. Other than the picnic blanket Alfie had brought along, they had nothing else to stave off the cold, but despite that she didn't want the evening to end.

Then, quite unexpectedly, the bracelet began to pulse red and Jenna felt an impulse to step outside. What could be happening out there at this hour, and why would it matter so urgently?

"Why are you getting up?" asked Alfie, surprised at her sudden movement as she fumbled around for her discarded clothing in the semi-darkness.

"Call of nature," she replied, stepping outside and immediately spotting a figure about a hundred yards away, heading towards the rocky outcrops at the far end of the beach.

"Alfie," she whispered as loudly as she dared. "Come and look at this."

Together, they looked at the man walking in the opposite direction from them. With the semi-moonlight and the brilliantly starlit sky, unspoiled by any light pollution, it was easy enough to identify him.

"That's Gordon," said Alfie, echoing Jenna's instinctive conclusion. She had sensed it was him before even getting a proper look. That was probably down to the bracelet again.

"Now what on earth would he be doing down here at this time of night?" asked Alfie.

"I've no idea but I think we should find out, don't you?" replied Jenna.

"Absolutely," said Alfie, pulling on his light jacket and handing Jenna hers.

They followed him towards the shoreline, where jagged rocks stretched out into the sea. Beyond lay a small cove, inaccessible on foot except for a couple of hours around low tide. That was where Gordon seemed to be heading. They crept along behind him, tracking his footprints on the wet sand recently uncovered by the receding tide, hoping he wouldn't look back.

He disappeared behind the rocks as they carefully made their way towards the outcrops that marked the boundary between this beach and the cove. They followed Gordon's path, which wasn't generally recommended, since getting caught on the wrong side of the rocks when the tide came back in could lead to being stranded there for hours.

"Can you smell that?" asked Alfie, as a whiff of smoke reached Jenna's nostrils.

"Someone's having a bonfire," she replied. They paused behind a large jagged boulder, some six feet high. After years of playing here as children, they knew every inch of these unchanging rocks, even in the dark.

Curious, they peered around the edge of the boulder, just as Gordon approached a group of several others, all wearing heavy robes and standing in a circle around a fire. One of them passed Gordon a similar set of robes, which he put on, joining the others as the fire lit up their outlines, casting flickering shadows. Notably, Gordon's robes were white, while all the others were brown, suggesting perhaps that he was their leader.

"What are they doing?" asked Alfie, as the figures began marching around the fire in a circle, chanting low, rhythmic words Jenna couldn't quite decipher.

"I think it's some sort of coven," she said, as the pungent smoke from the fire grew stronger. Then Gordon tossed something into the flames, which crackled and flared. The group's movements slowed, and then they cast off their robes and whatever clothing they had on beneath. Jenna could see there were both men and women present, about twelve people altogether. What followed might have made her blush, had she and Alfie not been doing the same thing less than an hour before.

"They're having an orgy!" exclaimed Alfie, watching the bodies entwine in every possible combination. Jenna wasn't sure who the woman was that Gordon was cavorting with, but she was certain it wasn't his wife. He was in his fifties, and this young woman couldn't have been any older than Jenna. As for the others, there were a couple of men she recognised from nearby villages, one of whom she was sure was District Councillor Vince Norton, from further up the coast. He came into the pub from time to time and acted every bit as entitled as Gordon.

The whole thing had a ritualistic, almost animalistic quality as if tapping into some half-forgotten folklore, with chanting continuing throughout. Not wanting to risk discovery or getting trapped by the tide, Jenna suggested they slip away, and Alfie agreed, so they retreated quietly to the village.

"That was unbelievable," said Jenna, once they had returned to the normality of the seafront. "If the parishioners knew about this, Gordon would be finished."

"Would he, though?" asked Alfie. "I mean, it was all rather sordid, but were they breaking any laws? Technically, they were only doing what we were doing in the shack."

"Yes, with women less than half their age, who were blatantly not their wives. We're a young couple in love which is a completely different scenario."

"Is that your roundabout way of telling me you love me, Jenna? You've never said it before."

"I guess it is," she said, and after the moment they had shared earlier, there was no question that she did.

"Then I love you too," he replied, and they shared a long goodnight kiss outside the pub. It was after closing time by now, so Jenna let herself in the back door, went up to her room, and pondered what to do next.

What Alfie had said was true. Gordon hadn't necessarily been doing anything illegal, but it was certainly immoral and the scandal would rock a community like Pencarven to its core. The trouble was, she had no way of proving it. Yet the bracelet was always a few steps ahead, and Jenna sensed that it would guide her towards finding the evidence she needed; she was right because it came good the very next day.

When she got up, she had a telephone number engraved in her head. It was a London number beginning with 01, though she had no idea who it belonged to. What she did know was exactly what the bracelet wanted her to say to whoever might be on the other end of the line. This included giving away the secret of her true identity and telling them about the bracelet.

She waited until her mother had gone round to see Shelly at the café and her father was busy bottling up, before retreating to the pub's private living room and dialling the number. It rang a couple of times, and then a male voice answered.

"Keith Diamond, *News of the World*, can I help?"

She didn't have to think, the words just came into her head, as if the bracelet were dictating them to her.

"Hello, Keith. My name is Jenna Rae and I am the custodian of the bracelet for 1983."

That was all she needed to say to get Keith's attention, and they spent the next few minutes chatting away, as Keith explained to Jenna that he had been through the same experience as her in 1980. He was intrigued to hear from her, having passed on the bracelet after his year was over, assuming that would be the end of it.

Once all the explanations were done, she hit him with it.

"I've got a story for you," she said, going on to outline all the details about what she and Alfie had seen, which Keith lapped up. It was exactly the sort of thing his paper loved, and as far as he was concerned, if the bracelet wanted to call on his services, it had to be for a good cause. She even knew the exact date and time when Gordon would be holding his next orgy because the bracelet had furnished her with the details. All Keith had to do was to come down to Cornwall and get the story.

"Just one thing," he said before he rang off. "I'll be bringing my photographer, Jimmy, with me. He doesn't know about any of this bracelet stuff so we'll need to keep schtum when he's around. Call me back in a couple of days and we'll finalise the details."

There was a week to go before all this would happen, and during that week, the bracelet went into overdrive, sending her here, there, and everywhere on fact-finding missions that would, to put it biblically, damn Gordon for all eternity. It couldn't have made it easier for her.

She was able to get into Gordon's office in the dead of night, thanks to a key left for the cleaner under a flowerpot. Then she opened his safe, the bracelet having directed her to where he had written the combination on the underside of a desk drawer with a felt-tip pen – an unbelievably idiotic thing to do. This laxness suggested he had complete confidence that he was above suspicion, and with the lack of crime in Pencarven, he likely assumed no one would ever have cause to break in.

If she had expected to find blatantly incriminating evidence, like an envelope full of cash and a note from a grateful donor, she was to be disappointed. No one would leave anything that obvious lying around, even in a safe, no matter how much they believed that they would never be investigated. What she did find was a red folder, tied up with a piece of string, which the bracelet encouraged her to open.

The folder was full of letters, receipts, and contracts, none of which looked untoward at first glance. Closer inspection revealed several invoices on headed paper

110

from a company called Cornish Coastal Infrastructure Advisory Ltd, a name Jenna didn't recognise. The fees listed were eye-watering for so-called 'market evaluation' services amounting to hundreds or even thousands of pounds in some cases.

All the letters were signed by Gordon, who was the head of this company, with the business address in Tintagel. That was odd since Gordon's official accountancy business was based in Camelford.

Jenna was no expert, but she was convinced these payments were far beyond whatever the legitimate going rate was for such services, and why would a local council official be accepting them anyway? Surely that was a conflict of interest? Of particular note was a payment from a building company working on a new estate in a settlement further up the coast. That area had received substantial sea defence investment the previous year.

The payment was dated three days after Gordon had voted against Pencarven's defences and was accompanied by handwritten scribbles including '£1,500 cash', the date of the council meeting, and the initials CA, JD, and VN, each with a tick next to them. She found similar cryptic notes on several other documents too. Jenna couldn't fully decode it, but she knew someone who could. She was certain that, pieced together correctly, this bundle of documents would paint a damning picture of corruption. In the hands of a savvy investigative journalist like Keith Diamond, it would be dynamite.

She couldn't take it with her right then. It was all about timing. She knew Gordon only came into the office on Fridays, so the papers needed to stay in the safe until the weekend. Keith was coming down on Sunday 24th, the date of the next meeting of the coven on the beach. All she had to do was slip into the office on Saturday night after dark, 'borrow' the file and give it to Keith to examine. So she replaced the folder in the safe, taking care to leave everything exactly as she had found it, apart from one thing.

Keith knew all about bugging offices and, at her request, had sent her some kit through the post, along with instructions on how to use it. This was something that the bracelet had suggested. She concealed the device as he had instructed, ready to listen in on Friday. Jenna thought this was probably another legal grey area, recalling a scandal over phone hacking sometime in the 2010s, but Keith seemed confident it wouldn't be a problem. According to him, it was only a problem if you got caught, and the bracelet would normally ensure that you didn't.

The bracelet knew what it was doing. On Friday, two members of the production team for the forthcoming movie visited Gordon to discuss permission to film in and around Pencarven. They had a budget set aside for this and were willing to pay handsomely for the privilege. Gordon was only too happy to offer his support, promising them a favourable deal with the council in return for an under-the-desk cash payment – something to which they eagerly agreed. And Jenna now had the whole exchange on tape.

By the time Sunday arrived, after a couple more telephone conversations with Keith, everything was in place. Jenna stressed how important it was that she and Keith were not seen together. Her involvement in all this had to remain hidden. Gordon's actions were reprehensible, but if Jenna's methods of exposing him came to light, it could damage her chances in the election too. Breaking into an office and raiding a safe, even for a good cause, wouldn't look great to voters.

With that in mind, Keith and Jimmy booked themselves into the caravan park, away from the village, arriving just before teatime. When Jenna went to meet them, they discussed their plans in detail. They had to be careful, given that Jimmy didn't know about the bracelet and Keith had warned they must keep that quiet.

"This is all well and good," said Jimmy. "But I still don't know how you figured out all this stuff in the first place."

"By keeping her eyes and ears open, Jimmy, something you could learn a thing or two about," said Keith. "Now, I expect you're hungry. Why don't you go into the village and pick us up something to eat? You do have a chippy in Pencarven, I assume?"

"Of course," said Jenna. "But it doesn't open on a Sunday except in high summer. There's a Chinese in Camelford open seven days a week."

"Lovely," said Keith. "Off you pop then, Jimmy. Get one of those banquet meals for three. You'll join us, won't you, Jenna?"

"Of course."

"Better make it a meal for four then, because Jimmy eats twice as much as everybody else. And don't forget the prawn crackers."

With Jimmy gone, Jenna and Keith talked freely about the bracelet and their past experiences. Jenna found it fascinating to hear what Keith had done back in 1980, and he was equally intrigued by her story and how she'd acquired the bracelet from Wendy Wood.

"Wendy Wood!" he exclaimed. "I ran a story on her last year, not a very flattering one, I'm afraid. I feel a bit bad about that now. The old Keith wouldn't have thought twice about it, but I'm kind of a reformed character these days. Some of the stuff that goes on at the paper makes me a tad uncomfortable, to say the least. Also, it was Jimmy who took that infamous photo when her bra popped off. Looks like the bracelet didn't see that one coming."

"I doubt she's bothered," said Jenna. "Things turned out well for her in the end. There is one thing I don't quite understand, though. If you were here for a year, and then went back to 2020, how come you remember all this?"

"That I don't quite understand," said Keith. "I believe part of me went back to the future, and part stayed here. I know that I was confused for a day or two after it happened, and I can't remember anything about the future and the other Keith's life anymore. It's as if there are two of us – quite difficult to explain, to be honest."

They got down to business, with Jenna showing Keith the documents she had taken from Gordon's safe, and playing him the tape recorded from the bug in his office.

"This Gordon Pentreath is a right villain," declared Keith. "It'll be a joy to take him down, and if this coven business is as juicy as you say, it's massive brownie points for me and Jimmy at the paper."

"Oh, it is," promised Jenna. "You'll see."

114

Getting the pictures they needed required expertise, and despite Keith's general disparaging of Jimmy, it was clear he knew his stuff when it came to taking pictures. They discussed the best way to go about this over the meal when Jimmy returned from Camelford.

"We can't use flash photography, obviously, or we'll give ourselves away," said Jimmy, as he munched on a spring roll. "What I can do is use high-quality black and white film, with a wide aperture lens, provided there's enough light from the fire to illuminate the members of the coven."

"It was clear enough last time," said Jenna. "And tonight's a full moon, according to my diary."

"Even better," said Jimmy, looking out the caravan window at the clear sky. "If it doesn't cloud over, conditions will be perfect."

"The most important thing is that we aren't seen," stressed Jenna. "But there are plenty of concealed places among the rocks. Can you zoom in from a safe distance? A hundred yards or more should do it. They won't hear us over the sound of the sea."

"You can count on Jimmy," said Keith. "And I don't say that very often. We've done this sort of night work before."

Jenna kept these plans secret from Alfie. She couldn't think of a way of explaining how she knew the exact date of the next coven meeting so told him she was having a quiet night in. Then, armed with the key he had given her after she helped him stock the new shack, she, Keith, and Jimmy headed there at sunset. They concealed themselves among the brand-new surfboards, having

115

lugged the camera equipment down from the park earlier.

It was a couple of hours before Gordon emerged, crossing the beach just as he had before. The three observers followed at a safe distance, finding a perfect vantage point where Jimmy could set up his tripod and angle the lens through a gap in the rocks, zooming in to get the best shots he could. Keith tried using his Dictaphone to record the chanting but admitted that from this far away it wouldn't pick much up.

"Doesn't matter," he said. "We don't need sound anyway."

They watched as the coven disrobed once again, the firelight revealing everything they needed to see. Jimmy focused on getting clear snaps of Gordon's face and as many other members as possible. The stronger flames and full moon helped produce better-lit shots than he had dared hope for.

"Put your eyes away, Jimmy," remarked Keith, as his companion gazed at the naked female bodies cavorting about. "He loves this sort of thing, Jenna. It's why he became a photographer. He used to work on Page Three on one of the dailies before we moved across to the *News of the World.*"

"We'll have to censor most of this before it goes in the paper," said Jimmy.

"Not a problem," said Keith. "We'll just black out the dangly bits. Though knowing you, you'll probably be keeping a few copies for your private collection, won't you? Better make sure Penny doesn't find them, though.

116

Didn't she make you get rid of your 'art' collection when you got married?"

Jimmy ignored him, concentrating on getting more shots. Once he was happy he had enough, they made their way back to the caravan where they enjoyed a celebratory drink and toasted a job well done. Before Jenna went home, Keith assured her that the story would be in the following week's paper, which was the last Sunday before the election. Then, he gave her back Gordon's files to return to the safe, having made copies of all the relevant material with a microfilm camera, a technique he claimed he had learned from a former secret agent known only as Locksmith Larry.

"There's just one thing," she said before they parted. "Do you need that tape of Gordon taking a bribe in his office? Because I'd like to hang on to that. I've got a feeling it may come in useful later, and it's always handy to have a card up your sleeve."

"I've got more than enough to hang, draw, and quarter him already," replied Keith. "You keep it, if you think you can make use of it."

"Oh, I will," she said, as she bade them farewell and headed home.

All things considered, this had been a very productive night's work.

May 1983

True to his word, Keith broke the story in the edition of the *News of the World* dated the 1st of May 1983. It was the day of Pencarven's spring fair, held annually on the beach to celebrate May Day.

The weather could not have been better with warm sunshine, a light breeze, and a brilliant azure sky. The beach was alive with colour and sound, with stalls lined up on the sand above the high tide line, and children dressed in traditional smocks and ribbons waiting excitedly by the tall maypole that had been dug into the sand for the occasion.

The official proceedings would begin at midday, when they would commence dancing in elaborate patterns, weaving their long colourful ribbons around the pole, in a tradition that went back hundreds of years.

Jenna, sadly, knew that this would be the last generation of children to do this unless she managed to make the changes needed to preserve Pencarven's traditions. By the new millennium, with fewer and fewer children being born to local families, and the proliferation of second homes, all of these events would cease.

The fair was in full swing, with local families, visitors from neighbouring villages and early-season holidaymakers mingling happily. The attractions included all the usual stalls: a tombola, and local people selling their arts and crafts, plus there were donkey rides and a carousel for the children.

It was a great opportunity for the locals to get the tourist season off to a good start. Shelly had closed the café for the morning and was instead serving pasties and selling her little baskets of seashells which she still foraged for on the beach most days.

Meanwhile, the colourful ice cream van with Chilly Willy's logo emblazoned across it was doing brisk business to queues of eager customers in the warm sunshine. With plenty of other food on offer, aromas of doughnuts, popcorn, burgers, and hot dogs mingled on the breeze, tempting all those present.

It was a good day's business for David and Morwenna too, who ran an outside bar in a beer tent that would do a roaring trade all afternoon, being granted a special licence to serve outside the normally restricted Sunday hours.

The stalls stretched down to the far end of the beach, where Alfie's surf shack was open for business for the very first time. The beach had a lifeguard employed from May to September, who placed flags on the beach to show the recommended swimming area, and Alfie had come to an arrangement with her for a small area to be designated for surfing. He was thrilled to see how many people were interested, hiring wetsuits and boards to try their hand at the sport which was increasing in popularity in the UK.

Jenna wasn't a vengeful person, she only wanted justice for those she perceived to have done wrong, but she couldn't deny she was relishing what was about to happen. Gordon had been invited to officially open the festivities, on the very day that millions of people across the country had woken up to sordid revelations about him being splashed across the pages of a major Sunday paper. But Gordon, who was presumably more of a broadsheet man, probably never stooped to looking at the tabloids. He appeared blissfully unaware, as he stepped up to a temporary dais, preparing to give his speech.

As usual on such occasions, he was all puffed up and full of his own importance, looking rather overdressed in his snazzy suit compared to the shorts and T-shirts of most of the men in the crowd. He always felt it was essential to ensure that they knew he was better than them.

He cleared his throat, adjusted the lapels of his jacket, and gave one of his fake beaming smiles as he prepared to speak. And then he noticed the crowd behaving oddly. In several places, small groups weren't looking at him as he expected, but were clustered around tabloid newspapers, engrossed in something.

This was happening in several spots, and then some of them looked up, stared at him, and in a few cases, pointed.

"That's him!" yelled out one young man.

"Dirty pervert!" called out a middle-aged woman.

Jenna watched, fascinated at the perplexed look on Gordon's face. That he didn't have a clue what was going on made this all the more delicious, as he attempted to begin his introduction.

"Ladies and gentlemen, as your local elected district councillor – and I do hope you're going to vote for me again this Thursday – it gives me great pleasure…"

That was about as far as he got before he was drowned out in a chorus of boos. It was time for Jenna to step in.

"Excuse me, can I borrow that a second?" she said, turning to a woman next to her who was clutching a copy of the *News of the World.* "I'll give it back."

The woman acceded to her request, so holding the paper tightly, Jenna weaved her way through the crowd until she was able to join Gordon, still bemused, on his makeshift podium.

"What's going on, Jenna?" he asked. "Who are all these people booing in the crowd? Your supporters? Rent-a-mob is an extremely underhanded way of doing politics, I must say and it won't work. This is Pencarven, not a picket line on Merseyside. You're still not going to win."

"Oh, I think I am," she said, stepping up to the microphone and addressing the crowd.

"Can we have a little hush, please?" she asked. Eager to hear what she wanted to say, the onlookers quietened down.

"Councillor Pentreath," she began, holding the newspaper spread out so he could see the damning images and headlines, "I'm sure we'd all love to know if you can explain this."

"What? That's not me," he tried to bluster, to no avail. Jimmy's incriminating photographs of his participation in the coven's orgy were as clear as day. There was no mistaking him, and as for Keith's summary of his shady financial dealings, they were as damning as they could be.

"Oh, I think it is you," she replied, as the crowd watched in awe before she turned to them. "Tell me, ladies and gentlemen, is this the sort of person we want representing us here in Pencarven?"

A thunderous "No!" erupted from the crowd.

"I thought not," she said. "Thankfully, there is an election in four days, and I'm standing against him. So you all know what to do."

They certainly did, chanting Jenna's name as Gordon made a rapid retreat, suitably humiliated. Jenna then took over proceedings, introducing the children's maypole dance. The accompanying folk musicians struck up a lively tune, and the crowd redirected its focus to the long-standing tradition in front of them.

Jenna knew now that she couldn't fail to win the election, with Gordon's disgrace being the talk of the village in the days ahead. An off-the-record conversation with Matt in the pub suggested a criminal investigation was to be launched into the exposed councillor's business dealings, though he couldn't go into details.

As for Gordon, although no warrant had been issued for his arrest, he had well and truly gone to ground. When the day of the election dawned, he was nowhere to be seen, having correctly surmised that the game was up and that he no longer had any chance of winning. Shelly, always on the ball with the gossip, found out that his wife had thrown him out, and took great joy in telling everyone who came into her café.

As Jenna stood outside the polling station at the church hall, she was gratified by the number of people who offered their support and told her she had their vote, and so it proved, with her winning in a landslide. It was another battle won and she was now the new district councillor. What with her commitments at the caravan park, her offer to help out at the surf shack when Alfie was giving lessons, and her shifts at the bar, she was going to have an extremely busy few months ahead of her.

Something had to give, and her next shift in the pub, a couple of nights after her election win, was enough for Jenna to decide it was time to hang up her barmaid's apron.

To begin with, she had been listening to Trevor, the middle-aged owner of the small amusement arcade on the seafront, moaning endlessly about the new pound coins introduced a couple of weeks ago. It started when he handed her a five-pound note to pay for his usual tipple, a double gin and tonic, and she gave him his change in the new chunky golden coins. These were still relatively rare, with only a few passing through the pub so far instead of the familiar green one-pound notes, but Trevor wasn't happy.

"Do you know how much trouble these damn things are causing me?" he asked. "I already had some stroppy woman in the arcade today asking why the fruit machines wouldn't take them."

"Can't you adapt them?" asked Jenna.

"I am, slowly, but it takes a lot of time and money," replied Trevor. "And what annoys me most of all is that I already went through all this hassle last year for the new twenty-pence coin. Now I've got to do it all over again. And what next? They'll be bringing out a two-pound coin before you know it."

"It must be a nightmare." said Jenna, trying to sound vaguely interested, although she wasn't. She wasn't fond of Trevor. He was boring and she remembered once being stuck behind him in the bank queue in Camelford while he paid in a weekend's takings from the arcade. That was a lot of coins to count and she had been there a good twenty minutes while he piled endless bags of copper onto the counter.

But it wasn't just the likes of Trevor who she was having to deal with. Since the election, Jenna had become the focal point for anyone with a minor complaint about anything going on in Pencarven. Being behind the bar meant she was a sitting duck and every few minutes, someone would sidle up to the bar and say something along the lines of, "Jenna, just the person I want to see," before launching into complaints about everything from dog poo outside the chip shop to weeds in the playground.

She tried explaining that she was working and suggesting they took it up with the Parish Council or save it for her Friday surgery – the sessions she was taking over from Gordon in his old office. Unfortunately they took the view that, since she was here, they might as well bring it up now. Striking while the iron was hot was an expression they frequently coined and not wanting to appear rude so early in her new political career, she felt obliged to listen.

At the caravan park she was spared these encounters, dealing mostly with holidaymakers who knew nothing of her council role. So the pub was the job that had to go. She only worked a few shifts in the summer anyway and hoped it wouldn't be a big deal. Yet when she brought it up at breakfast the following morning, it didn't go down well.

She broke the news just as her father opened an official-looking brown envelope.

"…so I'm going to give up working behind the bar, at least until the summer's over," she concluded.

"I don't believe this!" exclaimed David.

She hadn't expected enthusiasm, but she soon realised his reaction was driven by the letter he was holding rather than her announcement, as he started waving it in the air.

"What is it?" asked Morwenna, setting down the toast rack with four triangular half-slices of bread before him.

"Bloody annual insurance premium renewal for the pub! It's more than doubled!"

"It can't have," said Morwenna.

"It bloody has! How can they justify that?" He scanned the letter, looking for details. "Something about increased flood risk," he said.

"They've probably had some claims from that minor flood we had earlier in the year," suggested Morwenna.

"Which I warned everyone about," said Jenna. "Pity so many chose not to listen."

"Well, that's it, we can't afford it," declared David.

"You have to pay it, Dad," insisted Jenna, remembering what had happened before.

In the original timeline, at Christmas 1983, the flood striking the pub proved catastrophic when David, having failed to keep the insurance up to date, was left facing financial ruin. But it wasn't just that which led him to take his own life. Furious with David, Morwenna had confessed to an ongoing affair with Blake and that she was pregnant with his child – that child being Elliot who four decades later would evict Jenna from the caravan park.

That night, Morwenna had walked out and David drowned his sorrows in an entire bottle of whisky, then hung himself. There had been no one there to stop him. Jenna had accepted an offer from Morgan to stay up at the caravan park overnight due to the flooded state of the pub and to escape her parents' rows. It was she who found him the next morning, another event to add to the list of tragedies that had traumatised her during that dreadful year.

What neither of her parents knew was that Jenna herself had also been pregnant by Blake earlier that year in that old timeline. She had never been able to bring herself to tell anyone, being so ashamed and haunted by it all.

Back then, Blake had arrived in late May, all money and charm. On the very first night, he latched on to Jenna, who was young, impressionable, and vulnerable. She was also still grieving over Alfie's death.

That night, she lost her virginity to Blake in his luxury motorhome at the caravan park. It hadn't been pleasant. He plied her with drink and became forceful when she expressed reservations about whether she ought to be doing it. With time, Jenna came to understand that she hadn't given proper consent. Later, she learned she was far from the only one. When her old school friend, Janet, came back to Pencarven years later for a family funeral, she revealed that Blake had outright raped her.

After that first night, Blake had ruthlessly tossed Jenna aside, moving on to other women in the village, some even younger than her. When Jenna discovered she was pregnant, several weeks later, she approached him only for him to demand she get rid of it, driving her to a private surgeon in Exeter and paying for the abortion.

She had been given little say in this decision, and the experience had tarnished all her future relationships. Eventually, she was left with years of regret, particularly when she reached the age when she realised that it was unlikely she would ever have a child. That had been her only pregnancy.

When Morwenna announced she was with child, Jenna had expected Blake to spurn her in the same way as he had treated her. But that wasn't how it turned out at all.

By then, Blake had decided he wanted to settle in Pencarven, having become quite enamoured of the place. With David dead, and the pub in a sorry state with no prospect of reopening, he saw the perfect opportunity to get a foothold in the village.

He married Morwenna, who in a few months gave birth to baby Elliot. He then spent a small fortune restoring and modernising the pub, as well as contributing a large sum of his own money to finally building the sea defences that would prevent such damage from occurring again.

All of this, of course, made him incredibly popular in the village, where he could seemingly do no wrong and was now not only 'Blake the famous film star' but also 'Blake the local hero'. Only Jenna, and the other women who had been abused by him, knew the truth, and they were too scared to speak up, and even if they had done, it was doubtful anyone would have listened.

He soon had Gordon, who was still a councillor in that timeline, in his back pocket, controversially gaining planning permission for a huge mansion up on the cliffs, sweeping away habitats of rare sea birds in the process. Soon, he began to invite his friends to visit. Just as taken by Pencarven's charm as he was, they also decided they wanted to own a piece of it, and their yachts soon joined Blake's in the harbour.

At first, this benefitted the local economy but it was storing up problems for the future. Pencarven's gentrification had begun, leading to soaring house prices and rents, eventually pricing the original residents out of the market. It also attracted a new breed of holidaymaker – one who wanted tapas and cocktails, not chips and beer.

It was vital her father remained insured against disaster, so she took it upon herself to badger him into keeping up the premiums, even if she had to contribute herself. However, David was in no mood for her advice that morning, irritated not only by the letter but also by her announcement that she wouldn't be working behind the bar anymore.

The insurance was only half the battle – the biggest issue was to get the proper defences built so the pub wouldn't get flooded in the first place, insurance or no insurance. But how was she going to do that? At her first council meeting the following week, she raised the matter, leading to a detailed discussion and some hard facts and figures.

Put simply, the council couldn't afford it. The estimated cost of the work was around two hundred thousand pounds, and they only had money left in the annual budget for half that. She suggested fundraising for the remainder, but they considered it highly unlikely she would be able to raise that kind of money.

Not from fundraising, perhaps, but she still had that ace up her sleeve with the tape recording from Gordon's meeting with the two producers from the film company. So she put a proposal to the council: if she could acquire the other hundred thousand, would they pay the rest? Not expecting there to be a hope in hell of her actually achieving that, they agreed. Now all she needed to do was get the money, and she had already figured out exactly how she was going to go about it. She didn't even need the bracelet to help her.

When the producers, Brad and Harvey, returned, seeking Gordon out at the council office, she had a surprise in store for them. They didn't know anything about recent events and weren't expecting to see her. Although Blake was a British actor, this was a big Hollywood blockbuster movie, and her visitors were both Americans who didn't keep up with local Cornish politics.

Jenna had agonised long and hard about what to do about the production of this film, for she now had the power to prevent it from being filmed in Pencarven altogether. Brad and Harvey had come here hoping that permission to film in the village and the caves would all be green-lit by now. But those arrangements had only been made verbally with Gordon previously, and with his sudden departure, were now null and void.

She could stop the filming altogether, simply by threatening to reveal the tape's contents, incriminating not only Gordon but Brad and Harvey as well, unless they upped sticks and found somewhere else to make their movie. That way, Blake would never come to Pencarven, and the village's heritage would remain intact.

The downside to doing that was that with the lack of funding required, the village would remain exposed to flooding, and it would allow Blake to pursue his predatory activities elsewhere. This was not an easy decision, and she needed to think strategically, balancing the various risks to the village's future against each other and her desire to see Blake face justice.

In the end, she decided it was better to lure Blake here, so she could expose him for the monster he truly was, thus protecting a whole future generation of potential victims. How she would do this, she didn't know yet, but she had dealt with Gordon easily enough with the bracelet's help. She trusted it would guide her again when the time came. And at the same time, she could get the money she needed.

Brad and Harvey rubbed her up the wrong way from the start, talking down to her with a misogynistic swagger as soon as she explained who she was. This was not helped by Brad repeatedly addressing her as 'little lady'. They seemed unable to accept that it was possible that she, barely out of her teens, had replaced Gordon as councillor.

"We had an agreement with Gordon that we could start filming in the village later this month," insisted Harvey.

"Yes, I know all about your agreement," said Jenna; then she played them the tape, watching their arrogance drain away as it reached the part where after revealing their budget, Gordon had proposed a deal.

"Oh, I'm confident you'll be able to get away with paying a lot less than that," said Gordon via the mono speaker on the cheap Boots own brand cassette recorder Jenna had brought along. "Most of the others on the council haven't got a clue when it comes to this sort of thing. Let's say I go to them and propose that you've offered five thousand pounds for local community projects to compensate for the disruption the filming will cause. They'll bite your hand off."

"Really, is that all?" asked Brad, his voice clearly recognisable on the recording.

"Plus my cut, of course," said Gordon. "I'll need three envelopes, each containing two thousand pounds in cash. That's for me and one for each of the other two councillors we need to push it through. Then you'll get permission, no problem."

"How soon can we start filming?"

"The sooner the better," said Gordon. "By the end of May, I would say. I'll get it all through at the next meeting. You said you need about a month in the village and a couple of weeks in the caves. If you get all that done, you'll be finished before the school summer holidays in July and August. There's no way you can come here during that period. Pencarven will be packed out with holidaymakers."

Jenna stopped the tape at that point.

"Rather damning, don't you think?" said Jenna. "Of course, what Gordon didn't mention was the small matter of an election coming up between then and the next council meeting. I don't know if you know what he's been up to, but this should shed some light on it."

She handed them the newspaper that had destroyed Gordon's career, which they examined with distaste. Not being readers of British tabloids, this had also slipped past them.

"I was instrumental in bringing that story to the press, so I'd advise you not to take me lightly," said Jenna. "I could have given them this recording too, but I decided against it. Otherwise, you wouldn't have come out of it smelling of roses, would you?"

"Look, what exactly is it you want, little lady?" asked Brad.

"Well, for a start, you can stop calling me little lady," she said.

"Do you want more money?" asked Harvey. "We'll give you double what Gordon wanted to push the deal through. Incidentally, you don't know where he is, do you? He's got six big ones of our money."

"Oh, I didn't realise you'd already paid him," said Jenna. "I doubt you'll see that again, and as for the other councillors, they won't dare oppose me after what happened to Gordon. They're terrified of being incriminated and are lying low. That's why they didn't say anything at this month's meeting where Gordon was supposed to propose the deal. With me taking his place it wasn't even mentioned. So there's nothing more that can be done now until the next meeting in June."

"We can't wait until then," protested Brad. "We've got a tight schedule."

"You can't film in high season unless you want your seventeenth-century setting to have modern-day tourists wandering into shot, so you'll just have to wait," said Jenna. "But don't worry, all is not lost. I've got a new proposal for you. Want to hear it?"

"We don't have much choice, do we, Brad?" asked Harvey. "This girl's got us over a barrel."

"Shoot, lady," said Brad.

"OK, so the full deal is now this. You announce that you are going to donate one hundred thousand pounds towards sea defences to be constructed here, with the insistence they be completed before December."

"That's outrageous and way over our budget!" protested Brad. "We've never paid that amount of money out to film anywhere."

"How much are you paying Blake Cadwallader for this film?" she asked.

"That's confidential," said Brad.

"Don't worry, I already know," she said, remembering that Blake had bragged to her about it when he had been driving her to the abortion. "Don't ask me how, but it's two million pounds. So I'm sure you can find a hundred grand down the back of the sofa. In return, you'll get full cooperation from me and the rest of the council, plus a lot of positive press coverage."

"And what's your cut?" asked Harvey.

"Nothing," said Jenna. "I don't do business the way Gordon did. But you don't get the green light until that money's been paid. And you film in September, after the bulk of the tourists have gone home. Once the sea defences are finished, that tape I played you earlier disappears forever."

Brad and Harvey looked at each other.

"Doesn't look like we have much choice, does it?" said Harvey. "It's too late to look for somewhere else and in any case, we haven't found anywhere remotely as good as here."

Brad agreed, and the two men shook hands with her.

"You're one fine businesswoman, little…" began Brad.

"Don't say lady or the deal's off!" interrupted Jenna.

And that concluded their dealings, leaving her in a pretty good place. By putting off the filming until September, she would delay Blake's arrival, giving herself more time to get established in her council role and figure out how to deal with him.

It also allowed time for the logistics of building the defences to be organised. It wasn't just a case of hiring someone to stack a load of bricks in front of the harbour. There would be surveys, design work, and a host of other preparations, all taking months. It was May now. Perhaps the work could take place in October and November, after the filming was completed but before the flood.

"Did I handle that alright?" she asked, seeking the bracelet's approval, and was pleased to see a green pulse in return. She was getting rather good at this.

June 1983

With everything seemingly under control, Jenna felt able to take stock and give herself a breather. In five short months, she had accomplished a great deal and already massively altered the course of events. Saving Alfie's life, and delaying Blake's arrival, already meant the remainder of the year would be nothing like the 1983 she had left behind.

When Alfie suggested a weekend away in Newquay, she was all for it. He had friends there from his stint working as a surf instructor the previous summer and had been invited back to take part in one of their annual competitions. This would be a chance for the two of them to properly spend some time together. Much as Jenna loved Pencarven's close-knit community, it could be hard to find privacy at times. The phrase 'everybody knew everybody else's business' was extremely apt.

Since they had consummated their relationship in the surf shack, opportunities for intimacy had been limited. Aside from the challenge of finding times and places to be alone, Pencarven was still rather old-fashioned in its outlook, and Alfie's father wouldn't allow Jenna to stay overnight with him, despite them both now being in their early twenties.

They had got frisky on the sofa on a couple of evenings when Ned had been out at the pub, but after the second time, when he came back early, they were left in a frantic scramble to do up buttons and zips in a state of semi-undress. After that, they decided not to risk it again. Perhaps they would have been better off in Alfie's bedroom, but then they would have faced the problem of smuggling her out. In the small cottage, where the stairs descended directly into the living room, there would have been no way to get past Ned without being spotted, once he'd settled into his favourite spot in front of the telly.

Having Alfie stay over at the pub was also out of the question because David was even more Victorian in his attitudes than Ned. When Jenna broached the subject of their trip away over breakfast, he immediately voiced his disapproval, just as he was mopping up the stray yolk from a fried egg that was oozing across his plate like the tide coming up the harbour.

"Together?" he said in dismay. "For a whole weekend? I trust you'll be having separate rooms?"

"Dad, this is the 1980s," she explained, something which felt like a weird thing to say. She still hadn't fully adjusted to the idea that she had travelled back forty years in time. "Things have changed since you grew up, and anyway, I'm twenty years old and the local district councillor – not some precocious teenager trying to sneak off behind the bike sheds with her boyfriend."

"Bugger," said David, who had been holding his piece of toast in mid-air, mouth open in disbelief at his precious daughter's open admission that she was sexually active. He had paused too long, giving the yolk time to drip down the front of his shirt. "Look what you've made me do. Now this isn't on, Jenna. Dirty weekends away indeed – whatever will people say? There was none of this sort of business with me and your mother before we married, was there, Morwenna?"

"There's not a lot now," said Morwenna, in a tone thick with her lack of fulfilment, as she turned from the toaster to replenish the table once again. There never seemed to be enough toast, no matter how much she made.

"And that's not strictly true," she added. "Don't you remember the night of that barn dance over Davidstow way?"

"I'm sure Jenna doesn't want to hear about that," said David hurriedly, before turning back to his daughter. "Now look, you're barely here as it is, what with your job and all this council stuff. I'm still not happy about you giving up working in the pub."

"She works bloody hard, David, and deserves a break. You should be proud of her. As far as I'm concerned, if she wants to go away for the weekend with Alfie, she should go. We ought to be grateful she's courting a local lad who's setting up a business here. At least it means they'll both probably stick around, unlike Jacob. We haven't seen him since Christmas."

That effectively settled the argument, so on the second Friday in June, Jenna and Alfie set off for Newquay, borrowing Ned's van for the weekend. He hadn't been too happy about them going either, but Alfie had promised to help him out the following week when his father was due to take proud possession of his new boat.

They left straight after Jenna's regular Friday morning council surgery, in glorious sunshine and clear skies. They opted for the B3314 rather than the A39, a far more scenic route, and the winding road close to the coast offered frequent tantalising views out to sea. The waters shone brilliantly under the midsummer sun, glinting beneath a sky of vibrant blue. Jenna had heard it said that Cornwall had the best light in the country in the summer, which was why so many artists flocked to places like St Ives.

Every so often, the van would round a bend to reveal a fresh panorama of sweeping sands and rugged, rocky cliffs. It was this iconic coastline that defined her county, the only place Jenna felt she could ever truly call home. Here and there she could spot fishing boats out at sea, while swooping gulls circled above, their cries a perpetual backdrop to her life. They were noisy and woke her up early in the morning sometimes, but she would miss them if they weren't there.

They had Radio Two on to begin with, which was what Ned liked to listen to in the van, but all that was being discussed on Jimmy Young's show was the previous days' general election, in which Margaret Thatcher and the Conservatives had won a second term in a landslide victory.

Despite her role in local politics, Jenna wasn't remotely interested. She was going to Newquay for the weekend to get away from such matters, so she re-tuned it to Radio One, where Simon Bates was hosting his *Golden Hour*. He was playing hits from a year in the late 1970s which wasn't that long ago from Alfie's perspective, but it certainly was from Jenna's.

As they approached Newquay, Alfie's excitement visibly grew. They caught a glimpse of the beach below, dotted with wetsuit-clad surfers in the waves, no doubt practising for the competition ahead. Turning to Jenna, he explained what made the day's conditions ideal.

"See how the breeze isn't coming straight onshore?" he said, nodding toward the distant break. "It's a light offshore wind, which holds the waves up longer so they stand taller before they crest. The swell's coming in clean sets, about shoulder height. Perfect for manoeuvres but not so massive it's dangerous. And the tide's mid-turn right now, which shapes the sandbanks just right under the water. Basically, you get long, peeling waves you can ride for ages without them closing out too soon."

As he spoke, his voice brimmed with excitement and anticipation in the way people did when they were talking about their passions. Jenna didn't understand half of what he had said, but it hardly mattered. His enthusiasm alone rubbed off on her, and she was thrilled that she was going to be there to cheer him on in the weekend's competition.

She had been slightly concerned about what the reception might be like at the B&B, even going so far as to suggest they pretend to be married, using the classic old Mr and Mrs Smith ruse. But such fears were unfounded. Like she had explained to her father earlier, this was the 1980s, not the 1950s, and attitudes, outside Pencarven at least, were becoming more relaxed with every passing year.

They were too early to check in so went and grabbed some brunch, until they could gain access to the room after midday. It was noticeably old-fashioned even by 1980s standards, with no television or any other mod cons, and garish orange and yellow floral bedspreads with matching wallpaper. There was no toilet or shower either – these were shared facilities. All they had was a tiny sink in the corner.

After listening to *The Golden Hour*, and now this room, Jenna could have been forgiven for thinking she had travelled back a further five years to 1978. But the outdated décor didn't bother her. She was so excited at finally being alone with Alfie that she practically pounced on him as soon as they got into the room.

Afterwards, as she lay with her head nestled against his chest, admiring his lean, toned physique, he said, "You're full of surprises."

"I did say I wanted to make the most of this weekend away," she replied.

"As long as you're not going to wear me out too much. I've got two days of serious surfing tomorrow and Sunday."

"Better make sure we eat a hearty meal tonight then, to keep your strength up. Where do you recommend in Newquay?"

They ended up at a restaurant that had been Alfie's favourite the previous year, The Dolphin on Fore Street. Alfie was taking the competition seriously, so they didn't go wild on the booze, though they did share a bottle of Black Tower with the meal. This was a German white wine Jenna remembered wine snobs denigrating as being rather unsophisticated. They classed it in the same bracket as Blue Nun, the butt of many a joke. But she had always loved it for its distinctive black stone crock bottle alone, one of which she was using as a candle holder in her bedroom back home.

Later, back in their room, they got intimate again, more tenderly than the rushed, excited coupling of their first arrival, before falling asleep, looking forward to the big day ahead.

Saturday dawned bright and cool, the flimsy curtains of their modest room proving no match for the sun piercing through the thin fabric. Much as she was tempted, Jenna kept her hands off Alfie this morning, knowing the first heats were only a couple of hours away.

They made their way downstairs to breakfast, into a tiny dining room where four square tables were wedged into a space that would have felt snug just with two. The floral wallpaper was even more old-fashioned than they had in their room, but the smell of freshly cooked food was welcome, whatever the surroundings.

Their cheery hostess was a Mrs Watkins, who was nothing like the stereotypical stern landlady of the past. She was all smiles and jokes, putting them at ease as she deftly navigated the narrow gaps between the tables. She brought them orange juice, toast, and a generous plateful of scrambled eggs for Alfie – the perfect protein-rich fuel for a day's surfing.

They were the youngest in the room by far, all the other tables taken up by pensioner couples. This was typical for early June, with older visitors often choosing this time to get away when prices were cheaper compared to later in the summer when the school holidays began.

Outside, the world was full of early-summer promise: a sky with few clouds, and a gentle, cool breeze. There was no hint yet of the blazing temperatures soon to sweep the country. As they approached the beach, they heard music pumping out from the sound system set up for the day. The track playing was 'Temptation' by Heaven 17, which was about as 1983 as you could get. If Jenna remembered rightly, it had been on the first *Now* album.

It was only a short walk to the stretch of beach where the competition was to take place, which was fortunate given how weighed down they were with gear. Alfie, already in his wetsuit, was carrying his brand-new surfboard, purchased specifically for this event, with the orange and blue logo of his surf shack on it. Jenna wore a backpack which they had loaded up with drinks and snacks from a Martins just around the corner from their B&B.

One of the first things that caught Jenna's eye was that almost every kid on the beach, and a fair few adults too, were wearing deely boppers. These were plastic headbands with two colourful antennae, often with sparkly shapes attached by springs, that bobbled around when the wearer moved. This was a short-lived fashion craze that she had completely forgotten about that had been at its height in the summer of '83.

She could see a stall selling them doing a brisk trade but couldn't help thinking that the people wearing them looked rather ridiculous. It reminded her of another fleeting trend from the 1980s when for some inexplicable reason, everyone had begun wearing fluorescent-coloured socks, in colours more commonly associated with Staedtler highlighter pens. When had that been? A little later, she thought.

Overall, the beach had the feel of a summer fete and a grassroots vibe which was quite different to a couple of surfing events she had attended here in later years.

143

Those had been far bigger, with corporate sponsorship and professional organisation. She had a feeling she was going to prefer this more down-to-earth gathering.

"It's good this event is so early in the summer," said Alfie. "I wouldn't have been able to lose a weekend's business running the surf shack in high season. Even so, closing up this weekend is going to cost me."

"Let's hope you come away with some prize money then," she said. "What did you say first prize was?"

"£100," he replied. "OK, it's not huge, and there are bigger events, but it's still decent, considering it's only £3 to enter and it will be mostly amateurs competing, talented ones, mind."

He led the way to the registration area, a small canopy emblazoned with the name of the local surf club. The organisers had built a temporary stage on the sand consisting of a simple wooden platform fronted by loudspeakers, with an enthusiastic DJ calling out announcements between songs. Nearby, a large board displayed a scoreboard with handwritten surfers' names pinned to it.

"Alfie, mate!" called a friendly voice from behind them. A tall, blond surfer approached, clad in a sleeveless wetsuit, ready to go out. "I wondered if you'd be coming back this year."

"Lewis! Good to see you. Still living in Newquay?"

"Wouldn't go anywhere else. Surf's good, the money's half-decent in the summer, and I couldn't resist another crack at this. I came third last year."

He nodded politely at Jenna. "Aren't you going to introduce me?"

144

"This is Jenna, my girlfriend, from back home in Pencarven. You must come up and visit us sometime. I'm running my own surf shack now."

"Sounds awesome!"

Lewis's gaze shifted towards a small cluster of people behind the scoreboard, and Alfie followed his line of sight, spotting an unwelcome figure beneath a red baseball cap.

"Oh, no," murmured Alfie to Jenna. "That's Scott Ramsey – an Aussie who showed up last year. He's a great surfer but a total braggart."

"You can say that again," said Lewis. "After he won, he wouldn't stop showing off, banging on about how he had won so many trophies, he didn't know how he was going to fit them in his suitcase for the flight home to Brisbane."

Scott turned and spotted Alfie, strolling over with a casual, confident air. "Back for more punishment, mate?" he enquired in his strong Queensland accent. "I thought you'd have learned your lesson after last year. I hope you've improved since then."

Before Alfie could respond, Scott moved on, presumably to taunt someone else.

"Nice chap," remarked Jenna sarcastically, having seen enough in those few seconds to form an impression.

"Blokes like him just inspire me to do better so I can whip their arses," said Alfie, showing no sign of being rattled.

"We can beat him, mate," added Lewis. "He gave me some stick earlier too. It's time he was taken down a peg or two."

Jenna cast a glance at the bracelet to see if there were any clues she needed to follow. Was she meant to intervene somehow and sabotage last year's champion? The bracelet stayed silent. Perhaps it was letting her enjoy a weekend off, free from timeline duty, and she concluded she should just let events play out naturally.

Soon, the competition began. Each heat was around fifteen minutes, with four surfers in the water at once. Alfie was scheduled for the third heat of the morning – thankfully not in the same one as Scott, who was going out later. While he was waiting, Alfie prepared his board and kept an eye out for any change in the conditions. They stood close to the shoreline while a small crowd gathered around the PA system, where the commentator announced each surfer's scores.

When Alfie's heat started, Jenna felt her heart beating faster as he caught a rising swell and rode along a peeling right-hander, seemingly full of confidence. The announcer's voice crackled through the speakers, extolling his performance: "Nice bottom turn, good cutback – that's Alfie Trelawney, a talented lad from just up the coast at Pencarven who some of you may remember from last year."

He emerged top of his heat, beaming as he jogged up the beach, board beneath his arm. Jenna rushed over, throwing her arms around him.

"You looked amazing out there," she said, breathless with excitement. "It was like you weren't even trying. Everything flowed so naturally."

"It went perfectly," he replied, full of beans. "The next heat's this afternoon. I've just got to keep the momentum going."

They grabbed sandwiches from one of the food stalls and settled down on the sand to eat, washing them down with the cartons of orange juice Jenna had picked up from Martins earlier. As they watched the final morning men's heat, Jenna noticed both Scott and Lewis were in it and even from a distance, she could sense Scott's arrogance.

"Scott's a semi-pro surfer," Alfie explained. "Travels around for competitions here in the summer, then goes back to Oz to participate during the winter. He usually avoids the bigger events and mops up the prize money in these smaller ones."

"Well, I hope you wipe the floor with him," said Jenna.

"That's the plan," replied Alfie.

There wasn't just a men's contest taking place, and after lunch, they watched as the juniors and the ladies showed off their skills in their heats, before the men went out for their second sessions. Alfie performed equally well in the afternoon, making him one of the top contenders heading into Sunday's finals.

They made their way off the beach to the sound of Michael Jackson's 'Beat It' as afternoon drifted into evening. Alfie was tired yet elated as they headed back to the B&B to get showered and changed.

Later, they ambled along the promenade, past the busy harbour. This was Pencarven on a far larger scale, with dozens of small fishing and tourist boats bobbing gently in the evening sunshine, and the smell of fish and chips filling the air. Hungry after their day out, they went to a takeaway aptly named The Chippy and ate on one of the benches overlooking the sea. Jenna was relishing every moment of this weekend with no work, no stress, and not even the bracelet to bother her. It was simply a perfect time with the man she loved.

They rose early on Sunday morning. Alfie appeared calm, but Jenna couldn't help feeling nervous on his behalf, even though he seemed confident about his chances. Mrs Watkins was excited about his exploits in the surfing contest and beamed with pride when he recounted what had happened the previous day.

"The breakfast of champions!" she announced, presenting him with an even bigger mound of scrambled eggs than the previous day.

"Wow!" he exclaimed.

"Well, it worked yesterday," she insisted. "Go out and do us proud. Imagine the prestige – the winner of the surf contest staying here at the Seaview!"

"I'll do my best," he replied, starting to tuck in.

Down at the beach, the vibe was more intense than on Saturday. The also-rans had been knocked out and now things were getting serious. A bigger crowd had gathered, with deely boppers waving like crazy in the breeze which had picked up a little from the day before. The DJ had upped the ante, playing more inspirational tunes like 'Eye of the Tiger' as the remaining surfers prepared to do battle.

There was even a local bookie, chalking up odds on a board, for which Jenna noted Alfie was being offered

148

at 3/1. Those placing bets, though, all seemed to be backing Scott, the even-money favourite.

Alfie drew heat one of the semis, alongside another local surfer, a competitor from Tenby, and Lewis. Jenna planted herself close to the stage for a good view, scouring the shoreline as each surfer took to the water. Looking around, she spotted Scott chatting a few yards away, shoulders relaxed, wearing his usual cocky expression. Alfie had again avoided him, as he was in the other semi, but it seemed inevitable that they were going to clash in the final.

When the hooter sounded, Alfie paddled out in long, easy strokes, pausing at the line-up to catch a promising wave. He dropped in smoothly, powering along the face of it keeping a low centre of gravity, and slicing clean arcs. The announcer whooped approval, calling it "an absolute cracker of a first wave from Trelawney."

Lewis also rode solidly, stacking up consistent points. By the end of the heat, Alfie had done enough to qualify for the final, just edging out Lewis, with the other two eliminated.

Scott dominated the next semi in commanding form, and Jenna had to admit he looked good with his fast and aggressive style, which the judges duly rewarded. He finished top, meaning Alfie, Lewis, and Scott were set for the final that afternoon, alongside Joel Lawson, a Newquay-born competitor who was the local crowd's favourite, judging by the cheers when the scores were read out.

Jenna and Alfie gulped down a quick snack. He didn't want anything too heavy after all those eggs at breakfast. Then, it was time to prepare for the final.

"Good luck," said Jenna, planting a kiss on his lips as he readied himself, scanning the horizon for potential changes in the conditions. He turned and smiled at her, the gratitude for her love and support clear in his eyes, before striding off with his board beneath his arm.

She glanced at the bracelet again, noting it still lay dormant. Part of her wished she could help Alfie along somehow, but maybe it was better this way. If he was going to win, it ought to be on merit.

"Ladies and gents, this is the moment!" declared the excited announcer. "It's the men's final between Alfie Trelawney, Joel Lawson, Lewis Bradley, and Scott Ramsey. Fifteen minutes to decide our champion. Best two waves count, so choose them well, lads!"

The crowd watched expectantly as the four surfers splashed out into the water. Scott had strutted down the beach as if defeat were impossible, but today he was out of luck.

There had been no intervention on Jenna's part, but perhaps fate lent a hand when Scott's overconfidence undermined him. On the first big wave, he seized it confidently but in a foolhardy move, tried to show off by waving to the crowd as if he had already won and promptly overcooked it – resulting in a spectacular wipe-out. The crowd groaned, presumably led by those who had bet on him, but a few others broke into an ironic cheer, clearly not endeared by his brash personality.

"Ramsey going for gold too early," observed the commentator. "That could cost him."

It did cost him, well and truly knocking the wind out of his sails, and he never recovered. Meanwhile, Alfie caught a long, peeling right-hander, carving deft, controlled arcs. He capped it with a clean off-the-lip turn, spraying water like confetti. The crowd roared, and Jenna found herself screaming encouragement.

Lewis performed with precision, and Joel showcased his knowledge of the local waters, but none could match Alfie. When the final hooter sounded, he topped the points, with Joel trailing just behind. Lewis was third for the second year running, with Scott limping home in last place.

Jenna dashed to meet Alfie as the crowd cheered, nearly colliding with him in her eagerness. She threw her arms around his damp shoulders and practically screamed, "You did it!"

"We did it," he replied. "I couldn't have done it without you."

It sounded a little trite but he had no idea of how true his words were, given that his washed-up body would by now be rotting in Pencarven's cemetery, had it not been for her intervention. Yet she tried not to dwell on that, just as she tried not to think about having to leave this fairy-tale romance behind at the end of the year.

Today, she couldn't have felt prouder as he received his prize money and a small golden trophy in the shape of a surfboard for his victory. As for Scott, he was nowhere to be seen, skulking off as soon as he'd emerged from the water.

Mrs Watkins at the B&B couldn't have been more delighted at Alfie's win, insisting on taking a photograph of him holding the trophy to display in the hallway above the guest book, which she also insisted he signed. Later

151

that evening, they met up with Lewis, Joel, and a few of the other surfers to celebrate outside one of the harbour pubs.

It had been a simply wonderful weekend, and Jenna couldn't remember a time in either of her lives when she had felt happier.

July 1983

"Phew, what a scorcher!" announced David, reading the rather predictable headline on the front page of the tabloid paper that Morwenna had just plonked down on the breakfast table in front of him.

He swiftly turned the page, giving Jenna an unwanted glimpse of a topless Samantha Fox, who had become something of a Page 3 sensation in 1983.

"You know, you really ought to read something a little more intellectual," said Jenna, who didn't want to see bare boobs being flashed around at the breakfast table.

Quite how it had ever been acceptable for sixteen- and seventeen-year-old girls to objectify themselves this way in a national newspaper, Jenna had never quite understood. It was one aspect of 1980s culture which she was more than happy to see consigned to the dustbin of history.

"Shame he's not interested in mine anymore," said Morwenna, who had noticed David gawping at the paper. The bitter tone in her voice which Jenna was hearing so often these days was again prevalent.

What could she do to help her parents' marriage? It was a huge concern, even if she managed to keep her mother away from Blake when he eventually arrived. But that alone wouldn't fix the underlying problems.

Perhaps it couldn't be fixed. If two people didn't want to be together anymore, there was no easy solution. There was no magic wand she could wave, or in this case, magic bracelet. Her ever-present companion on her wrist helped solve practical, everyday problems, even saving lives, but it couldn't alter people's basic feelings.

"Give it a rest, will you," said David, who was nursing a cup of black coffee in front of him. "I'm feeling a bit rough this morning."

"I'm not surprised," said Morwenna. "He had another lock-in last night. He's been at it nearly every night this week."

"It's the hot weather," he protested, wiping his forehead theatrically as if to mop off some sweat, even though there wasn't any there. "You know I find it hard to sleep when it's like this. Staying up an extra hour or two makes all the difference."

Jenna was relieved that the heatwave she had been forecasting for months had arrived on schedule. By now, in the third week of July, it was blazing hot sunshine and blue skies every day. She'd had a brief worry at the start of the month that it might not happen, after reading a piece in one of the Sunday papers about chaos theory. The article explained how the mere act of a butterfly flapping its wings could spark a hurricane on the other side of the world.

She hadn't given it much credence but if it were true, could the fact that she had been walking around and breathing in and out in different directions for the past six months lead to changes in the weather patterns?

Of course it couldn't. She might influence people's lives, but fundamentally altering the entire planet's atmosphere was a pie-in-the-sky idea. Her contribution was the equivalent of a drop in the ocean. And so it proved when the sun began shining in early July and didn't let up. So much for the butterfly effect.

After breakfast, Jenna walked up to the caravan park where the children's entertainment began at ten o'clock. The heat hit her the moment she stepped outside, the sunlight so intense she found herself blinking at the glare. She really ought to buy some sunglasses, even if it was only a cheap pair from the tourist shop on the front that sold buckets, spades, and beach towels. Mirror shades seemed to be the in thing at present but she wasn't keen. She thought it made the wearers look like they had something to hide.

The harbour was already packed with tourists queueing for boat trips, some of them with noticeably shiny complexions from the copious amounts of sun cream they had slathered on. She was pleased to see Ned proudly ushering a group of middle-aged men, all eagerly clutching their fishing equipment, aboard his new boat. *The Saucy Nancy* was resplendent in blue and white and she hoped he would take better care of it than he had the previous one.

She then walked along the packed seafront, having to dodge between families clutching their extensive collections of equipment encompassing everything from towels to cool boxes and windbreaks. It could never be said that the British holidaymaker didn't come fully prepared for a day at the beach. That phrase about bringing everything but the kitchen sink just about summed them up.

Shelly's Café door was propped open in a forlorn attempt to keep the air circulating, but the only things circulating were the flies and wasps hovering around the cakes and scones. It might have been only mid-morning, but the temperature was already in the mid-twenties and forecast to climb as high as twenty-eight degrees later. That was over eighty on the Fahrenheit scale that a lot of people still used, particularly newspapers when they were trying to hype up the high temperatures.

It wasn't as hot here as in other parts of the country, where temperatures were exceeding thirty every day at present, but Cornwall's coastal nature always kept it a few degrees cooler in the summer. Jenna thought about how oppressive it must be in London right now, having seen footage on television the previous evening of tarmac melting in the city and people frying eggs on car bonnets. She knew where she would rather be.

She passed the beach, the sand baking under the powerful sun as it rapidly dried out in front of a receding tide. It was already filled with holidaymakers who had arrived early to stake out their spots, and she had scarcely seen it as busy as it had been the past week. It all boded well for Pencarven in the short term but such weather couldn't be expected every year and Britons were increasingly being tempted by the promise of holidays abroad where the weather was practically guaranteed.

She caught a glimpse of Alfie, busy hiring out boards, and the new female lifeguard who was chatting eagerly to him outside the shack. Jenna had hardly seen him over the past week as they had both been so busy but she was determined to get down to the beach at the weekend, when the kids' club didn't run, to lend him a hand.

Someone else who was busy was Willy, who had never had it so good, to the point he was struggling to keep up with demand. There was only so much stock he could carry on the van for one day, and he had been back and forth to the cash and carry in Bodmin more times than ever before. It was more than an hour's round trip every morning, and even then, he often ran out by mid-afternoon.

The only local who didn't appreciate the hot weather was Trevor from the arcade, whom she overheard bemoaning his ill fortune in the pub on Friday evening. She was having a drink with Alfie, as the usual suspects gathered at the bar.

"Bloody hell, I'm knackered!" exclaimed Willy, as he came in around sunset after another lucrative day on the van. "And thirsty. Large orange juice and lemonade, please, David."

"Still off the sauce, that's what I like to see," observed Matt, enjoying an off-duty pint. Jenna knew that David would be hoping he wouldn't be hanging around all night. There were no lock-ins when the local bobby was on the premises. Breaking licensing laws was a sure-fire way to loss of livelihood.

"I'll have plenty to spend on beer come October if this weather holds, you wait and see," said Willy. "Things have been so good I might be able to spend the winter drinking champagne cocktails! You do sell champagne, don't you?"

"I think we've got a bottle left over somewhere from the royal wedding in 1981," replied David.

"Excellent," said Willy. "Let the good times roll!"

"Alright, don't rub it in," said a disgruntled Trevor, perched on the stool next to him. "This has been my worst summer since 1976. People don't come to the arcade in the daytime when the sun shines. I want rain, and lots of it."

"Well, you're in a minority of one there," said David. "But I'm sure you're not going to be headed for the poorhouse any time soon. I know you still have some customers because only last night there was some bloke in here moaning that your bandits are all rigged."

"Of course they're rigged," said Trevor. "How do you think I make any money?"

"Oh, really?" asked Matt, his ears pricking up. His favourite motto was that a good copper was never off duty, and there were plenty of loose lips in the pub. "Are you confessing that your fruit machines are bent?"

"No, of course not," said Trevor. "By rigged, I mean that they are designed to pay out less than goes in. Amusement machines with prizes have a 70% payout, a legal requirement that I'm sure you will know, as a custodian of the law. But if no one's feeding them because they'd rather be on the beach all day, then I'm not making any profit, am I? So the sooner it starts pissing down again, the better."

"Blimey, and there I was thinking I was the most miserable old git in here," said Ned, from the next stool along. "I'm sorry, Trev, but you're not going to get any sympathy from the rest of us. So why don't you just put up and shut up about it? It'll be raining again soon enough. This is Cornwall, after all, not Corfu!"

The banter rumbled on, as it always did. Then, that night, Jenna found out that Trevor's dream of angry black clouds emptying their contents over the beach was about to come true.

A few forecasts had mentioned a small risk of thunderstorms, but nothing concrete. The location and timing of such storms were notoriously hard to predict, yet when Jenna woke up on Saturday morning, another of the bracelet's dream predictions had lodged itself solidly in her head.

She knew with certainty that at half past one in the afternoon, there was going to be a colossal thunderstorm over Pencarven Bay, sending sunbathers scurrying away from the beach, desperately seeking shelter.

While the dream didn't suggest anyone would come to any harm, it wasn't going to be pleasant for those caught in it and she felt duty-bound to warn as many people as possible. She had already established a reputation in the village for having her finger on the pulse, thanks to her uncanny knack for predicting events. She managed this carefully, mindful there was a thin line between being perceived as being exceptionally astute, and possessing impossible levels of perception, bordering on the supernatural.

Her knowledge had allowed her to advance the new sea defence project at an unprecedented pace with the bracelet nudging her at just the right moments, helping her navigate the swathes of red tape and reach the right people at the right time. All this was enabling her to push through a scheme that could have dragged on for years within the seven-month window available to her.

No one had yet questioned her supreme efficiency in getting this, and other things done. All she had received had been a great deal of praise, including from the local mayor who had already suggested that her bright start in politics might one day lead to her holding the role.

Away from council duty, there were little tasks she performed with the bracelet's help almost every day, mostly unnoticed because there was nothing to see when a crisis was averted. Whether it be a tray of drinks that didn't go flying in the pub, the small boy on the beach she prevented from treading on a weever fish, or the grandad who didn't break a hip when she alerted him to the state of the rickety deckchair he was about to sit on, it was all in a day's work for her and the bracelet.

When her good deeds did draw attention, she brushed it off, saying it was just what anyone would have done. Among those had been the rescue of two students who'd sneaked off to the next cove, got carried away with what swimming pool signs used to label 'heavy petting', and ended up cut off by the tide. Her claim that she had spotted them climbing over the rocks while she was helping Alfie pack away the surfboards was plausible enough, and accepted by everyone.

Another time, she was drawn to a small child separated from her parents among Pencarven's crowded cobbled streets on a sweltering afternoon packed with tourists. Taking the sobbing girl's hand, she let the bracelet guide her through the heaving throng to her two grateful parents, who by that time had become distraught. One minute their daughter had been looking at sticks of rock in a sweet shop window, and the next she had vanished, swept up in the crowd.

When the father of the girl called into the pub that evening, he saw Jenna with Alfie, and she found herself, not for the first time, being publicly hailed as a hero.

No one seemed to begrudge her the adulation coming her way, though at times she wondered if she might end up being perceived as too saintly for her own good. If she kept this up, surely someone was going to question her ability to always be in the right place at the right time. But what was she supposed to do – just ignore people in need?

Making her little corner of the world a better place had been one of the prime reasons she had been sent back here in the first place, hadn't it? That was certainly what Wendy, and more recently Keith, had suggested. So she vowed to carry on and that included trying to warn people about what was on the way this afternoon.

Certain that the storm was coming, she made her way down to the harbour, determined to catch the former fishermen before they set out for their first trips of the day. There were four of them running tours now. Jack and Ned had been joined by George, who had planned to retire but reversed that decision when he saw how much money the other two were earning.

The fourth vessel belonged to Marcus, a newcomer from Tintagel who ran a glass-bottom boat. Unlike the others, it had a specially designed lower deck set just below the water's surface, fitted with wide panels of reinforced glass on either side. Holidaymakers could walk down a short flight of steps, and gaze through these windows to observe the marine life below the surface.

Although she was unaware of there being any risk to life, Jenna disliked the idea of these boats being out on the water amid lashing rain and lightning. One bad experience like that could put a nervous holidaymaker off returning to Pencarven for life, not to mention how traumatising it might be for any children on board. And what Pencarven needed, more than anything, was happy, loyal visitors who would come back, year after year, to support the local economy.

Three of the boatmen needed little persuading, despite the official forecast suggesting storms were only a remote possibility. Jack had learnt over recent months that it was wise to listen to Jenna, and when she told him, he wasn't at all surprised.

"You know, I did wonder," he said. "Despite what the forecast says, I've been working these waters long enough to know when to be wary. I know every inch of this coast, every subtle nuance in the wind, and the colours in the sky in the morning. When I first came down here today, I had an inkling something might be brewing. Now you've said as much, I'm convinced."

"It's going to strike at half past one," she said. "You normally take a trip out at one, so why not delay that trip today? Schedule it for two instead. Then, if it's still coming down, you can wait until it stops. Better that than being caught out there."

"It won't affect me," said George. "I'll be back from my eleven-thirty trip by then, and I don't go out again until half past two."

"We agreed to stagger our departure times," explained Jack. "Going out at ninety-minute intervals, doing virtually the same tour. That way, we can fit in six trips a day, we're not competing with each other, and no one's ever waiting more than an hour and a half."

Marcus was happy to accept Jenna's advice too, but true to form, there was one sailor who refused to listen.

"Poppycock," said Ned. "What would you know about it?"

"For goodness' sake, Ned, haven't I proved myself by now? All year you've been trashing my advice, but how many times have I been right?"

"Lucky guesses, that's all. You may have persuaded these idiots, girl, but I'm not falling for it. I've got a party of ten booked in for my twelve-thirty. They're part of a deep-sea fishing club from Stoke-on-Trent."

"Really?" asked Jenna. "I didn't know there was a lot of coastline near Stoke."

"There isn't, which is why they've come here, obviously," retorted Ned. "It's their annual members' holiday."

"Oh, well, on your head be it," she said, sensing no point in arguing with the stubborn old coot. "You can't say I didn't warn you."

"Nothing to warn me about," said Ned. "If a drop of rain falls from that sky today, I'll eat my hat."

"I won't hold you to that later," she replied. "But I will say 'I told you so'."

"You won't because it won't happen," he insisted.

Most of the other people she warned were more receptive. None was more delighted than Trevor, whom she went to see in the arcade to deliver the good news. She found him standing in the change booth, shoulders slumped, watching a single granny playing the penny falls. Despite the man's frequently annoying persona,

163

she couldn't help feeling a little sympathy seeing him in this sorry state.

"You're not normally in the booth," she said. "Where's Jean?" she added, referring to the lady who usually dished out the change.

"I've given her the day off," said Trevor. "No point paying her if no one's coming in. She'll be back at seven tonight when things pick up."

"I'd get her back sooner if I were you. You're going to have a lot of drenched holidaymakers desperate to take shelter and gamble away their holiday money in a couple of hours. There's a big storm coming."

"I hope you're right, Jenna," he said.

"Aren't I always?" she said, then immediately worried that might have come across as a bit cocky. Sometimes it was hard not to act that way when she had all the answers.

"It seems so," he replied.

Her next stop was the beach. There was no point trying to warn the tourists, and what good would it do anyway? They were hardly going to give up their day on the sand just because some woman they didn't know told them there was a storm coming later.

At least she could give Alfie the heads up. However, as she approached the shack, she was irritated to spot Karen, the new lifeguard, hanging around again. A pretty, tanned blonde who wouldn't have looked out of place in *Baywatch*, had that existed in 1983, her presence made Jenna uneasy. Even though she never doubted Alfie's fidelity, it had become obvious over the past couple of weeks that the girl had designs on him.

As Jenna drew near, Alfie cracked a joke and Karen laughed exaggeratedly, obviously trying to flatter him. Well, she would soon put a stop to that.

"Hello, Karen, what are you doing here?" she asked. "Shouldn't you be up on your highchair, keeping an eye on the water? That is what the council, of which I am a member, pays you for."

"I'm here on official business, as it happens," replied Karen. "Just checking the tide times with Alfie and making sure we've got the flags in the right place."

"You don't need to check that with anyone. It's your job to know and do all that. Can I have a word, Alfie?"

"Uh-oh, someone's in trouble," teased Karen, flouncing off before turning back and blowing him a kiss, parting with, "See you later, surfer boy."

"I don't like her," said Jenna. "She's blatantly after you."

"But I'm not after her, and never will be," said Alfie, keen to reassure her. "So you've nothing to worry about."

Jenna wasn't naturally insecure and trusted him implicitly. She was further reassured by a gentle green pulse from the bracelet. Still, it didn't do anything to alter her dislike of Karen and she had already decided not to warn her about the storm after their earlier exchange. But she didn't want Alfie getting caught up in it.

"Listen, you'll have to trust me on this. Shut the shack for a couple of hours at lunchtime. There's a massive storm coming between one and two, so don't rent out any boards. You can reopen once it's passed. And don't tell Karen."

"And you know this how?" he asked. "Actually, don't tell me. I swear you've got some sixth sense."

"It's my spidey senses," she joked. "Take an hour off and watch the storm from the café with me. We'll have lunch together – my treat."

When the storm arrived it was truly ferocious, just as Jenna's dream had foretold. Mercifully, as also predicted, it harmed no one. The most striking part was how swiftly it struck: the beach went from blazing sunshine to blackened skies in barely ten minutes. One moment, sunbathers were lying half-asleep on baking sand, soaking up the rays, the next they were scrambling in panic to get off the beach as a jagged fork of lightning tore across the horizon out at sea.

A gusty breeze whipped up from nowhere, straining the colourful stripy windbreaks that the holidaymakers always insisted on putting up, even on the calmest of days. Beach balls, loose pages from newspapers, and anything else that wasn't weighed down blew across the beach, and then came the rain. It began with heavy droplets that pockmarked the sand, swiftly followed by a pounding deluge that left everyone desperate for shelter, dragging their sodden belongings behind them as they fled.

Jenna and Alfie watched from inside Shelly's Café, listening to the sky rumbling ominously overhead, but even there they weren't immune to getting wet as several drenched tourists barged in for refuge, dripping water all over the place.

Through the window, she could see the street temporarily transformed into a gleaming, rain-lashed stream, as rivulets of water poured in from everywhere. And she couldn't help feeling a flicker of glee when she spotted a thoroughly soaked Karen hurrying along, her perfectly styled blonde hair reduced to a flat, wet mop plastered around her face.

Out at sea, Ned cursed Jenna's uncanny foresight, hating that she had been right yet again. Heavy raindrops hammered his new boat's wooden deck as he steered his way back to shore, with ten thoroughly sodden members of the Stoke-on-Trent Deep Sea Fishing Society, all hunched together against the downpour, glaring at him.

Thunderclaps erupted above them, following each flash of lightning which lit up their miserable faces in the gloom. Ned wasn't particularly worried about the storm because he had been out in worse conditions than this before. His greatest fear was that the fishermen might ask for a refund.

For one man in Pencarven, the sudden deluge was a boon. Trevor beamed from ear to ear inside his arcade as the machines rang and beeped like they hadn't in weeks. Drenched visitors, children and parents alike poured in to escape the storm, pockets heavy with change they were only too happy to spend. But this welcome boost to business would not last long. The storm passed as quickly as it had begun, and within an hour of the first clouds gathering, it was all blue skies and sunshine again.

"Don't even think about it," stated Ned that evening, shuffling sheepishly into the living room to find Alfie and Jenna curled up on the sofa watching *Nationwide*.

He had spent a long while soaking in the bath, only just feeling human again after staggering off *The Saucy Nancy* with sodden clothes clinging to every inch of him. The last thing he wanted now was Jenna rubbing his nose in it.

As for his fishing enthusiasts from Staffordshire, they had made their displeasure blatantly clear in the kind of coarse Anglo-Saxon that left Ned in no doubt there'd be no repeat business. Fortunately for him, TripAdvisor was still decades away.

But Jenna couldn't resist having a dig. Struggling to keep a straight face, she asked, "Are you looking for your hat? Or have you already eaten it?"

"You and I need to have words, boy," said Ned, grumpily stomping off toward the kitchen in search of something to eat.

"Don't worry about Dad," said Alfie. "He likes you really."

"No I don't," came Ned's voice from the kitchen, before he reappeared. "She's too darned clever for her own good. However, I might reconsider my position if she pops out and gets me some fish and chips. There's nothing in the fridge, and I can't face the queue at the chippy after the day I've had."

"More like you're worried about running into those fishermen from Stoke again," said Alfie. "Remind me, where it was they said they wanted to stick their rods?"

"I don't want to think about it," said Ned. "Best I lie low for a while. They're all going home tomorrow. Here, I'll give you a tenner. You two haven't eaten yet, have you?"

168

He handed it over, more than enough for three portions of fish and chips at 1983 prices, and Jenna went out to get them. Once Ned had a full belly, he grew far more agreeable, and despite his earlier claim that he didn't like her, Jenna wasn't perturbed. She knew that much of his grumbling was exaggerated and just part of his over-the-top belligerent act that she generally found amusing.

That evening, he decided to skip his usual trip to the pub, wary the men from Stoke might be there. They had been angry enough in the afternoon while sober, so he certainly didn't fancy running into them with a few pints inside them.

Instead, they stayed in and played Monopoly, which went surprisingly well – especially once Jenna let Ned bag Mayfair at a bargain price during an auction. That completed his set, ultimately leading to him winning. Jenna felt it did no harm to flatter his ego a bit. If he was destined to become her father-in-law one day, they would have to learn to get along.

August 1983

As the summer wore on, Jenna found herself becoming increasingly irritated by Karen constantly sniffing around Alfie.

It wasn't that she doubted Alfie's loyalty – their relationship felt deeper than ever, and she was confident he could never be swayed by another woman. Yet Karen's blatant contempt for Jenna, founded on a smug assumption that she was a prettier, sexier, and more fun option, grated on her nerves. She seemed convinced that if she flashed her eyes at him long enough, she could win him over.

Unlike some of the problems Jenna had faced before, this wasn't one she had any foreknowledge of because none of this had happened in the old timeline. She couldn't recall ever meeting Karen. By August 1983 the first time around, she had undergone a termination at Blake's insistence and, depressed in the aftermath of that on top of Alfie's death, had avoided the beach altogether through that long hot summer of misery. So Karen hadn't even been on her radar. But now here she was, making a nuisance of herself, and Jenna wanted rid of her.

It was the bracelet that enabled her to do just that. The moment came during her lunch break at the caravan park, in the gap between her morning sessions with the younger children and the afternoon activities for teens. The day, like every previous one for weeks, was bright and clear, the sun searing down from another cloudless sky as the record-breaking summer continued.

Jenna sat outside on one of the picnic benches, savouring a cheese-and-pickle sandwich bought from the shop on the site, washed down with a can of Lilt, while scanning the newspaper. Headlines continued to trumpet the ongoing heatwave, describing how Londoners were melting in record temperatures and that there were going to be hosepipe bans. Up here on the cliffs of Cornwall, by contrast, the sea breeze took the edge off the midday heat, making it just about perfect.

Then, she felt a sharp pulse from the bracelet, accompanied by a red warning flash. An urgent image of a small girl struggling in the sea flashed through her mind and she knew at once that this was a call to action. It was almost as if she were an additional emergency service. Abandoning the rest of her lunch, she sprang to her feet and dashed toward the front gate of the caravan park.

As she rushed off down the bone-dry path, each step sent dust swirling around her sandals, but she barely noticed in her haste to mount a rescue. She sprinted down the hill until the path reached the point where it overlooked the beach. There, she came to an abrupt halt and scanned the scene below.

The official flags, two bright red-and-yellow boundary markers, were in their usual positions near the middle of the bay, indicating the safest swimming area. Here, the beach was at its most crowded, children splashing in the waves while their parents sat on tartan picnic blankets or in striped deckchairs.

She could see that Karen's lookout chair, placed in the centre of this zone, stood unoccupied, as so often seemed to be the case lately. Jenna couldn't see Alfie's shack from this angle, due to a rocky outcrop obscuring that part of the beach, but she would have bet her bottom dollar Karen was there, still pursuing her futile quest to sink her claws into him.

Jenna froze upon spotting, just beyond the flagged zone, a small figure floating on the surface, drifting slowly out to sea. A child, perhaps four or five years old, wearing bright orange armbands of the standard variety that kept her afloat. Each retreating wave nudged her further from shore and towards the edge of the flagged area, yet no one seemed to have noticed. Those on the beach were too absorbed in rummaging through cool boxes for their lunch, or keeping an eye out for the seagulls who were always on the lookout for food they could snatch out of their hands.

"Hey! Someone help!" yelled Jenna in vain, too far away for anyone near the shore to hear her over the crashing waves. She tore her gaze away and resumed her run, covering the last couple of hundred yards downhill toward the beach. There, she flung off her sandals and dashed across the sand, glancing sideways as she ran to confirm what she had guessed: Karen was indeed chatting with Alfie by the shack, her back turned to the sea.

"Alfie, Karen! There's someone in trouble in the water!" shouted Jenna, speeding up as she crossed the boundary from the dry, powdery sand onto the firmer wet stretch where the tide had been. She continued running as she entered the sea, then, when the water was up to her waist, she plunged forward, swimming front crawl faster than she ever had in her life.

The child had drifted at least fifty yards out to sea, and now Jenna could hear her cries. She was younger than Jenna had first thought, perhaps only three, and was only now, it seemed, realising what was happening. Thank goodness she had the armbands. All sorts of thoughts were going through Jenna's head but she tried to put her fury at Karen, and questions about the whereabouts of the parents, to one side for now as she concentrated on the rescue. There would be plenty of time to apportion blame later.

Nearing the girl, Jenna heard her sobbing, tears streaking her face. Though the armbands kept her afloat, she was outside the safe zone and the undercurrents on this section of the beach could easily pull a panicked child under. That was why they had flags and lifeguards in the first place. She reached her just in time, looping an arm around her waist to steer her back toward shore.

"It's okay!" said Jenna, "I've got you."

She was out of her depth this far from shore and found it difficult to manoeuvre with a frightened child clinging to her. Each surge of the tide seemed determined to pull them both further out, but help was coming. Alfie was swimming toward them, with Karen floundering in his wake. A couple of other bystanders, realising what was happening, also swam in to assist, and soon the danger was over.

When they reached the shore, a frantic couple came dashing forward. The mother had a crying infant slung on her hip, with a half-fastened nappy trailing below. The father clutched the remains of a kite string in one hand, face drained of colour, while two older boys stumbled along behind them.

"Mary!" cried the mother, scooping the little girl into her free arm, with a mix of relief and fear at the realisation of what might have happened etched on her features. "Oh my God, oh my God, are you alright?"

"She was drifting outside the flagged zone," said Jenna, breathless after her run and frantic swim, leaning on Alfie for support. "She's okay now, but she might not have been. How could you let her go off on her own like that?"

"I only turned my back for a moment," replied the mother, tears streaming. "The baby's nappy needed changing."

"I was flying the kite with the boys," explained the father. "I honestly thought Mary was with her mum."

"Kids do wander off," said Jenna, before turning on Karen, who stood sheepishly behind Alfie. "Which is exactly what you're employed to watch out for. Where were you? This could have ended in tragedy!"

Karen, guilt plain on her face, tried to justify herself. "I was just checking the flag positions with Alfie," she said, refusing to meet Jenna's gaze, and casting her eyes down at the sand instead.

"More like you were flirting with him," snapped Jenna, adrenaline still surging. "You left your post again. You've been doing it all summer. Well, that's it. As soon as we're done here, I'm on the phone to your manager. I want you removed from this beach."

A small group of onlookers had gathered, some shaking their heads in disgust at Karen's neglect, others murmuring sympathy for the family. Then the father spoke up.

"Thank you so much," he said, in a voice overwhelmed with relief. "No matter what the rights and wrongs, the most important thing is that Mary is safe, and we can't ever thank you enough. You're a hero!"

Applause broke out among the onlookers. Jenna felt her cheeks warm, despite the lingering chill of the sea. She saw Alfie flash a proud smile, sliding his hand into hers.

"Yeah, she's making a habit of that," he said, "You've saved the day again."

"Well, it's taught me a lesson. I won't let her out of my sight in the future," declared the father, placing an arm around his daughter, who was now clinging to her mother's waist. Jenna was confident he would keep that promise. The memory of a shock like the one he had just experienced stayed with people for life. Lesson learnt.

News of Jenna's latest heroics spread fast, and the following week's *Cornish & Devon Post* ran the story on its front page beneath the headline LOCAL COUNCILLOR SAVES DROWNING CHILD.

This was a bit of an exaggeration since the little girl hadn't been physically drowning. Still, that might well ultimately have been the outcome if she had gone unnoticed much longer so Jenna was happy to take the credit, however it was worded. She was also pleased that the paper was highlighting the importance of staying safe on the beach with a few dos and don'ts added to the article for good measure. The locals would already know all this but if a few holidaymakers read it and it made them more vigilant then it was all well and good.

As for Karen, Jenna stayed true to her word and rang the council official who was responsible for hiring her. Jenna had tolerated her flirting and casual neglect until now, but with a child's life put at risk, she felt she had no alternative. The next day, a new lifeguard occupied the lookout chair, and that was the last they ever saw of Karen.

With that drama out of the way, the long lazy days of summer resumed for some, though Jenna was as busy as ever. Between council matters, her bustling kids' club at the caravan park, and evenings devoted to spending time with Alfie, she had become so wrapped up in this new life that she had almost forgotten she was only here for a year.

The bracelet was still giving her good deeds to do, often to help the locals. Willy had been finding it impossible to keep up with demand, frequently running out of ice cream, leaving the peals from his Chilly Willy van to fall silent. Trips to the cash and carry in Bodmin were often proving fruitless, as every ice cream man in the area was cleaning them out as soon as they opened every morning.

At the bracelet's suggestion, Jenna redirected him to a much larger depot on the outskirts of St Austell. She also tipped him off about a large second-hand chest freezer up for sale in the local paper. It meant a far longer round trip to stock up, but with the additional storage space, he was able to keep enough stock at home to see him through even the hottest days.

He was grateful, and the business was thriving again thanks to her input, even though she knew he would ultimately probably spend it on beer. Still, that would benefit the pub's takings, and keeping the holidaymakers well fed with ice cream and lollies would keep them happy too. She was thinking long-term. Just like companies offering good customer service to generate repeat business, Jenna knew that for the future of the village, she needed to encourage repeat visits. It was often little things, like being able to get an ice cream when you wanted one, that made all the difference when people were weighing up whether to come back next year or go somewhere else.

Some days, Willy brought his van up to the caravan park which was bursting at the seams with visitors. There were so many kids staying there in August that she reluctantly had to turn children away from her sessions on occasion as she simply did not have room for them. Morgan couldn't have been happier about the park's success, and he had some big news to tell her one afternoon, right as she was preparing to leave.

"Jenna," he began excitedly, "while you were off running the French Boules contest, a couple of people from the film company came by. Guess what they told me."

"What?" she asked, instinctively glancing at her wrist in case the bracelet delivered one of its red pulses. She suspected she already knew. If it was what she thought it was, it was something that had happened before, albeit earlier in the year, in the old timeline.

"Blake Cadwallader wants to stay here, right on the site in his luxury motorhome. Apparently, he doesn't fancy any local hotels, because there aren't any places up to his standards. He says he wants to get a proper feel for the community. Think of the attention that'll attract, especially in September when the park usually starts emptying out for the year."

"Great," said Jenna, stifling a sigh. There was no sense arguing; if Blake wanted to stay at the park, he would. He always got what he wanted, something she knew from bitter experience.

"A shame he felt the need to slag off our local hotel trade, though, isn't it?" she added. "Clearly, we're not good enough for him."

"He's an international star, what do you expect? He's probably used to the five-star treatment all over the world, not cheap guest houses."

"And you're going to give him that here, are you? Roll out the red carpet next to the bubble-gum machine by the front entrance? Deliver champagne and caviar to his caravan, twenty-four-seven on request? Order in prostitutes for him, on demand?"

"If it makes money, yes," replied Morgan. "And as for your last, rather crude point, I'm sure a man with his looks and fame wouldn't need to pay for sex."

"You'd be surprised," said Jenna, who knew a lot more about Blake than Morgan did, but there was no point arguing with her uncle. He was star-struck and had pound signs in his eyes.

The rest of the village was also buzzing with excitement over the news, none more so than Morwenna, who wouldn't stop going on about it at breakfast. David hadn't come downstairs yet, so her mother had free rein, talking non-stop until Jenna, her ears unable to take any more punishment, removed herself and her half-eaten

178

toast to the living room. There, at least, she could watch Roland Rat on TV-AM in peace.

David hadn't been up, because once again he had been drinking late, and Jenna felt she ought to do something about it, she just didn't know what. He had been getting progressively worse as the year had gone on, and Morwenna seemed past caring. She just let him get on with it now, which did not bode well as it suggested she had stopped being concerned. She'd also reached the point where she was openly expressing her admiration, bordering on desire, for Blake, right in front of her husband, and she hadn't even met him yet. How much worse would it be when he was right here, in the pub?

To escape having to put up with listening to it every morning, Jenna tried going to Shelly's for breakfast on the way to the caravan park. But if anything, there it was even worse. Wherever she went, the unmerited worship for Blake followed her around, and no one would hear a word against him. But why would they? They didn't know what she knew.

In addition to Blake's imminent arrival, Pencarven was also putting itself on the map in other ways. This included the village's first official surf contest, organised by Alfie from his beach shack. Compared to the Newquay event at which he had triumphed in June, this event was tiny, contested mostly by local amateurs and a few holidaymakers fancying a go, but, as Alfie liked to say, "From little acorns..." He hoped he could grow it into a major annual event.

By far the biggest draw for holidaymakers in the area was the impending Radio One Roadshow, scheduled for the final week of August. By Jenna's time in 2022, this had long vanished from the radio schedules, but in 1983 it was a national institution, traversing Britain's coastline each summer and broadcasting a lively ninety-minute show from dozens of seaside resorts. She had attended a few in her teens, trekking to Bude and Newquay just to catch a glimpse of the BBC's top DJs.

Pencarven had never hosted one before and nor would it have in the old timeline because, as Jenna discovered, a few years previously the BBC had asked if they could bring it to the village, only to be turned down.

Gordon had told them that he didn't approve of pop music, believing it would lower the tone and attract the wrong sort of people at a time when there was much hysteria about the behaviour of punk rockers sweeping the country. Jenna, by contrast, had nearly bitten the station's hand off when they rang again this June to say a regular venue had fallen through and they were seeking an alternative. She promised to do everything in her power as a councillor to secure the event.

There was much excitement when it was revealed that Pencarven was getting a visit from one of the station's biggest names, who had built a huge following with his innovative, humorous afternoon show. This guaranteed a substantial crowd on the day, and so it proved. Even though the hot weather had eased by late August, the beach looked busier than ever with tourists flocking from miles around, with widespread deely boppers adorning heads again and mirror shades aplenty. There were also many eager locals present, excited to have a major radio station broadcasting live from their home village.

On the morning of the show, Jenna watched the roadshow lorry rumble onto the beach. A team of technicians bustled about, unfolding the sides to form a temporary stage adorned with the station's distinctive red, white, and blue logo, proclaiming "275 & 285 MW" referring to the AM frequencies on which the station broadcast.

In 1983, it was all still quite basic, lacking the colossal stages and major band performances that would feature in later years of the show. This had a more down-to-earth, almost local-radio vibe that Jenna appreciated. She had cancelled the morning sessions at the park for the day, rightly assuming that the kids and their families would be more interested in attending this than arts and crafts in the clubhouse.

The show was set to begin at 11am, but the host appeared beforehand, greeting fans and signing autographs. He then warmed up the crowd with some light-hearted humour on the mic, as they responded with cheers and laughter. Then, at the appointed hour, he kicked off the live broadcast, his distinctive friendly tone booming out from the speakers.

"Good morning, Pencarven! This is BBC Radio One, coming to you live from this beautiful Cornish beach. Let's hear a cheer if you're having a good holiday!"

A roar of excitement rolled through the crowd, as the first tune kicked in, the current number one, 'Give it Up' by KC and The Sunshine Band, which was one of the definitive hits of summer 1983.

The show ran about ninety minutes, at least half of which was devoted to music, with short interviews, features, and games filling the links. The highlight was a music quiz called *Bits 'n' Pieces*. Four audience members were selected to come up on stage, each interviewed beforehand. Jenna watched as the first contestant climbed the steps, a tall, lean man in a yellow Ocean Pacific T-shirt.

"So, our first contestant today is Barry, from Oxfordshire. Tell us, Barry, what do you do?"

"I'm in the army," said Barry. A thunderous cheer broke from the onlookers and there were even a couple of wolf whistles from female admirers.

"The audience like that, and from that reaction, you'd have to say that the women here do love a soldier! So what brings you to Pencarven?"

"I'm here on my honeymoon," said Barry, to a ripple of good-natured groans from some of the women in the crowd.

"Ladies, do you hear that? He's off the market, I'm afraid," replied the DJ, feigning disappointment, and eliciting a groan from the crowd. "So who's the lucky lady?"

"Her name's Jane. She's down there, waving," said Barry, pointing into the crowd.

The host moved on to greet the other contestants, and then the quiz began. It was quick-fire in nature, consisting of ten short clips from pop songs of the last couple of years, each just a few seconds in duration. The contestants had to scribble down their answers quickly, and then present them for marking at the end.

To the delight of the crowd, Barry was the clear-cut winner, correctly identifying all ten. Jenna reckoned she had got eight, including Spandau Ballet, Adam Ant, Siouxsie and the Banshees, The Cure, Eurythmics, The Style Council, Rod Stewart and Kajagoogoo. The only two she failed to name were Freeez, with their hit 'I.O.U.', and New Edition's 'Candy Girl'. She remembered both songs but couldn't name the bands, which was poor form in the latter case, as it had been number one earlier in the summer.

Barry won a Radio One T-shirt for his troubles, which he elected to change into straight away. This prompted more cheers and wolf whistles from the crowd as he removed his other shirt and pulled on his new prize, showing off his tanned, bare chest in the process.

When the show ended around half past twelve, the crowd gradually dispersed, many in search of lunch or some liquid refreshment which brought good business for both the café and the pub.

The host lingered a little longer, posing for more photos and praising Pencarven for its warm welcome. He had put on a fantastic show, and Jenna felt the satisfaction of another job well done. She had brought something new to the village, and it had been such a hit that perhaps it could become a regular fixture.

She couldn't imagine that something popular among the masses, like this roadshow, would be to the taste of Blake and his rich friends, who would probably look down their noses at Radio One. So that was all the better. Anything that put them off wanting to move here was to be welcomed.

The general feeling in the pub that night was that the event had been a huge success, but as always, there were one or two detractors. One thing council business had taught Jenna was that it was impossible to please everyone.

"Didn't do me any good, did it?" complained Ned to Jenna and Alfie, as he puffed away on a Woodbine. "Do you know how many turned up for my eleven o'clock fishing trip?"

Alfie opened his mouth to reply but never got the chance. Ned had this habit of asking questions he didn't want answered, preferring to supply the answer himself so people wouldn't break his narrative flow.

"I'll tell you how many. None. That's the first time I've ever had none. And do you know why?"

Jenna and Alfie again kept silent, knowing their input was not required.

"Because they were all down at your bloody radio show listening to that awful modern pop music. What you see in that dreadful racket, I will never know. Then there are all these trendy DJs who are way too fond of their own voices. Whatever happened to Pete Murray? Now there was a man who knew how to conduct himself on the radio."

"I thought your boat looked packed when it came back in this afternoon," observed Alfie.

"Aye, in the afternoon, maybe."

"You said the afternoon trips were usually quieter," said Alfie.

"They are as a rule, boy."

"There you go, then. The roadshow brought hundreds more people here today, and they were looking for something else to do this afternoon."

"You probably had more people on that trip than you'd usually get from the two sessions put together," added Jenna. "So you've benefitted, just like everyone else."

"Are you two ganging up on me?" said Ned. "All I'm saying is that music's not what it was in my day. And I'll thank you not to keep retuning my radio and turning it up so loud every time you borrow my van. I got in there this morning, started her up, and nearly split my eardrums. It took me ages to get it back to Terry Wogan."

Strangely, Jenna could sort of see where he was coming from, thinking of how she felt about the music of the 1980s compared to the uninspiring offerings of the 2020s. Then, she had been about the same age that Ned was now.

Nostalgia was a funny thing. Ned loved the 1950s, Jenna loved the 1980s, and perhaps the middle-aged people of the 1950s had once pined for the 1920s. But Jenna had a unique advantage over them all.

While most people could only look back wistfully on their lost youth, she was living it again, day by day, moment by moment. It was an experience few could even dare to imagine, and with each passing week, she was reminded just how extraordinary the gift she had been given truly was.

And if it all played out against a soundtrack of the music from the era she had loved the most, well, that was just a bonus.

September 1983

The tourist season tended to end more quickly each year than it began, with the crowds rapidly vanishing from Pencarven in the early weeks of September.

The first Saturday of the month was the turning point when new arrivals were far outnumbered by those departing ahead of the new school term. After that date, it reverted to being mostly pensioners and families with toddlers, making for a quieter atmosphere compared to the hustle and bustle of July and August.

The afternoons still retained a pleasant warmth, but an increasing crispness had begun creeping into the mornings, and the daylight was now noticeably fading earlier each day. The beach was looking rather spartan now, dotted with only a handful of windbreaks from those hardy souls who refused to accept that summer was over.

The drop-off in visitors eased the strain on Jenna at the caravan park, where her kids' club continued only in the mornings for the pre-schoolers. The surf shack was still open but was doing a fraction of the trade it had been in August, though Alfie remained hopeful of coaxing a few more weeks of custom out of the dwindling visitor numbers before he would have to close for the winter.

Jenna had wondered if the upcoming film shoot might draw extra sightseers into Pencarven, but that didn't seem to be the case. Although there had been a fair deal of publicity about the production in the local newspapers, hardly anyone outside Cornwall appeared to know it was taking place.

Without social media or national news coverage, there was no easy way to spread the word, which was probably the way the film company wanted it. The time to promote the production would be when the paying public could go and spend money watching it in the cinema, not when they might make a nuisance of themselves by getting in the way of filming.

Shooting was scheduled to begin mid-month, and Morgan, expecting Blake to arrive shortly beforehand, was busy with preparations. The first job was clearing out the camping field so Blake could have the privacy he had demanded. He wasn't allowing any more tents in, even though that meant turning away paying customers in the days leading up to his famous visitor's arrival.

He wasn't bothered by the loss of earnings, boasting to Jenna about how much Blake was paying him. It was ten times the going rate. That didn't surprise her because that was his style. He effectively bought people and everyone had their price – a phrase she remembered him being fond of uttering.

She was dreading his arrival, still not quite sure how she was going to handle it. It was also another reminder of the ever-present worry of the state of her parents' marriage. She felt guilty for neglecting them during the summer rush, and with her reduced hours at the caravan park she planned to spend more time at home.

She began by offering her services behind the bar again, especially in the evenings, since that was when David's drinking was at its worst. If she was pulling the pints, she might at least be able to curb how much he consumed. She could also ensure that the pub stuck rigidly to the licensing laws, ensuring not a drop was served after eleven and that everyone was out the door by twenty past.

These changes did have some beneficial effects, including ensuring her father went to bed at least semi-sober more often than not, but they didn't do anything to fix the overarching problem. The frosty atmosphere at the breakfast table persisted, no matter what she tried to say to lighten the mood.

One tack she used was to try to get them to focus on the business. Once again, she raised the question of the pub doing food, thinking if she could get them working together on that it might help. It was to no avail because they remained stubbornly entrenched in their positions on opposite sides of the debate. Morwenna was keen on the idea, but David wasn't.

Meanwhile, the days slid further into early autumn, the sky still bright but with the gradual dropping off in temperature hinting that winter was on the horizon. It was also a reminder for Jenna that her days here were numbered, something she didn't want to think about, most of all because of her romance with Alfie. She was completely in love with him and the thought of leaving him behind at the end of the year was unbearable.

Trade for the other locals in the tourist trade was also falling away, which became the main topic of conversation in the pub on the second Monday in September, Jenna's first night back behind the bar. Ned, Jack, and Willy were already perched on their usual stools as the conversation turned to their winter prospects.

"You see, I told you this would happen, boy," said Ned to Alfie, who had just come in. Ned had arrived much earlier than usual, not long after evening opening, rueing his lack of business for the day. "It's all very well you and your girlfriend saying, 'let's embrace the tourist trade', but what happens now? I didn't even bother going out this afternoon. Only one bloke turned up – and that was just some old pensioner in a flat cap so I'd have had to give him the concession rate."

"You turned him away?" asked Alfie. "You shouldn't turn away paying customers. It creates a bad impression."

"That's easy for you to say – if only one surfer turns up, you can give him a board and a wetsuit and off he goes. Costs you nothing. I can't take the boat out for one person. I'd spend more on fuel than he'd pay me for his fare."

"I suppose you've got a point," replied Alfie.

"I know I've got a point, and here's another. What am I going to live on for the next seven or eight months until the tourists come back? And the same goes for you, while we're on the subject. I can't imagine you're going to have crowds of surfers queuing up in November, desperate to get out on the balmy Atlantic waves."

"We discussed all that in the spring, Dad, when we started this. You were raking it in during high season – three or four times what the fishing used to make. The idea was to make hay while the sun shone and put it away for the colder months. I've set aside a fair bit, and yes, the winter will be lean, but I'll muddle through. I can give you some extra every month plus I'm still paying you back for lending me the money for the shack in the first place. Don't worry, you won't starve."

"Still won't be enough, though," insisted Ned. "Trying to cram a year's earnings into four months is not a good business model if you ask me. What about you, Jack?"

"It'll be tight," he admitted. "But my boat is still rigged up for deep-sea fishing. I was thinking of going out once or twice a week, just to keep the wolf from the door."

"That doesn't help me," said Ned. "All my gear went up in smoke on *The Buccaneer*. I never bothered outfitting *The Saucy Nancy* for mackerel. It'd cost me a packet to convert it now, and it's not worth it."

"Well, I'll be fine," said Willy, sipping his orange juice. "Just had my best summer ever. Know what I did today?"

"Not much, I'd guess," said Ned. "It rained most of the afternoon."

"I know, so I drove the van into Bodmin, popped down to Lunn Poly, and booked a fortnight on the Costa del Sol. Four-star hotel, full board – just the job. All paid for by selling 99s, Mini Milks, and Lemon Sparkles. In two weeks from now, it'll be sangria all the way!"

"It's alright for some," said Ned.

"We'll be alright, Dad," said Alfie, but Jenna couldn't help noticing the slight look of concern on his face. She could guess what he was thinking. His dad hadn't blown the year's profits already, surely?

"If you say so, boy," said Ned, easing his concern. "Though we'll need to plan better for next year."

"Tell you what, Ned," said Willy, "I could bring you back some Woodbines from Spain, duty-free. Save you a few quid. Since you're struggling, like. I'll split the difference with you."

"Don't put yourself out on my account," said Ned, scowling. Hearing Willy boast about his good fortune while he wasn't doing as well was dispiriting. It was also bad form, as far as he was concerned.

"Do they even do Woodbines in Spain?" asked Alfie. "You're the only person I know who still smokes them. They are a bit old-fashioned."

"Perfect for Ned, then," remarked Willy, triggering laughter from everyone except the butt of his joke who did not see the funny side.

Later, when Jenna talked with Alfie, he confided that he had put aside more than he had revealed to his dad during the summer. He felt confident about surviving the off-season, even if he had to support Ned through some of it. His first year's takings were better than he'd forecast, thanks to the hot summer, and with all he'd learnt, he was sure 1984 would be better still, especially if they were blessed with decent weather again.

The pub, too, had profited during the long hot months but Jenna's efforts to persuade her father to invest more in the business while they were in better shape fell on deaf ears. He also refused to discuss the subject of insurance, and she suspected he still hadn't paid it.

That left her relying on the new sea wall to save the pub. Though the plans were in place for completion later in the autumn, she knew from experience that such projects could be held up by anything from bad weather to strikes or contractual squabbles. She felt that she'd covered every angle, but there was no telling when a rogue spanner might land in the works.

Over the following few days, Pencarven became a hive of activity due to the members of the arriving film crew meticulously scouring the village for the best places to exploit its 'olde world' charm. They spent hours wandering the cobbled lanes leading up from the harbour. Some of the narrow, crooked passageways between the oldest cottages were perfect for scenes in which smugglers would skulk through the shadows by lantern light. They also mapped out the route for a dramatic chase scene on horseback when the authorities were hunting down the smugglers.

Unlike most places in Britain, Pencarven had retained its traditional lampposts around the harbour, even if they were no longer gaslit. In the alleys where they planned to do much of the filming, there was barely any lighting at all, so they would be able to use flaming torches which always added an authentic touch to these period pieces.

Modern shopfronts that betrayed the current era were easily covered, and the production team negotiated with Shelly to convert her café for a few days into a blacksmith's, explaining how they would bring in rustic furniture, props, and heaps of straw – as well as redecorating the front of the café to fit its new fictional purpose. In return, she would be generously compensated for the loss of trade, which she naturally overestimated, using August's peak sales figures as a guide.

There was an opportunity for the pub too, set to be turned into a 17th-century tavern under the temporary name of The Smugglers' Rest, with all filming to take place in the afternoons when the pub was closed. Because the interior was already so traditional, only minimal changes were needed: they simply covered the modern taps, brought in some wooden barrels, and removed any conspicuous contemporary signage. A few bits of old sackcloth draped over the optics hid any modern brands on display.

Allowing filming at the pub posed another dilemma for Jenna, aware that it would inevitably bring Blake into contact with Morwenna. Yet she realised this was bound to happen sooner or later anyway, and the extra money from the film crew was tempting, so she convinced her father it was worthwhile and arranged to handle the negotiations herself. If she didn't, she knew that they would go and talk to James Pascoe up at The Anchor, and why should he benefit? She still hadn't forgiven him for messing her about at the parish council meeting earlier in the year, since when he had consistently proven to be useless as a parish councillor.

Discussions over the use of the pub were led by the set designer and director, rather than Brad and Harvey, the two producers she had coerced into funding the sea defences back in the spring. It was a relief not to deal with them as Jenna suspected they wouldn't be thrilled at her extracting yet more money out of their production. Together with her mother and father, she struck a lucrative deal, and she was pleased that at last the three of them had achieved something positive for the business together.

Some of the other modern trappings outside in the village were more troublesome, with television aerials posing the biggest issue. They couldn't simply airbrush them out with CGI – such technology didn't exist in 1983. In the end, a combination of clever camera angles and temporary removals did the trick, with assurances the aerials would be reinstalled and a modest payment made to any homeowners upset that they might be missing some crucial developments in *Emmerdale Farm*.

Down at the harbour, local children were thrilled when a replica pirate ship took up residence, with *The Saucy Nancy* and the other modern boats moved out of the harbour and moored in the next bay. After lamenting the state of his finances just days earlier, Ned was only too happy to cash in by shifting his boat for the duration of the filming. By claiming he took out fifty people a day on it, he too was able to claim a healthy compensation from the film crew, which all boded well for the Trelawney family's winter finances.

Meanwhile the rest of the harbour required surprisingly little dressing, already cluttered as it was with ancient nets, rotting timber, and the other battered remnants of the once-bustling fishing trade. A rusty old anchor half-buried in sand, and encrusted with barnacles, provided a nice touch, which the director planned to feature prominently in an opening panoramic shot of the harbour.

As the start of filming approached, a palpable buzz spread across Pencarven. The film crew mingled freely with the locals, who, despite the inevitable disruption, were thrilled at the idea that, in just a few months, their little village would be starring on the big screen.

With everything arranged, Jenna knew it was time to face her nemesis, an encounter that took place earlier than she was expecting.

She had finished her Friday morning shift at the caravan park but Morgan had asked if she could mind the front desk for an hour over lunch. His usual receptionist had cried off sick and he needed to pop into Camelford to do the banking. Despite a red pulse from the bracelet, she agreed, unable to think of a valid excuse not to, and reasoning that nothing particularly catastrophic could happen behind a reception desk. Even if it did, at least she had been warned.

Almost an hour after Morgan left, she discovered the reason for that warning. The park had been gearing up for Blake's scheduled arrival on Saturday, but now the low, heavy rumble of a large vehicle announced someone coming up the track. Leaning forward on her chair, she peered out of the window and felt nauseous at what she saw.

A hulking motorhome, one she recognised only too well from her past life, was grinding its way up the gravel slope, engine working overtime with the gradient as it negotiated the sharp turn leading to that gate. It was far larger than the usual touring vans that holidaymakers brought, with a glossy beige-and-brown exterior and huge blacked-out side windows framed with shiny chrome trims.

It resembled something from an American road movie rather than a sleepy corner of Cornwall. The driver's cab alone was large enough to dwarf a typical family car and she was amazed it had even got up here. She had seen delivery trucks smaller than this struggling.

The heavy tyres crunched the gravel loudly beneath them, and with the windows of reception closed against the stiff breeze and squally rain showers, she could feel them vibrate from the engine's deep growl.

She took a moment to compose herself, trying not to think about what had happened to her in that vehicle before – the place where she had lost her virginity, possibly against her will. She still struggled with processing what had occurred that night, even after all this time.

So much for avoiding contact with Blake until she had figured out a plan. Not only had he turned up a day early, but now she was going to be the first person he encountered on his arrival, scuppering her plans to be nowhere near this place on Saturday.

He stopped right outside reception, completely blocking the road and the entrance to the car park, which was typical of Blake. It would only inconvenience the 'little people', as she recalled him referring to the public, and to him, they were of no consequence.

That was unless one happened to be a woman he could potentially fuck, of course. Then they interested him, right up until he got what he wanted.

It had been raining heavily shortly before his arrival, and because of that, there was nobody about. The park's dwindling number of residents had retreated to their caravans for shelter, where they were now having lunch and gazing out at the gloomy skies, probably wishing they had been able to afford to come in the summer instead.

Blake opened the cab door, jumped down to the tarmac, and walked with purpose up the path to reception. He was in his early forties, with the kind of commanding presence that made it obvious why the tabloids were speculating about him replacing an ageing Roger Moore as James Bond. His stride was confident, radiating the self-assured poise of a man who was totally at ease with himself.

He had dark hair, neatly trimmed and brushed back, with not a hint of grey, giving a youthful edge to his mature, assured persona. His skin was tanned and smooth, and then there were his eyes – piercing, blue, almost hypnotic, just as Jenna remembered. He could seduce a woman at fifty paces with those eyes alone.

Blake's attire consisted of a tailored suede jacket over a red cashmere sweater. Slim-fitting trousers in deep charcoal and polished leather shoes with discreet buckles completed his outfit – smart yet casual, the perfect choice for his drive down from London. Whatever Blake did, or wherever he went, he always looked immaculate.

She braced herself as he reached the reception door. How could she turn this situation to her advantage? Right now, she knew him, but he didn't know her. That gave her an edge, right? She was still trying to persuade herself of that as he flung open the door and strode up to the desk, immediately making and holding eye contact.

Jenna knew from experience this was one of the tricks he used on any woman he saw as ripe for seduction, but she wasn't going to be intimidated. She

197

gave as good as she got, returning his gaze, unblinking. She could already see the animal look of desire in his eyes and knew exactly what he would be thinking. But she was determined to seize control of the situation and had thought of the perfect way to put him on the back foot.

"Good morning, sir. Can I help you?"

"I believe you've been expecting me," he said, flashing a smile of impossibly white teeth. He must have had them done.

"And you are...?"

His smile faded momentarily, and she knew she would have triggered his egotistical nature. He was one of the most famous film stars in the world, he would be thinking. How could she not know who he was?

"Blake Cadwallader. I'm surprised you don't recognise me."

"Should I?" she replied, making a show of thumbing through the booking folder in front of her and deliberately taking her time to make him sweat.

"Yes, you should," he said. "I'm a famous film star. You do have cinemas down here in the sticks, right?"

"Ah, yes, here you are, Mr Cadwallader. It seems we have a bit of a mix-up. Your booking doesn't start until tomorrow."

"Maybe it does, but I'm here now. I'm sure you can find a way to accommodate me, can you not?"

He locked eyes with her as he said this, phrasing it in such a way that the implied double meaning was obvious. He was trying it on already, but that was nothing she hadn't been expecting.

"Well, I'm not too sure about that, Mr Cadwallader. We've got a couple of abattoir workers from Swindon camping in the field we were going to allocate to your vehicle, and they're not leaving until tomorrow. Perhaps you could come back then?"

She had fabricated this simply to gauge his reaction, the truth being that Morgan had cleared the field days ago. She wasn't disappointed by his response.

"This is outrageous," he said, losing his cool. "I'm an international star, shooting a multi-million-pound movie here next week, and you expect me to wait another day for the sake of two blokes who chop up animals for a living! Do you know how much I'm paying for this pitch?"

That was exactly what she wanted to see: Blake, the man who always got what he wanted, losing his temper when encountering opposition, particularly when it was over something so trivial from someone menial like Jenna. He expected the likes of her to instantly yield to his commands – whether they be related to business or pleasure. Usually, he only had to click his fingers to get everyone around him dancing to his tune.

The more she thought about, it, the more she realised this could be the key to his downfall. He simply couldn't bear not getting his way and that was a weakness – one she could exploit.

"Of course, Mr Cadwallader, you should have said. Let me see what I can do for you."

199

She made a further show of browsing through the book, spinning it out for as long as she dared before it became too obvious she was leaving him dangling.

"You're in luck. We do have a spot for you. Come with me, please."

Subsequently, she showed him the way to the field he had always been destined for anyway, acting as though she was doing him a huge favour. Once he was parked up, he had regained his composure and turned on the charm once again.

"Thank you, Miss..."

"Rae's the name," she replied. "Jenna Rae."

It amused her to deliver it in the manner James Bond often introduced himself, knowing how much Blake coveted that role, yet she knew something he didn't. He was never destined to secure it, because the next James Bond would be Timothy Dalton.

"Well, Jenna, I can't thank you enough for finding me this pitch."

"Not at all," she said. "I'm just surprised you want to stay in our humble park instead of a hotel or with the rest of the film crew."

"The thing is, Jenna, I like my privacy."

I'll bet you do, she thought, but didn't dare say it. She didn't want him getting any inkling that she had his card marked. Not yet anyway.

"Speaking of which, how would you like to come in and look around the motorhome? It's luxurious and has everything you could ever want. I've even got some champagne on ice, just in case anyone special should happen to drop by."

She wasn't remotely surprised by this invitation but swiftly declined it.

"That's most kind of you, Mr Cadwallader, but I really must get back to reception," she replied. "We are very busy today."

"I don't think you are," said Blake, once again fixing those cold blue eyes on her. "I haven't seen another soul since we got here. No one's going to miss you, so come inside. You won't regret it."

Even knowing all she did about him, Jenna could see how easily he had seduced so many women, including her in the old timeline. He possessed an indescribable allure that cheap romance novels described as making heroines swoon, or go weak at the knees. Whatever it was he had, certain pheromones or something else that she couldn't put into words but only feel, she could feel it exuding from him right now. But there was no way she would fall for it a second time.

"Oh, I think I would," she said. "Now I must get on." Then to her alarm, he grabbed her arm just above her wrist in a vice-like grip. He was muscular and very strong and she realised if it came to having to fight him off, she would probably be unable to.

"Just ten minutes," he urged. "I absolutely insist."

This was getting out of hand. Had she made a mistake by putting herself in this situation? And why hadn't the bracelet warned her that something like this might happen? Then she recalled that it had, back when Morgan first asked her to mind the front desk. She hadn't taken it seriously and that had been a mistake. Things had been going so well lately, she had become over-confident, and now she had put herself in danger.

Fortunately, salvation was at hand as she spotted Morgan's car turning in through the gate. He instantly clocked the motorhome and drove past the clubhouse towards them. Simultaneously a couple of young women, emerging from a caravan in the adjoining field now that the rain had stopped, passed the entrance and spotted the two of them.

"Look, it's Blake Cadwallader!" shrieked one of them excitedly, and she rushed into the field through the gate they had neglected to close on their way in. Blake had demanded strong locks and security but they were no good if he left the gate wide open. He had no choice but to release his grip.

"Looks like your fan club's arrived," said Jenna as the women approached, followed by Morgan's 1977 dark blue Ford Cortina.

"Let me tell you something," said Blake, speaking quickly to get out what he wanted to say before the new arrivals came within earshot. "Firstly, I always get what I want. Secondly, I never take no for an answer. Remember that."

Then the two women were upon him, one of them fishing a notepad out of her pocket to demand an autograph, as Morgan pulled up, practically stumbling out of the car in his haste to fawn over his celebrity guest.

In all the excitement, Jenna slipped away, though she could feel his gaze burning into her back as she got out of there as fast as possible.

What had gone wrong? She had felt so in control while winding him up at reception, but after that, somehow he had turned the tables. He was far more menacing and dangerous than she remembered, and now she had rebuffed his advances, she had made him view her as a challenge. That hadn't been very clever.

All in all, this had not got off to a good start.

October 1983

Blake's presence in Pencarven had made Jenna's life extremely uncomfortable in the weeks following his arrival. Not only was he doing all the things she remembered him doing previously – including sleeping his way through the village's women – but now, seeing seducing Jenna as a challenge, he was constantly in her face.

Any attempts she made to convince the other villagers that Blake was not the wonderful man they believed him to be fell on deaf ears. It was infuriating. Telling other women he was a sexual predator had little impact when they desired him to the extent that they dismissed her claims out of hand. She had expected better of them, but they were all acting like giggling teenagers, reminding her of those women who routinely threw their knickers onto the stage at Tom Jones concerts.

Even the menfolk of the town, whom she'd suspected might resent this rich upstart swanning around like a ram in a field of ewes, seemed unbothered. They were as much in awe of him as the women.

It put Jenna in mind of a film quote. She couldn't remember exactly who had said it or where it was from but it was along the lines of 'women wanted him and men wanted to be him'. Maybe it was Austin Powers, but since that film wouldn't be out for another fourteen years she had no way to check.

It was an apt enough phrase for the situation, though. She knew for a fact that Blake had slept with at least two married women in the first week after his arrival, because Shelly had told her. She wondered if their husbands knew. Would they even care if they did? It was all very peculiar, particularly in a community that was generally rather Victorian in its attitudes. She tried not to dwell on it but thoughts of Morwenna and David were never far from her mind. Would her mother be next on his list of conquests?

Every attempt at trying to expose his immorality, even if she mentioned his forcefulness when he had grabbed her arm outside the motorhome, fell flat. In some cases, she almost felt it was encouraging those she warned. A prime example was what happened after a conversation she had with Shelly in the café.

"But don't you think it's a bit sleazy?" argued Jenna, tucking into a Cornish pasty over lunch, on her way back from her final kids' club session of the season. "All those women he's slept with – aren't they worried they might catch something?"

"Oh, I'd risk it for a roll in the hay with him," replied Shelly, infuriating Jenna.

"How can you degrade yourself like this? Do you really want to be some rich man's plaything? Come on, Shelly, you're better than that."

"I'll be his plaything any time he wants," said Shelly. "I'm a free agent. And if he's as randy as you claim, it must be my turn soon."

There was no point trying to dissuade her, and sure enough, a few days later Shelly turned up to see Morwenna one afternoon, positively glowing and bursting to spill the beans about what she'd been up to.

All the gory details came out over tea and some leftover scones she had brought from the café.

The gist of it was that she had seen Blake passing the café just as she was opening up that morning before any customers had arrived. She had invited him in for coffee, flipped the sign on the door over to 'Closed', and made it blatantly obvious by walking around behind the counter, bending over and sticking her bottom out with the pretence of getting something out of the oven, that there was more than coffee and cake on offer.

Her protruding posterior was an open invitation, and seconds later he was giving her a good seeing-to over the counter, sending scones and pasties flying in all directions. When Shelly related that part of the tale, Jenna almost choked on the scone she was munching, wondering exactly where it had been while this sordid act had been taking place.

When Blake left, Shelly gave the counter a quick wipe and reopened the door, pulling her clothing back into shape as her unsuspecting clientele wandered in. For someone who had been single for years, and almost given up hope, she likened it to a thunderstorm in a drought-stricken desert.

As far as Shelly was concerned she had done nothing wrong, and technically that was true. Jenna couldn't judge her too harshly for it. It was more the way Morwenna was lapping up the details, eyes sparkling with unbridled lust, that unsettled Jenna as she listened to Shelly's confession. Her face was full of excitement along with a hint of jealousy that gave out a vibe of 'I wish it had been me'.

Perhaps it soon would be. With Blake tearing through the local womenfolk like a starving man at an all-you-can-eat buffet, he was bound to target Morwenna sooner or later, especially given the history between them in the other timeline.

Finishing work at the park for the season was a relief. After their fractious encounter on the first day, it hadn't taken Blake long to work out Jenna's daily routine. He swiftly developed the unwelcome habit of appearing around the time she finished her shift, even requesting filming breaks to facilitate it. One of his favourite tricks was to accost her on her way back down to the village, first attempting to woo her, then turning borderline aggressive when she rebuffed him.

She had considered asking Alfie to walk her home, but that would require explaining why, and she didn't want to create conflict between him and Blake. In her previous life, she had heard rumours of sticky ends coming to the few men who dared to oppose him. These included whispers about a couple of high-profile deaths – one who had allegedly shot himself and another who had been the subject of a hit-and-run.

In both cases, there had been circumstantial reasons to suspect foul play, but Blake had friends in high places and ensured any association connecting him to the deaths was swiftly quashed. She wasn't sure how true any of it was, but she wasn't about to risk Alfie's safety. The bracelet had also suggested, with a red pulse when she thought about it, that it was a bad idea.

The only option was to bite her tongue for now, and hope things might get easier now she no longer had to go to the caravan park. She couldn't stop Blake from turning up at the pub though, which he frequently did, often accompanied by other actors or members of the production crew. His mere presence made her skin crawl, but she still went out of her way to serve him whenever he approached the bar.

She reasoned that if she got to him before Morwenna did, at least she was protecting her mother. The biggest issue with that was that Morwenna didn't want mollycoddling from her daughter and made her annoyance plain whenever Jenna elbowed her aside to get to Blake first.

Thankfully, filming in the village was nearing completion, with the crew set to move over to the caves in the middle of October. Hopefully, that would mean Blake wouldn't be around the village quite so much. In the meantime, to take her mind off her issues with him, the bracelet had a new task lined up for her.

It had been some time since Jenna's last bracelet-inspired dream, and to begin with, she wasn't even sure if this was one of them. It could just have been a normal dream brought on by observing costume-clad pirates wandering around all over Pencarven for weeks. It would have been nothing out of the ordinary for her subconscious to fashion some night-time scenario out of that.

When it came to pirates and buried treasure, the obvious trope that sprang to mind was of a bulging chest, buried somewhere shown on a map where X marked the spot. Some fevered digging would uncover the prize, and the lid, once opened, would reveal a rich trove of gold, jewels and other ill-gotten gains.

That was how it was usually portrayed in books and films. Whether this film they were making contained such scenes she had no idea. From what she had gathered from the crew members in the pub, the plot focused more on smuggling in historic Cornwall than the traditional parrot-on-the-shoulder, walking-the-plank, pieces-of-eight sorts of pirates.

That was why the crew had been so keen to film in the caves. They were perfect for portraying smugglers landing in the dead of night to spirit away their goods through the extensive network of caves and tunnels that ran through the cliffs behind the neighbouring cove. This was the same cove in which Gordon and his fellow cult members had carried out their rituals and orgies before Jenna exposed them. Since that unsavoury debacle, the locals had nicknamed it 'Devil's Bay', a moniker that seemed to have stuck, and it was this place that her dream was imploring her to visit.

She didn't need a treasure map with an X on it because, in her dream, she had been shown exactly where she needed to dig.

"Is this for real?" she said out loud shortly after waking up, and glancing down at the bracelet, which pulsed green at her. That was all the confirmation she needed, and she sensed the need to get to the caves with some urgency. She had to get to the loot before anyone else, the most likely candidates being the film crew. If any digging or burying was going on in the story, then there was a possibility they might discover by chance whatever was down there.

She had kept Alfie in the dark about Blake's harassment but had no hesitation about involving him in this. It was Sunday, so neither of them was working, and after checking the tide times, she called round to see Alfie, who was intrigued at what she had to say. With Ned out enjoying a Sunday lunchtime pint, they were able to talk freely.

"We're going on a what?" he asked.

"A treasure hunt!" she declared, trying to conjure up an air of mystery by clasping her hands in front of her chest.

"You mean like one of those where you drive from place to place looking for clues? We did one around the Newquay area last year."

"Much better than that," said Jenna, trying to maintain the suspense. "One with real treasure! I don't have time to explain now as I need to get back to the pub. I'm supposed to be on the lunchtime session and it's already ten past twelve. Meet me outside your shack at six o'clock tonight, and bring a shovel. I'll bring the torches. We will need them where we're going."

Low tide was at seven, and she knew they would have only a couple of hours to get around the rocks into the caves and back. She wasn't sure how long the digging might take.

They met outside the shack at the appointed time and made their way round into the newly named Devil's Bay, with Jenna filling him in on where they were going and why as they walked across the sand. Already the light was beginning to fade on what had been a cloudy and dull day.

"But how can you be so sure this treasure is there?" asked Alfie. "I mean, someone must have told you."

210

She had been expecting this question and had already prepared her answer.

"You must remember the rumours when we were kids? About treasure in those caves?"

"Yeah, but that was just our childish imaginations, surely. And besides, I remember digging in there with some friends for just that reason, and I never found anything."

"Perhaps you weren't digging in the right spot. My grandad was convinced there was something there, he used to go on about it all the time. Now, the film crew are going to be all over those caves for the next few days. If there's anything there, we need to get to it before they do."

"If there was something buried, surely someone else would have found it by now. I mean, we've lived here all our lives. The caves have been thoroughly explored and there have been plenty of folk who have gone looking with metal detectors. Why are the film crew likely to find something that no one else ever has?"

"I don't know, just call it a hunch, but last night I dreamt of the exact spot where we need to dig. What harm can it do to go and have a look? It's better than staying in and watching *Highway*."

Alfie looked at her, eyes full of curiosity at how she seemed to know so much. How many more times could she pass off these things as luck or hunches? They were in an intimate relationship and deeply in love; she couldn't keep hiding things from him. If she did it much longer, what guarantee was there he wouldn't feel resentful at her for not confiding in him all these months?

There and then, she resolved that before the year was out, she would tell him everything. But now, as they walked up the cove, was not the time. They had some treasure to find.

Usually this cove was deserted, but not today. The film crew had been shipping gear by boat and had erected a temporary canvas shelter near the cave entrance to store what they'd be using over the next few days. As they entered the caves, they also discovered a scattering of props: wooden torches on the walls, presumably to be lit during takes, along with a few old barrels and boxes.

"When did you say filming was starting?" asked Alfie, as they switched on their battery-powered torches.

"Tomorrow," said Jenna. "So it looks like we got here just in time."

"That's if there's anything here," said Alfie, as they walked deeper into the tunnel.

"Oh, there will be," she replied, then paused, her ears catching something from further ahead in the caves. "Listen – did you hear that?"

"Hear what?"

"Stand still and be quiet a minute," she said.

He complied, and there it was again. The faint scrape of metal on rock echoed through the gloom, followed by a larger clatter and shout of, "Bloody hell," from an unseen man. The shovel must have caught on something. Then the digging continued.

"I think someone's got here before us," said Jenna, creeping forward.

212

"Careful," cautioned Alfie, taking her arm. "They could be dangerous."

"You don't think it's real pirates, do you?" asked Jenna, who was looking at the bracelet for guidance. It was green, which didn't suggest they were in any danger.

"That would be a turn-up, wouldn't it?" said Alfie. "Perhaps they time-travelled here from the seventeenth century."

"Stranger things have happened," remarked Jenna, thinking about how she had come to be here in the first place. Then she thought about the man she had heard cry out. She felt instinctively that she knew him, but couldn't quite place him.

"You know, there was something familiar about that voice."

"You're right," said Alfie. "Do you think it could be someone we know?"

"Only one way to find out," she said. "Come on, let's be brave."

"And end up buried next to the treasure?"

"We'll be fine," she said, and as soon as they rounded the corner and recognised who had been doing the digging, she knew they had nothing to fear.

The man had brought his own torch, set on a rock to illuminate where he was digging. With that light, and the two new torches now on him, it was easy to identify him, and as he turned, startled by the fresh beams of light hitting his suntanned face, they exclaimed his name in unison.

"Willy!"

213

"What are you doing here?" added Jenna. "Aren't you meant to be in Spain? You certainly look like you've been abroad. Did you know your nose is peeling?"

"I... I got back last night," he said, clearly startled by their unexpected arrival.

"And just popped down to the caves for a spot of archaeology?" asked Alfie.

"Yes, well, it looks like I'm not the only one!" said Willy, as they moved closer and he spotted the shovel in Alfie's hand. "How did you two find out about the money?"

"And what money might that be?" asked Alfie.

"You must know, or you wouldn't be here. Though how you know is beyond me. He told me he hadn't told a soul before he confided in me."

"And who is he?" asked Jenna.

"Don't play the innocent, Jenna, you know very well. You seem to know everything else that's going on around here. I'm guessing he must have left some clue behind at the office and you found it."

"Here's a suggestion," said Jenna. "Why don't you tell us everything you know, and then we'll give you our side of the story."

With any luck, he would tell them everything so she wouldn't have to say anything, particularly since she had nothing to go on but her dream.

"Fine," said Willy. "So, you knew I was going to the Costa del Sol, right?"

"Of course. You were going on about it long enough in the pub, flashing your money around," she replied.

"Yes, and boasting how you were the ice cream king of Cornwall," added Alfie.

"Right, well, I flew down there a couple of weeks ago and stayed in a lovely little hotel in Marbella."

"That was an odd choice," said Jenna. "I thought Torremolinos would have been more your scene."

"I could afford to go upmarket, so why not? Anyway, while I was there I started going into a few expat bars. There are loads of Brits down there – many of them not able to come back, if you know what I mean. Thanks to the current extradition situation, the law back here can't touch them."

"That's why they call it the Costa del Crime, isn't it?" asked Alfie.

"Exactly. So I wandered into one of these British bars one afternoon and who should I run into but none other than your predecessor, Gordon Pentreath himself."

"So the IRA didn't get him after all?" asked Alfie, recalling the ludicrous theories floating around the pub a few months back.

"No, but the Old Bill will if he comes back. He explained it all over several drinks, which were all on him, incidentally. He seemed remarkably pleased to see me, which was a surprise. When he lived here, the bastard treated me like something on the bottom of his shoe. Anyway, I soon found out why he was being so nice."

"Would that reason have anything to do with why you're here now?"

"Spot on," he said. "The thing is, he had to get out of Pencarven in a hurry, which meant leaving something behind."

"The something you're digging up now?" asked Jenna.

"Got it in one. There's fifty grand in a suitcase buried down here. He can't come back and fetch it, so he wants me to take it to him."

"That's a bit risky, isn't it?" asked Alfie. "What if customs stop you at the airport?"

"I was going to hire a car, take the hovercraft from Dover and drive down. There's far less chance of getting stopped that way."

"What's in it for you?" asked Alfie.

"I get to keep five grand," said Willy. "That's worth the risk, in my opinion."

"But you've blown it already," said Jenna. "Never mind being caught by customs, we've already rumbled you, and you haven't even dug it up yet."

"Perhaps we should get on with it, then," said Alfie, shovel in hand, as he joined Willy and the two of them resumed digging together.

"Try a couple of feet to the left," suggested Jenna, recalling her dream and noticing Willy hadn't been in quite the right spot.

Soon, they unearthed a battered black leather briefcase containing the ex-councillor's shady earnings. Brushing off the dirt, they opened it with the code Gordon had given Willy, who had refused to cooperate unless he was able to take out his share first. That was remarkably trusting but since Gordon didn't have any other options, he had no choice. Now, the three of them found themselves staring at fifty thousand pounds in used notes.

It wasn't buried treasure in the way she had imagined, nor had it been there for centuries as her grandfather had suggested, but it was treasure nonetheless.

"What do we do now?" asked Willy, echoing the thoughts of all three of them. Doubtless he was hoping that he was still going to get his hands on some of it.

"Well, Gordon's not getting it, that's for sure," said Jenna.

"And my cut?"

"You don't have a cut. And you don't need it, anyway. You said yourself you made a fortune this summer. Do you want the risk of getting caught with any of this? Five grand of dirty money? What would happen if Matt found out?"

"He won't find out unless you tell him. Will you?"

"I haven't decided yet," she replied.

"What do you suggest, then?" asked Willy. "Handing it in is a mug's game. The authorities won't give it back to the people Gordon ripped off to get it, most of whom were probably bent anyway. And I wouldn't put it past the coppers to slip a few notes into their own pockets while they're counting it."

"I'm not going to hand it in," said Jenna, reaching a decision. "But we're not keeping a penny. I've got a much better idea where it should go and I can't see either of you disagreeing."

She explained her plan, which Alfie was wholeheartedly behind. Willy was a little harder to convince, having just kissed goodbye to five thousand pounds, but in the end he grudgingly accepted. At least the money would be going to a good cause.

"What about Gordon, waiting for me in Spain?" he asked.

"He'll have a long wait," said Jenna. "But I doubt he'll go hungry. And he can hardly come after you, can he? Just don't go to Marbella on holiday next year."

"You're right, he'll be fine," said Willy. "He's got a villa down there with a pool and everything. The greedy bastard can whistle for it."

"We're all agreed, then," said Jenna. "This money's going to a far better place."

True to her word, she and Alfie spent the next couple of days carrying out her plan. They split the money, mostly in used twenty-pound notes, into ten bundles of five thousand each and toured Cornwall's coastline, from Port Isaac to Penlee, stuffing the RNLI's charity boxes at every station. With the organisation relying solely on private donations, Gordon's ill-gotten gains might just save a few lives.

Jenna's little treasure hunt had provided a welcome distraction from the unresolved Blake issue. Although filming was taking place in the caves for a fortnight, he still appeared in the pub most evenings, remaining as popular as ever. Ned, Trevor and others refused to hear anything against him. Why would they, when Blake was buying rounds for everyone every night? Willy was back on the sauce now he was back from his holiday and eagerly joined in too. As for the business of the money, that was never mentioned again between him, Jenna and Alfie. The three of them had agreed to draw a line under it.

The only person in the pub who wasn't happy was David. Despite the extra money coming into the tills, he couldn't fail to notice the attention Blake had started giving Morwenna. She didn't bother trying to hide her attraction, and Blake went out of his way to be flirtatious with her, especially in front of Jenna. It all came to a head one night at the end of October when David and Jenna were scheduled to work together and Morwenna had the night off.

Filming in the caves had finished, and the film crew were packing up now that all the location work was done. There was still a lot of studio filming to do back at Pinewood, but that wouldn't start for another month or so. This left Blake with a few weeks to kill, and on the evening after the crew had left, he surprised the locals by reappearing in the pub and announcing he planned to stay on for a while.

This was no surprise to Jenna, nor was his declaration that Pencarven was the loveliest place in Britain and he intended to make his home here. The locals were delighted, especially as he celebrated by buying "drinks all round."

How easily they were bribed and taken in, she thought. Then again, how could they know that decades later their sons and daughters would be forced to move away, unable to afford homes in the village where

219

generations of their ancestors had been laid to rest in the churchyard? They didn't see what she saw – that they were drinking with the devil.

This was exactly how things had played out before, so she was unsurprised by his next announcement that he planned to build a huge mansion on the cliffs. It was a structure that Jenna knew inside out because she had lived there briefly after Morwenna married Blake in the old timeline. Not much later, after Elliot was born, it became clear that she was surplus to requirements.

At least that was something she could fight. He hadn't had any problem getting permission to build the mansion before when he had Gordon on the payroll. Jenna, on the other hand, would do everything in her power at the council to block his plans. She soon discovered he had already begun laying the groundwork, with surveyors and architects already on the case. He had submitted his application and it would be up for review in November. She would fight it, but first, she had her mother to worry about.

It was the final day of the month, the Monday after the weekend the clocks went back when the final holidaymakers went home after the half-term break. Morgan had now shut the caravan park for winter but Blake and his motorhome remained. Morgan had told him he could stay as long as he liked, and with the site now deserted, Blake would be free to get up to as many shenanigans as he liked, undetected. What he had in mind for that night was what concerned Jenna right now.

David opened the pub at 5.30pm, with Jenna due behind the bar an hour and a half later. Upstairs, when she stepped out of her room onto the landing, she caught the unmistakable smell of Opium by Yves Saint Laurent. It was her mother's favourite perfume which she wore only occasionally when she was going on a big night out.

The bathroom door was ajar, and inside she found Morwenna, in a slinky red dress, the sort of thing she would never normally wear, applying lipstick in the mirror.

"Mother, what are you doing? Why are you getting all tarted up?" She was so used to seeing Morwenna in her traditional rural attire that this was a shock to see.

"Oh, it's a night out with Shelly and a couple of her friends," she said hurriedly. "One of them is turning forty, and we're going into Bodmin to celebrate."

"What friend? I didn't know anyone had a birthday. And why didn't Shelly mention this to me in the café this afternoon?"

"Oh, yeah, er, it's her cousin, actually. She lives in Camelford."

"I don't believe you," said Jenna. "You're going to meet Blake, aren't you?"

"How dare you!" exploded Morwenna. "What do you think I am, some cheap whore?"

"Well, you're certainly going out of your way to look like one," retorted Jenna. Then it hit her out of nowhere: a stinging slap right across the face.

"I don't know who the hell you think you are, Jenna, but stay the fuck out of my life."

With that, she pushed her daughter back and slammed the bathroom door, leaving Jenna, red cheek burning from the pain, stunned by what had just happened.

Her mother had never laid a finger on her or sworn at her before, and now tears pricked the corners of her eyes before overflowing and rolling down her cheeks. She ran to her room, threw herself on her bed and sobbed, overwhelmed by what had just happened.

"I can't do this anymore!" she wailed, eyes drawn to the glowing red bracelet. "I can't stop him destroying everything."

All the stress, the pressure, and the pent-up helplessness of the past weeks poured out of her as she lay there in tears, despairing, for several minutes.

How could she fight Blake? He was going to do all the same things again that he had done before. She had achieved so much against the odds this year but this seemed an impossible task.

Then, from somewhere deep down, she felt her resilience begin to return. She had allowed herself a moment of weakness, but she refused to be beaten. She would pick herself up, dust herself down, and find a way, with or without the bracelet's help.

By the time she got up, it was dark and Morwenna had gone. She stepped into the bathroom, washed her face, and examined her cheek in the mirror. There was still a hint of redness streaked with tears, so she washed her face again with cold water and prepared to act.

She went downstairs to the bar, where her father was behind the bar, and asked if he had seen Morwenna. He hadn't, which didn't surprise her. Dressed as she was, she would have slipped out the back so he wouldn't see her.

"I'm sorry, Dad, but I can't work until later tonight. Something's come up."

"You can't leave me behind the bar on my own! I'll be run off my feet!"

"It's Monday night, you'll be fine," she assured him. "The caravan park's shut, so there won't be any tourists. And I have a feeling Blake won't be in tonight, so this lot won't drink as fast as they do when he's buying. Just hold the fort and I'll be back as soon as I can, okay?"

She pulled on her coat and headed out into the chilly autumn air. Where might her mother be? Was Blake wining and dining her? If so, it wouldn't be in Pencarven. Even at the height of summer, there wasn't much in the way of fine dining in 1983, and she couldn't imagine he would take her to the chippy.

Looking to the bracelet for guidance as she wandered towards the harbour, she saw it was glowing red. She turned and set off in the opposite direction, towards the caravan park, at which point the jewel turned back to green.

Of course, it was obvious. Blake didn't need to take her out to wine and dine to get what he was after. Morwenna must have gone straight there. If Jenna was going to stop anything from happening, she needed to get there fast, remembering Shelly's sordid tale of him taking her over the café counter within minutes.

She passed a few kids out trick-or-treating but once she was out of the village she didn't encounter another soul. It was slightly eerie, out here in the cold and dark as she climbed the track to the park, and she quickened her pace as much as she dared, aware that time was of the essence. She didn't run, though, not wanting to risk slipping on the even ground or being short of breath by the time she got to the top. She needed all her energy for whatever lay ahead.

The lights at the park were off and it was hard to see if there was anyone in the motorhome as she approached, since Blake's blacked-out windows didn't give out any light. But as she reached the door, she could hear laughter and clinking glasses from within. Without delay, she began hammering on it, much as Elliot had on hers, back at the start of all this.

Everything went quiet, and then Blake emerged in a silk dressing gown covered in Japanese writing.

"Jenna," he began, suave as ever, with no hint of surprise at her sudden arrival. "How lovely to see you. I'd love to chat, but I'm rather busy."

"I bet you are," said Jenna, deftly slipping past him and darting through the spacious interior toward the bedroom. She'd never set foot here in this timeline, but she knew its layout. She threw open the door, and there was her mother, sitting up in the bed and clutching a silver satin sheet around her upper body, eyes wide like a rabbit caught in the headlights.

"I knew it!" exclaimed Jenna. "You should be bloody ashamed of yourself. Don't you know where he's been? He's been up half the women in Pencarven, including your best friend Shelly."

224

"I know, and I don't care," said Morwenna, defiantly. "Your father pays me no attention, and you've got Alfie. Why shouldn't I have some fun for a change?"

"He's using you, can't you see? Did you know he tried it on with me?"

As she spoke, Blake appeared behind her, stepping into the room without so much as a flicker of concern at this turn of events, even when Jenna turned to rage at him.

"I bet you didn't tell her about that, did you? And how you didn't like it when I wouldn't play ball. Because I'm the only woman in Pencarven who's turned you down."

"So far," he said.

"And it'll be staying that way. Is this your way of getting back at me? You couldn't have me, so you thought you'd have a crack at my mother instead?"

She turned again, fixing her gaze on Morwenna.

"Don't you see what's going on, Mum? He doesn't want you. He's only got you here to get at me."

"Go home, Jenna," said Morwenna. "You don't know anything about it."

"Oh, I don't think there's any reason for her to rush off," said Blake, relishing the moment. "Why don't you join us, Jenna? I rather fancy a mother/daughter combo. It wouldn't be the first time."

Jenna looked at her mother, seeing her face fall. Surely this was a bridge too far. Blake had crossed an unacceptable boundary and now she needed to press home her advantage.

225

"Do you see what sort of man he is?" she said. "He's seriously suggesting having sex with both of us in the same bed at the same time. For God's sake, Mum, get a grip. This isn't right and you know it."

She looked imploringly at her mother, desperately hoping she would come to her senses. If she didn't baulk at this, then she was lost, probably forever. But thankfully, sanity was about to be restored.

"You're disgusting," said Morwenna, casting a look of distaste at Blake, his spell broken at last. She leapt out of bed and to Jenna's relief, she saw she was still wearing her bra and knickers. They were both black lacy numbers, no doubt purchased especially for the occasion, a far cry from her usual modest white cotton.

"Oh, don't go," said Blake mockingly. "Just as we were all getting to know each other."

"You're not getting to know any more of me," said Morwenna. "Come on, Jenna."

They couldn't get out of there fast enough, not that Blake seemed rattled in the slightest, even shouting after them as they hurried away from the motorhome, "You know where I am if you change your mind."

"In your dreams," shouted back Jenna.

As they hurried back towards the village, Morwenna couldn't apologise enough.

"I'm so sorry, Jenna. I don't know what came over me. I can't believe he would suggest such a thing. And even more, that I was taken in by him."

"You and every other woman around here, it seems. You didn't...you know...did you?"

226

"No," she said. "But if you'd turned up ten minutes later, I probably would have."

"Thank goodness for that," said Jenna, thinking about Elliot, and how she had just effectively erased him from existence. She felt no remorse. Blake's son had grown up to be just as bad as he was.

"And earlier – you know, when I slapped you. Can you forgive me? I'm so sorry."

"Don't worry about it," said Jenna. "I'm just glad you've finally seen his true colours. That man is bad news, and we've got to get rid of him. Are you with me?"

"Absolutely," said Morwenna. "Listen, about Dad. He doesn't need to know what happened tonight, does he?"

"Probably not," said Jenna. "But you two have got to sort yourselves out. You wouldn't have got into this mess tonight if you'd been happy at home."

"Maybe not, but he's so inattentive. And then there's the drinking. It wasn't like this when we were first married. We were happy, then."

"And you could be again. But none of us will be in the long term unless we deal with Blake."

"Agreed," said Morwenna.

Jenna still didn't know how she was going to achieve that, but at least she was now making progress.

Blake had failed to take possession of her mother. Now she had to ensure he didn't get his filthy mitts on Pencarven.

November 1983

Morwenna went straight up to bed, via the back door, following the shocking scenes in Blake's motorhome. By doing so she avoided having to face David and she also told Jenna that she didn't want to talk about it any further that night because she needed time to think.

Jenna returned to the bar, much to her father's relief, and resumed pulling pints for the locals as if nothing had happened. No one knew where she had been, not even Alfie, who was contentedly enjoying the convivial atmosphere with Ned and the rest of the regulars.

The following morning, Morwenna was in a reconciliatory mood. She was feeling more than a tad guilty about the previous evening's events and was ready to explain what she planned to do over breakfast.

"I know I said that I didn't want Dad to know about what happened last night but I've changed my mind. I'm going to tell him everything," she declared, as they watched Wincey Willis giving out the day's weather forecast on TV-AM.

"Is that wise?" asked Jenna, wondering what effect such revelations might have on her father who needed little excuse to reach for the bottle. Something like this could tip him over the edge into full-blown alcoholism.

"Very," she said. "We can't go on like this. If it hadn't been Blake it would have been somebody else. There are fundamental problems in our marriage, and we can't keep sweeping them under the carpet forever."

"I suppose not," was all Jenna could muster by way of a reply. She was fearful of the outcome, given the consequences of her parents splitting up in the other timeline. But at least Blake was out of the picture this time.

"Last night was a wake-up call," said Morwenna. "So when he comes down for breakfast, we're going to have a proper talk. Therefore, I'd appreciate it if you made yourself scarce. It's not that I don't want you here, and I still feel bad about what went on between us before I went out last night, but let me sort things out with him first, okay? Then we can work on what's best for us as a family, ongoing."

"Fair enough," said Jenna, thinking she might go and see Alfie since she had the morning free. Now that November had arrived, Pencarven was falling back into winter hibernation mode. Other than working in the pub and her council commitments, she had little else to occupy her, in sharp contrast to the hectic summer months.

Her mother's choice to come clean with David led Jenna to a decision of her own: it was high time she put Alfie in the picture about what had been going on. Not the time-travelling part – she still wasn't quite ready to talk about that – but the situation with Blake.

Alfie wasn't doing much of anything that morning, either, just pottering about at home. He had said he was going to try to think of a way to make money in the winter, and was working on an idea for setting up a mail-order business to sell surf wear through small ads in specialist magazines. It was only an idea, and in the fledgling stage, but it had merit.

Ned was sitting on the sofa, watching *Picture Box*, one of many school programmes that TSW showed in the mornings after breakfast television had finished. That meant they couldn't talk at his place. They thought about going to the café but it would have been impossible to speak there also, without Shelly eavesdropping or interrupting, so Jenna suggested they head out for a walk along the coast path where they could speak freely.

Outside, the air was filled with the noise of the construction team who were now busy working on the new sea wall. The incessant drilling had been going on for days, echoing off the cliffs and through the narrow streets, disturbing Pencarven's usual off-season tranquillity. There had been much complaining about the noise and the dust in the pub from the usual suspects who disliked the disruption, but as Jenna kept pointing out, it was all for a good cause.

The new month had brought a bracing chill, with grey clouds drifting over the cliffs, and the wind coming in from the north-west. There was plenty of hawthorn and blackthorn growing on this part of the coast, and their recently shed leaves were blowing around everywhere in the brisk breeze.

The ever-present gulls were circling overhead, issuing their raucous cries over the now-deserted beach, almost as if they were pleading for the tourists to return. They had figured out that there were richer pickings on land than in the sea, and their behaviour had noticeably changed in recent years as a result. This was not helped by tourists littering leftover food or even feeding them.

Jenna and Alfie followed the path up past the caravan park, thankfully not encountering Blake, and continued around the headland. It was about four miles to the next village, although it would have been less 'as the crow flies', or more accurately in this part of the world, 'as the gull flies'. The path was winding and it wasn't wise to stray off it to cut a corner to try to save a few yards, not unless you wanted to risk a sprained ankle on the rocky terrain or, worse still, a tumble over the cliffs.

Up on the heights, Jenna told Alfie everything that had happened since Blake's arrival, hoping he would understand. They walked side by side, and she held his hand as she spoke, though she avoided looking directly at him. If she saw anger or disappointment in his eyes, she might falter. These things had to be got off her chest and she would deal with his reaction when she finished.

"You're not angry, are you?" she asked once she'd unburdened herself, finally meeting his gaze.

"No," he said, though he didn't look particularly pleased. "Not with you, anyway. Though I am a little disappointed that you didn't feel you could confide in me."

"I wanted to," she replied. "But everyone here thought Blake was the best thing since sliced bread. I didn't want to drag you into a battle I wasn't sure we could win because I knew my opinions were unpopular. I realised that much when I tried to warn other women about him. So I decided to keep it to myself and try to handle him my way."

"It doesn't sound like that's been going too well," he said. "Especially after the stunt he pulled last night. I can't believe he suggested what he did. You know, if I could get my hands on him, I'd…"

"You see, that's one of the reasons I didn't say anything," said Jenna, cutting him short. She paused, remembering how laid-back Alfie usually was. "You're not the sort of man who goes looking for a fight, nor would I want you to. Blake's used to people gunning for him, and he's got money, power, and an army of lawyers behind him. You might think by landing a punch on him you'd be defending my honour, but if it lands you in prison, who's the real winner?"

"Well, what are you going to do, then? If he's as powerful as you say, how can any of us stop him?"

"By exposing the truth. My mother was the first to see him for what he is, apart from me. If we can open more people's eyes, we might stand a chance."

"Maybe, but I can't imagine that's going to be easy. You've seen what my dad and the others are like in the pub when he's splashing his money around buying them drinks."

"We can but try," she said. "His planning application's up for review tomorrow, and I'm going to do everything in my power to stop it going through."

Determined she might have been, but disappointment was looming. By getting on the planning committee, she'd hoped to block Blake's plans and was armed with a stack of objections, some moral, and some legal, ranging from the damage to local wildlife to the rerouting of the cliff path. Then there was the ugly modern design, all glass and metal, that didn't fit with the local architecture or landscape at all. She couldn't see how it could possibly pass.

But pass it did, by a convincing margin, with hers the only dissenting vote. Blake did not attend the meeting in Camelford but was waiting outside the offices afterwards, wearing a smug grin as she emerged with a face like thunder.

"I take it the vote didn't go the way you hoped?" he smirked, fuller of himself than ever.

"You know damned well it didn't," she snapped, unsure who she was angrier at: him, or the quislings who'd so easily rolled over to do his bidding.

"You know as well as I do that no sane councillor would ever have approved that application. How much did you have to bung them to get it through?"

"Really, Jenna, I wish you wouldn't use common parlance like 'bung'. This isn't an episode of *Minder*. I prefer to think of it as an investment. Everyone's got what they wanted, so everyone's happy. Except you, it seems."

"You haven't won yet," she said. "I'm convinced building this monstrosity contravenes at least two laws. I'm going to appeal and expose you for the charlatan you are. I've done it before, and I can do it again."

"Please. I know all about Gordon Pentreath and how you brought him down. Do you honestly think I'm remotely on the same level? Pentreath was strictly non-league at best. Me? I'm top of the first division. I've got enough legal people to tie you up in knots for years."

"We'll see," she said defiantly.

"Look, there's no need for all this. Why don't we have a nice drink and see if we can't patch things up? You know your life would be so much easier if you were my friend, not my enemy. And much more fulfilling too. I can do things to you that'll make you squeal louder than the seagulls. I bet your surfer boy can't do that."

"Like my mother said, you're disgusting," she said. "And I'm going to stop you, whatever you might think."

"Yeah, good luck with that," he said, as she turned to go. But he wasn't ready to let her leave just yet. "Why don't you let me give you a lift back to Pencarven?"

"No thanks, I'll get the bus."

"That's not very befitting of a councillor, using public transport. Come with me. I insist."

Just as on the day she first met him, he gripped her arm. But this time, they were in a busy high street with people around, and she could see the bus approaching.

"Get your hand off me, or I swear I'll kill you," she shouted, a little louder than perhaps she should. A few passers-by, startled by her outburst, glanced their way.

He relaxed his grip and watched her dash onto the bus, then turned away, smiling for a couple of autograph hunters. They were both young women, and from the bus window she could see him already working his charm on them.

When she got home, it was teatime. Her family always ate early, around five, before opening the pub for the evening. She was keen to tell Morwenna about the encounter in Camelford, but it seemed her mother and David had something to share first.

She'd been giving them space for a couple of days, aware that they had been having a series of heart-to-hearts, and now they were ready to talk. Morwenna was dishing up pork chops as Jenna walked in, and once she was seated, and spooning a dollop of apple sauce onto her plate, Morwenna began to explain what they'd decided.

"I've told Dad all about what happened the other night, and about how I've been feeling this past year or so. We've discussed it at length, and we're going to give it another go."

"The first thing I am going to do is stop drinking," said David. "I realise it's becoming a problem, and it's time I did something about it. I know it won't be easy, what with running a pub, but I'm going to try."

"And I'm going to help him," said Morwenna. "Then, we're going to have a real shot at making this place a profitable, thriving business. Including doing food. We've got quite a few ideas, and we're going to work together and turn things around."

"That's wonderful," said Jenna. "You know I'll be behind you all the way. I have a few ideas of my own."

"And there's one more change I'm going to make right away," said David. "Possibly tonight. Make sure you're both around this evening because you won't want to miss this."

He wouldn't elaborate, but they soon discovered what he meant when Blake came swaggering into the pub later. It was his first time back since the incident at the motorhome a couple of nights before, but that didn't seem to have deterred him.

It was a quiet evening as most chilly midweek nights were, with David behind the bar and half a dozen locals around, including Willy, Ned and Trevor. Alfie wasn't there yet, which was probably just as well. Despite his promise not to confront Blake, Jenna didn't want to risk anything kicking off between them.

"Double gin and tonic, please, my good man, and make sure it is a proper double. I don't trust you country types not to water it down," said Blake, displaying his customary contempt for his hated 'little people'.

"I'm sorry, I'm afraid we don't have any gin," said David, keeping a deadpan expression.

"Yes, you do. I can see it right there," said Blake. "Are you blind as well as illiterate? It's the bottle marked Gilbey's behind you."

"No gin, no whisky, no vodka, no anything," said David. "Not for you, anyway, because you are now barred."

"You what? You're not serious. If I'm barred, how am I going to buy all my friends here a drink?" he said, gesturing at Willy and the others with a flourish of the arm.

"He's got a point," said Willy, whose glass was almost empty. He was a good month into his new drinking season now, and knocking it back like it was going out of fashion.

"No he hasn't, Willy," said Jenna. "You don't need his money. None of us do. His money's what's going to destroy Pencarven and impoverish us all unless we stop him."

"Oh, trust you to pipe up with your scare stories," said Blake. "She's just annoyed because she lost a council vote today that went in my favour."

"We don't need you and we don't want you," said Jenna. "You're an arrogant sexual predator who buys and uses people, then tosses them aside. Willy, Ned, Trevor, if you carry on accepting drinks from him, you'll be signing away your own futures."

"Don't listen to her. She's the past, I'm the future. If you want to keep living in this village, you're better off sticking with me. This isn't the only pub in Pencarven. James up at The Anchor will be only too happy for my custom. Ditch this place, come with me now, and I'll keep your glasses full all night. You don't need these losers."

"Looks like it's decision time," said Morwenna, joining David behind the bar in a show of solidarity. "Are you going with him?"

The three men looked at one another, weighing up their options. All of them had demonstrated their shallow nature over money numerous times in the past, but this time, old loyalties won the day.

"We're going nowhere," said Ned, to Jenna's relief. He had been critical of her countless times over the past months, but when it came to the community sticking together against an outsider, he was showing that he could be a decent sort after all.

"We don't need you," said Trevor.

"So why don't you just fuck off," added Willy, perhaps the finest line he had ever uttered, particularly since it had initially seemed like he was going to take Blake's side. David and Morwenna weren't keen on swearing in the pub and even had a sign up to say so, but on this occasion, it was entirely justified.

"You're all finished, do you know that?" snapped Blake, making for the door. "Give it a couple of months and I'll own this shithole. Then we'll see who's barred – all of you lot for a start. It's about time this place started attracting a better class of customer."

He slammed the door behind him to a spontaneous round of applause from all present.

Jenna was on cloud nine, witnessing the tide turning against Blake so suddenly, but she knew it was far from over. As local opinion began to shift, he only increased his intimidating campaign against her. Wherever she went, he seemed to appear. Seeking advice from Matt on this continued harassment was of little help. He hadn't seen any evidence of Blake's true nature, and as Jenna discovered to her dismay, stalking hadn't even been defined as a crime in 1983.

Soon after the barring incident in the pub, she discovered she wasn't the only one Blake had been pursuing against their will when the bracelet sent her out late one night. It was closing time when it caught her attention with its ominous red warning, flashing rapidly to suggest an urgent problem. It didn't define the nature of the emergency, only where she needed to go, up to the top of the village, near Blake's new local watering hole.

It was dark up there, with no modern lighting, one of the reasons why the film crew had liked it so much. In one of the dark narrow alleys that criss-crossed the village, Jenna heard hushed sobbing. She followed the sound, as the bracelet guided her into the gloom.

She soon discovered the source. There was just enough light from a nearby bedroom window to identify her friend Janet, in a crumpled heap on the cobbles, her clothes dirty and torn. In the dim glow, she could see bruises beginning to form on one of Janet's arms, where her dress had been ripped away. It was the same spot on her body where Blake had grabbed Jenna, twice before.

"Janet, it's me, Jenna, what's happened?" she asked, stepping forward cautiously.

Far from seeking comfort, Janet recoiled, pulling herself upright with a sharp intake of breath. "Leave me alone," she cried out, as she staggered off down the lane towards home.

No matter what Jenna said, she wouldn't speak to her. When they reached Janet's front door, she hauled her bedraggled frame inside and slammed it firmly behind her, leaving Jenna alone in the silent street.

Jenna lingered in the deserted, almost pitch-dark alley, troubled by this latest outrage, knowing she couldn't let it go. There was no doubt in her mind who was responsible and if Blake had assaulted her friend, she needed to know just how far he had gone. She already knew he had raped Janet in the other timeline – had history repeated itself? If so, was it her fault? Should she have talked to Janet sooner to warn her she was in danger?

The next morning, Jenna tried calling at Janet's house again but got no answer. She remembered that she worked in Camelford, so she was likely there, though how she could face a normal day's work after the trauma of being attacked the night before was beyond Jenna.

She felt guilty for not having spent more time with Janet since returning to 1983. They had been good friends in their schooldays but had drifted apart over the years. Worse, Jenna should have been prepared for this eventuality, due to Janet confiding in her about it in the original timeline. But with everything else that had been going on, it had slipped her mind.

Now, even though the timeline was different, some things remained the same and Blake simply couldn't be allowed to get away with this. How many more victims had there been, and how many more might there be in the future? He needed stopping, here and now.

Later that day, she accosted Janet as she got off the bus but her friend made it clear she still didn't want to talk, hurrying up the hill away from her. For a moment, Jenna considered leaving her alone because surely the last thing she wanted was more unwanted attention, but her desire to get to the truth won out.

Eventually, Janet relented and let Jenna come in for a cup of tea after she pleaded through the letterbox. It was her mother's cottage and was small but tidy, with a two-seater floral sofa taking up most of the living room. She had an old-fashioned kettle, the sort you put on the hob which whistled when it boiled.

They settled on the sofa and Janet began to speak. She explained how Blake had been fixated on 'bedding' her, just as he had with Jenna, and ultimately attacked her when she refused to accede to his demands. To Jenna's immense relief, he hadn't raped her this time; a dog barking and a light coming on had startled him into running off. Even so, his hands had gone where they shouldn't, and he'd threatened that he wasn't finished with her yet.

When Jenna confided her own bad experiences with Blake, Janet seemed to relax a little, realising she was not alone. Then she came out with an unexpected confession. The main reason she'd been one of the few to resist Blake was because she wasn't attracted to men full stop.

"I had no idea," said Jenna.

"It doesn't bother you, does it?"

"Of course not. Why would it?"

"This is Pencarven," replied Janet. "Nobody here knows. It's hardly the most enlightened community in the world, is it? If I came out, I'd be ostracised."

She had a point. Jenna knew how ignorance still ran deep in 1983, and she had heard more than her share of slurs from Ned and others in the pub.

"Maybe, but the world's changing. Trust me," said Jenna. "You'll be free to be who you want to be in the future. You'll even be able to marry a woman if you want to."

"I hope that's true. I only stay here because of my mum. She's on her own now. I know she's got her Women's Institute meetings and her book club, which is where she is right now, but she needs me. I do manage to get away some weekends. I've got a girlfriend in Newquay who is a fair bit older than me, and she's got her own flat. People are more open-minded there. But I haven't told her about any of this. She'd go spare and come up here after Blake."

"I know who you should tell, and that's Matt."

"I can't, Jenna. I threatened to go to him when Blake was harassing me before, and he said he'd never believe me. And if I did, I'd have to make a statement and I don't want to go through all that."

"We ought to try. Matt's more likely to take these allegations seriously if he hears them from both of us."

"You go if you want, but keep me out of it. I don't want my mum finding out about any of this. She's not been the same since Dad died. The upset over something like this could kill her."

No matter how hard Jenna tried, she couldn't persuade her. Even so, she decided to speak to Matt again anyway. She had got nowhere before, but perhaps things might have changed. She and Janet might not be the only two. If anyone else had complained since she had last spoken to him, perhaps a pattern would emerge and even some evidence to build a case.

She marched up to the police house with its reassuring blue lamp outside but she had no more success than before. She told him all about the assault on Janet the other night, but Matt said unless her friend was willing to make a statement, there was nothing he could do. Worse, he scolded Jenna as she left.

"You can't keep coming here with these baseless accusations, Jenna. For some reason, you seem to have it in for Blake, but until you can bring me something concrete, please don't waste any more police time."

The locals in The Fisherman's Arms might have turned against Blake, but by all accounts he had made himself much at home in The Anchor, spreading goodwill with free drinks, splashing the cash and writing out cheques for large rounds. Yet he still sought out Jenna at every opportunity. He was cunning in how he timed it, always catching her alone so no one overheard. Then he would taunt her with threats and dirty remarks about what he wanted to do to her, using the filthiest language imaginable. Even when she told him she knew about his attack on Janet, it didn't faze him. He just asked her where her proof was, and of course, without Janet's support she had none.

As the days and weeks passed, Jenna felt as if everything was building towards a final showdown. The bracelet's red warnings kept flashing whenever Blake was nearby, suggesting she was in constant danger. Then, one day at the end of November, the reckoning she had been expecting finally arrived.

She'd spent the night with Alfie at his cottage, a rare occurrence made possible by Ned going to visit his sister in Penzance for a couple of days. He didn't get on with her and only visited once a year for her birthday. On departure, he explained to Jenna and Alfie that he would be back by the weekend, warning them not to get up to any 'funny business'. Of course, as soon as his van turned the corner and disappeared out of sight, that's exactly what they did.

Jenna awoke early the following morning in Alfie's single bed, and couldn't get back to sleep. It was almost dawn and she felt an urge to get up and go for a walk. She wasn't sure why, and looked to the bracelet for guidance, but it lay dormant. That was odd because she felt like this was a bracelet-inspired impulse.

She left Alfie sleeping, dressed quietly, and headed out into the deserted village, past the harbour and the reams of tape and cones protecting the area where the building of the sea wall was still ongoing.

Soon, she picked up the coast path and made her way up towards the top of the cliffs, as the sky grew steadily brighter from the east. It might have been the final day of November, but the dawn chorus was still lively with the harsh cries of the crows giving the gulls a run for their money. Soon, she was approaching the site of Blake's proposed mansion.

She could see why he had singled out this location as it had a stunning view of the bay and there was a good couple of square acres here of relatively flat land, running right up to the cliff edge. The coast path ran through this patch of scrub, which was dominated by hawthorn and blackthorn twisted by the Atlantic winds.

Their leaves were all gone now, but clusters of hawthorn berries still clung to the bare branches, tiny flashes of red providing food for the birds that flickered in and out of them. The blackthorn too, was sporting plenty of the dark sloe berries that she remembered her grandfather once collecting to make gin.

There were many different types of small birds already darting between the bare twigs and branches looking for breakfast. Jenna wasn't an expert on birds but had heard Trevor, who was a keen ornithologist, talk about there being choughs and finches up here. He even claimed that he had once seen a cirl bunting, though there was no proof that they had ever settled anywhere outside their small habitat in Devon.

The rest of the terrain consisted of hardy grasses and patches of gorse filling the gaps between the bushes, providing a year-round sanctuary for wildlife. It was why part of this area had been designated as a nature reserve many years ago, but that hadn't stood in the way of Blake's application. If she was unable to stop him, all of this would soon be swept away to be replaced by concrete foundations, then the house and manicured gardens that looked good but weren't conducive to the native wildlife. She knew because she had seen it all before.

From the edge of the cliff, she could look down at the harbour and see the bulldozers and cranes from the construction work. What could she do to prevent machines like these from being deployed up here? As she gazed out to sea, wondering what to do as the new day burst into life, she felt a rough pair of hands grab her from behind.

"Now I've got you," said Blake, who had crept up behind her with the stealth of an assassin.

"Get off me," she yelled, trying to wriggle out of his grasp.

"Not this time," he said, as she turned, catching a glimpse of his cruel face. His piercing blue eyes caught hers in a look that she could only describe as pure evil. She could see lust, hate, and anger, all rolled into one, a devilish combination that told her all she needed to know. He was going to do to her what he had tried to do to Janet in the alley.

He pushed her roughly down into the shallow gorse, barely six feet from the cliff edge and fumbled for the button to her jeans. She tried to scream out for help, but as she did, he shocked her by grabbing her by the throat. Was he going to strangle her too?

"Shut up, bitch," he yelled. "Not that anyone's going to hear you from up here, anyway."

She was desperate to resist but he was so strong it was impossible, and to her horror, she realised he'd got her buttons undone and was pulling down her jeans.

"Ever since I got here, you've been a thorn in my side, Jenna. Resisting my advances, trying to blacken my name, and then having the audacity to oppose my planning application. I told you the day we first met that Blake Cadwallader always gets what he wants. And I'm about to get what I want from you, right now."

He was on top of her now, pulling at her knickers, and in despair, she realised he was right. And where would this end? Was he planning only to rape her or was there even worse in store? Was she even going to come out of this alive?

Why hadn't the bracelet warned her about this? It had always protected her before, yet it hadn't given her any indication of what coming up here at the crack of dawn might lead to. If anything, she suspected it had led her here, even without the usual indicators. There was no denying the pull she had felt – the strange, insistent urge that had drawn her to this place.

What was going on? Had this whole thing, right back to when Wendy had first given her the bracelet, been nothing more than a cruel trick, designed to bring her formerly miserable existence to an abrupt and violent end?

Thankfully not.

Just as her fate appeared sealed, Blake was wrenched away from her and knocked sideways as a third figure slammed into him. Stunned, Jenna scrambled up, her breath coming in ragged gasps. It was Alfie. He must have woken up and followed her.

The two men grappled violently, feet skidding on the damp gorse coated in early morning dew, as they wrestled dangerously close to the cliff's edge.

"Oh, look, it's your little boyfriend coming to rescue you," shouted Blake, trying to get a grip on Alfie as they twisted and strained against each other. Blake was stronger, his movements forceful and aggressive, trying to force Alfie back, inch by inch, towards the sheer drop behind them. Jenna watched in rooted terror as Alfie fought against him, his slender frame no match for Blake's brute strength.

Blake shoved him hard. Alfie stumbled but managed to break free, ducking beneath Blake's arm. He might not have been as strong, but he was nimble, scampering out of reach as Blake lunged at him again and missed.

Caught off balance for a fraction of a second, Blake lost his footing, and a small section of the cliff edge gave way beneath him. He grappled desperately for a handhold, but there was nothing there.

The last they saw of him as he fell backwards was those cold blue eyes, staring at them in disbelief.

Then he was gone.

A strangled cry echoed through the morning air, cut short by the sickening crunch of impact.

For a moment that felt like an eternity, neither of them spoke, frozen in shock against the sound of the waves crashing against the rocks below, as the gulls circled and called to each other. What could they see that Jenna and Alfie couldn't?

Slowly, hesitantly, they edged forward, their hearts hammering with the inevitability of what they were about to witness. Then, at last, they summoned the courage to look over the edge.

Sixty feet down sprawled grotesquely across the jagged rocks, lay Blake's shattered body. Blood pooled around his split skull, seeping into the cracks in the stone below.

December 1983

Thirty-six hours later, Jenna was sitting in the police station at Camelford, waiting for the next in what was proving to be an interminable number of repetitive interviews.

She wasn't under arrest, and in theory, was free to go whenever she chose. Helping police with their enquiries was the way she believed it was termed, and there was no doubt that both she and Alfie were under suspicion. That was hardly surprising, given that they had been the only two witnesses to Blake's demise, and the events leading up to it.

Jenna's dislike of Blake was no secret around Pencarven, and as soon as his body hit the rocks, she knew she was potentially in the frame. Those first few minutes after she had seen his lifeless body had been overwhelmed by emotion, as she sobbed with relief, guilt, and fear of the potential consequences all coursing through her veins. Even with the presence of Alfie wrapping his arms around her while reassuring her that everything was going to be alright, it had taken a good quarter of an hour before she could think rationally again.

Things were not alright, not by a long chalk, no matter what soothing words Alfie could muster. Whatever the rights and wrongs, and however big a monster Blake had been, there was one undeniable truth. A man was lying dead below them, one who had not died before. Changing the timeline for the benefit of all was what she'd been led to believe she was signing up for when she had taken the bracelet. Neither Wendy nor Keith had said anything about that involving killing people. It didn't matter whether Blake's death was an accident or not. Simply by being part of the chain of events that had led to his tumble over the cliff, she was at least partially responsible.

As soon as she came to her senses, she told Alfie the full story about her trip back in time. She simply couldn't hold it in any longer. Whether he would believe her or not, she had no idea. For all she knew, she could end up getting carted off to the funny farm, but to her great relief, he accepted her story. How could he not, when she quoted back so many examples of the things she had foreseen over the past year? From the minor flood to the loot in the caves to rescuing the child from the sea, her record of knowing what was going to happen in advance spoke for itself. There were just too many examples for them all to be deemed lucky coincidences.

She even confessed to being the one who had set fire to *The Buccaneer*, thus saving his life in the process. If he was unhappy with her for keeping all this from him for so long, he didn't show it because, in their current predicament, they had more pressing things to worry about.

Blake was no more, and she had been a part of the process that had led to his death. Or perhaps the bracelet had been responsible, but the notable absence of any green or red signals from it beforehand left that as a grey area. It was almost as if the device was wriggling out of taking any blame for what had occurred, but she knew damned well it had planted the idea for her to go up to the cliffs that morning. If the bracelet wanted him dead, why couldn't it just have been honest with her?

Was it because it knew she might have refused to cooperate if she was aware of its true intention? Or was it to protect her from prosecution when later questioned? If she had no prior knowledge of what was about to happen, then she couldn't confess to a premeditated attack if the police tried to pin it on her.

The device on her wrist had wanted him dead, as simple as that, and she had just been the instrument to enable that to happen. Had this been its plan all along, and the sole reason for her coming back to Pencarven? Had all the other things she had done to try to make a better life just been window-dressing leading to this, the main event? If that were the case, she couldn't help feeling a little used.

She tried to look at the upside, if it was possible to establish one for a man's death. She had seen far more of the dark side of Blake in these past couple of months than she had in her original timeline. If he had been allowed to carry on, how many more victims might he have claimed? Yes, in that other timeline, he had in theory settled down by marrying Morwenna, but she knew for a fact he had only done it to get his grip on Pencarven. After the marriage he continued to cheat on her, especially when he was away filming.

No matter, it was over now, and the important thing was to ensure she and Alfie didn't have his death attributed to them. Murder and manslaughter weren't words she wanted thrown in her direction, nor Alfie's. Up on the clifftop, they debated what to do, a discussion on which the bracelet was now more than happy to give its opinion, flashing red and green at her various suggestions. The overwhelming verdict was that they needed to come clean and be totally honest about what had occurred.

They went back into the village, and up to the police house where Matt had just finished his breakfast. When they related the tale of what had gone on, he explained that this was way above his pay grade and that he would need to call in his superiors – something she had fully expected. First, he alerted the Coastguard and then the regional office in Bodmin, who sent down a detective inspector, several other officers, and a forensics team.

Jenna was concerned that they would be arrested on the spot, but that wasn't the case. However, Matt strongly suggested that they stay with him while they waited for the Bodmin team to arrive. He wouldn't be drawn on his opinions as to the role they had played in events, but she sensed that he believed her story, despite ticking her off the last time she had tried to seek his help over Blake. Whether his superiors would come to that same conclusion remained to be seen.

By the time the pub opened that lunchtime, the police were swarming all over the clifftop, and rumours were rife. She spent most of the day being interviewed by them, and although she was allowed home in the evening, the grilling she had received from DI Kelly, the officer heading the investigation, had left her in no doubt that she and Alfie were in trouble.

With Ned still away, she had planned to stay with Alfie again that night, but in the end, went home. They knew they would both be wanted for questioning again the next day and needed a decent night's sleep, if that were possible, given all they had been through. If they stayed together they would only sit up talking all night. Besides, there were other people she needed to speak with, beginning with her parents.

She didn't dare go into the bar, where she knew the watchful eyes of the regulars would be upon her, but managed to speak to Morwenna in the kitchen. She confirmed what she had suspected; that the news of Blake's death was already common knowledge and that the locals were speculating about the cause and whether it might be murder. Willy, Trevor, and the others were in their element, and although Jenna's name hadn't been mentioned in front of Morwenna, it was clear who they were alluding to when they were discussing suspects.

It was inevitable that the press would soon get wind of it. Jenna wouldn't have put it past the likes of any of the locals in the bar to go ringing the papers, seeing if they could cash in, so she decided it was time for a pre-emptive strike and called Keith on his home number in London. He hadn't heard a thing about it and promised to drive down overnight to help. He was grateful for the scoop on the story but that wasn't the only reason he was coming. With the bond that united them, from their mutual ownership of the bracelet across the years, he felt duty-bound to support her.

Despite Keith's early start she didn't get to see him that morning, because her day began earlier than expected when the police came knocking before breakfast. While they emphasised she wasn't under arrest, it was made clear that if she didn't come along, she would be, so she asked Morwenna to look out for Keith when he arrived and let him know where she was.

DI Kelly, the man from Bodmin, was a dour man in his mid-forties, with a face set into a permanent expression of disapproval, as if he regarded every potential miscreant he came across as guilty until proved innocent. His dark hair was greying at the temples, his suit looked in need of a dry clean, and Jenna noticed the waft of stale coffee and cigarettes around him the minute he entered the room at Camelford police station. As soon as he sat down, he pulled out the instantly recognisable gold livery of a packet of Benson & Hedges, took out a cigarette, and lit it, without either asking permission or offering her one, not that she would have accepted if he had.

He exhaled slowly, watching Jenna through the drifting smoke, saying nothing for a moment before nodding at a uniformed constable, who placed a notepad on the table and readied his pen. At that point, Kelly stated the date and time for the record, his tone flat and weary like a man who had done this too many times before. She was getting used to this routine by now, having been through it a couple of times already on the previous day. She had been half-expecting a tape recorder the first time, but perhaps they didn't do that yet in 1983.

She had been offered a solicitor but, at the bracelet's suggestion, had declined. If it didn't think she needed one, then presumably she didn't. That encouraged her that any accusations that were going to be levelled were not going to stick.

The first part of the interview was spent going over familiar ground, with the constable diligently recording each of Jenna's answers in longhand. Every so often, he

254

paused to read back a statement for confirmation, before continuing. Then Kelly started to get stuck in.

"Let's cut to the chase, Councillor Rae. I know all about the history between you and the deceased and have testimonies from local people that prove it."

"What people?" asked Jenna, wondering who in Pencarven might have dropped her in it. Might it have been Willy? She knew he was still annoyed at her for not letting him keep any of the money they had found in the caves.

"Well, one in particular from a woman right here in Camelford, who claims she heard you screaming at the deceased in the street a few weeks ago that you were going to kill him."

"And did she also tell you that he had hold of my arm at the time and was trying to drag me off somewhere? Because that is his style. He bruised my wrist doing it, and not for the first time."

Kelly's reaction was to ask her to roll up her sleeves before replying, "I don't see any bruises."

"It was three or four weeks ago. They've healed. But what about these?"

She pulled down the neckline of her thick roll-neck jumper to reveal the fresh marks where Blake had grabbed her around the neck.

"He was trying to rape me when he did that. And he may well have strangled me afterwards to shut me up if Alfie had not arrived in the nick of time."

"Ah yes, the gallant boyfriend, racing to your defence. Now, that does interest me. Do you know what

I think happened? I think he came along, saw what was happening, and in a fit of rage, grabbed Mr Cadwallader and threw him over the cliff."

"That is rubbish," replied Jenna. "I already told you what happened, and I'm sure Alfie has too."

"Oh, I'm sure you got your stories straight before we called you in. Tell you what, let me come at it from another angle. What if the deceased was not attacking you at all? What if you and he were in fact lovers, and your boyfriend just happened to catch you at it? Would that not be grounds enough for him to commit murder? The rich film star, coming down to your humble Cornish village and stealing his girlfriend? I imagine that could make him very mad indeed – perhaps mad enough to kill."

The interview dragged on, with Kelly probing continually, making it clear the direction he was taking. Jenna soon rumbled that he wasn't after her at all. He was gunning for Alfie.

Eventually they let her go, and outside in the foyer she found Keith waiting for her, much to her relief. Keen to see the back of the police station, they hurried away, grabbed a coffee at a nearby café, and compared notes. She wasn't surprised to hear that Keith had found out they had taken Alfie in that morning too, and he was still there.

"They can't hold him indefinitely," said Keith. "If they had any real evidence, they'd have charged him by now."

"They see him as the main suspect," said Jenna. "And when I told Kelly what happened, he kept twisting it around, trying to make it fit his warped version of events."

"Yeah, they tend to do that. They are much more likely to believe the pair of you if we can get some more people to come forward to corroborate your story of what Blake was really like. That way, they can establish a pattern of behaviour. You mentioned this girl Janet."

"Yes, but he so terrorised her, she was too traumatised to speak to the police."

"That was Blake's modus operandi, alright. There are rumours about him in Fleet Street, and it has been talked about more than once over a few pints. But he has always been adept at shutting people up with threats or bribes, including my editor at the *News of the World*."

"But he can't do it anymore," said Jenna.

"No he can't and while I'm down here, I have got Jimmy up in London on the case, but it is going to take some time to pull together all the information we need. If we can get your friend Janet down here to tell her story today, that could make a difference and help get you two off the hook."

"The bracelet agrees with you," said Jenna, noting the green pulse on her wrist. "Though I still cannot quite believe it has put me through all this."

"Me neither," said Keith. "In my time as custodian, it was all about saving lives, not taking them. But then I never came up against anyone like Blake."

"I guess we had better go and talk to Janet, then," said Jenna, prompting them to finish their coffee and head back to Pencarven.

It was not easy, but by emphasising that Alfie's liberty was on the line, Janet agreed at last to go and talk to Matt, and the wheels were set in motion from there.

A post-mortem confirmed Blake had died from the fall, with no evidence to suggest he had been pushed or injured in any other way beforehand. With no further leads or evidence, the police were left with no choice but to release Alfie later that same day. They simply didn't have enough to build a case.

For the following week, Blake's death was all over the papers. At first the stories focused on the nature of his demise, but as Jimmy, Keith and the reporters at the other papers uncovered more, the stories shifted towards the dark side of his personality.

The inquest, held on the 22nd of December in Bodmin, concluded that Blake's death was accidental, to a huge sigh of relief all around.

By this time, the police had already abandoned any attempt to pursue either Jenna or Alfie. The coroner's ruling was simply a formality, one final procedural step to close the matter.

The biggest losers were the film company, who could not possibly put the film out now, given what had come out about Blake, and the entire project ended up being abandoned. Jenna didn't have a great deal of sympathy since she hadn't cared for Brad and Harvey when they had come to see her earlier in the year. But she had got what she wanted out of them and was delighted, less than a week before Christmas, when the new sea defences that the film company's donation had enabled were finally completed.

Her work here was almost done. All she could do now was hope that the new sea wall did its job. But then, a couple of days before Christmas, she had something else to think about.

She had been to see the family doctor in the village a few days earlier because she had been feeling off-colour. It hadn't escaped her notice that she had missed her period, which should have come around the time of Blake's death. At the time, she had put it down to stress, with so many things on her mind, so when the call came through from the surgery informing her she was pregnant, it came as something of a shock.

Jenna had never had children in the other timeline after her aborted sole pregnancy, and in any other circumstances, she would have been overjoyed. But this was a highly unusual situation. In just over a week, she would be going back to the future, to a time when that baby would be in its late thirties. Was she to miss out on all the joy of seeing the child grow up?

She phoned Keith in search of advice. After all, he had supposedly gone back to the future at the end of 1980 but the version she knew was still here. He had talked about this before, and she wanted further clarification. He repeated what he had told her before, namely, that he had become confused for a day or two at the end of the year, and now remembered nothing of the life he had experienced in the former timeline.

All he knew was that there had certainly been one and that he had been brought back to 1980 for a second chance. But the part of him that had come from the future had seemingly gone back. Since then, he had simply continued living a normal life albeit one that he considered was much changed from the one he had lived before – hopefully, in a good way.

That didn't fully explain things, but at least it suggested some version of her would still be here to raise the child. She was willing to accept that, and at sunset on Christmas Eve, she took Alfie for a stroll along the beach and found a quiet moment to tell him that he was to become a dad.

He was thrilled and proposed on the spot, even producing a ring there and then to her great surprise. At first, she wasn't sure. Marrying someone just because you were pregnant wasn't always the smartest move, but as he explained, he had been planning to ask her on Christmas Day anyway. Her little announcement had just brought matters forward by twenty-four hours.

They decided to keep the pregnancy to themselves for the moment but were so excited at the prospect of marrying that they couldn't wait to let on about the engagement. The quickest and easiest way to do that was in the pub that very evening, in front of all their friends and family. Even Jenna's brother Jacob, who was home for a Christmas visit, was there to witness their announcement.

It was a perfect moment, and the reaction was overwhelmingly positive, including from Ned, who raised his glass with all the others, declaring that he was happy to have her as a daughter-in-law. It seemed that despite his initial lukewarm attitude to their relationship, she had won him over during the year. Or perhaps he just liked the idea of having in-laws who owned a pub.

To celebrate this union of the families, Morwenna spontaneously invited Ned and Alfie to Christmas dinner, an offering eagerly accepted. As she helped prepare on Christmas morning by peeling extra spuds, Jenna couldn't help thinking back to the original, miserable version of this day when there had been no Alfie, Morwenna had run off with Blake, the pub was destroyed by the flood, and her father had taken his own life. Truly she had turned things around, and today the final piece of the jigsaw would fall into place when the pub would hopefully be protected from the sea.

The storm was rolling in, and the tide was getting up, just as she remembered. At least the shipping and weather forecasts had correctly predicted it, and the residents were able to take precautions, which largely meant getting the sandbags out. Jenna had a feeling they were still going to need them, even with the new wall in place.

It was blowing a gale out front, and with high tide due at 11:46, Jenna was becoming severely worried by eleven when the waves were crashing higher up the beach than she had ever seen them. They had already reached Alfie's shack, which was normally well above the waterline. There was no equipment in there at this time of year, and hopefully it would survive, but of more concern was the harbour. Even here, where it was partially sheltered, the waves were several feet high, crashing into the new sea wall with incredible force, sending plumes of spray high into the air and huge swathes of water over the top of the wall into the road in front of the most vulnerable properties.

Ned and the others had been warned to secure their boats strongly, but even so, it was a nervous hour or two as they watched them being tossed about like toys under the onslaught.

The funding they had for the sea wall had been substantial, but not limitless, and they had commissioned the best design they could with the money available. Would it be enough? If the water continued to slop over the wall as it was already, they could be in trouble.

The real danger was if the height of the swell breached the top of the wall. If it started flowing freely over, as opposed to just splashing when the waves struck it, then it would all have been for nothing. Jenna had not been pleased to discover, a few days previously, that despite all her warnings, David still hadn't renewed the pub's insurance. After this storm, when he would see how close they had come to disaster, surely he would finally see sense.

Despite the wind and rain many of the villagers were outside, fascinated by the display, though Morwenna missed it, busy as she was cooking dinner for six people. With the water from the spray lapping at the sandbags in front of the door, Jenna suggested to David that he delay the planned noon opening by an hour until the danger had passed.

It was a close call, a matter of a couple of inches between safety and disaster, but at last, the water began to retreat. As it did, praise once again came Jenna's way, as the residents contemplated what would have happened if the new wall had not been in place. The lower part of the village would have been inundated. It had been money well spent, as the locals discussed over a couple of festive pints when David opened the pub just before one o'clock.

Thankfully, despite a small amount of water getting in which they swiftly mopped up, and the high winds that had accompanied the storm, there had been no disruption to the electricity supply. This meant the whole family was able to sit down and enjoy a belated festive lunch after David had managed to get the last of the regulars out of the pub.

All of them, that was, apart from Alfie and Ned, the latter getting in an extra pint just before closing to bring out the back to the kitchen. He obviously intended to make the most of his new in-law status.

Watching the happy faces around the table, Jenna could only reflect on what had turned out to be a job well done. Three of those present at the meal hadn't even been alive by the end of the old 1983, and as for the rest of them, they had been forever tainted by the events of that devastating year.

All that had been erased now, confined to a past that existed only in her mind. She had made life better for them all and even had high hopes that her parents might have a future together. David seemed serious about his vow to stop drinking and Morwenna, after her brush with Blake, had realised just how close she had come to losing her family.

But what of Pencarven's fate? What was going to happen to the village? Had stopping Blake in his tracks prevented the changes that would blight the future, or could she have done more?

The part of her that would be left here was going to have a baby, but that didn't mean she had to give up her council duties. Other wealthy folk would come, not just here, but to Cornwall as a whole. She knew because she had already seen it. What could the part of her she was leaving behind do over the next forty years to preserve her county's culture?

January 2023

Alfie and Jenna had decided not to stay in the pub to see in the New Year, slipping away an hour or so beforehand to steal a few final, precious moments together. They weren't entirely sure what to expect at midnight – all they knew was that it would be a disorientating experience, and she didn't want to be standing behind the bar with a drink in her hand when it happened.

Keith had explained this process to her but what he didn't know was what was going to happen to the part of her that would return to the future – because, from his perspective, that hadn't happened yet. There was no way of knowing where she would turn up, all she knew was when. When she discussed it with Alfie, they had agreed that when that moment arrived in the future, they would prepare for it. She could only hope that they would still be together – and both still be alive.

As the clock ticked down the final few seconds, she kissed Alfie for the last time, squeezed his hand, and then she was gone, transported across the decades to the exact moment she had left, twelve months before.

And then she was back, instantly reassured as she found herself looking straight into the face of the man she had married, rugged and weather-beaten from his years of surfing, but still handsome. They were sitting at the table in the kitchen of the pub – a kitchen that was much changed, redecorated and modernised, but undoubtedly the same room. From the bar, she could hear a raucous crowd shouting out, "Happy New Year!"

"Okay?" asked Alfie curiously, searching her face for signs of recognition.

"Umm… I think so," she said.

"Do you remember anything?"

She thought hard, but there was nothing – not since she left at the end of 1983. Were the last forty years lost to her forever?

"Nothing," she admitted.

"That's what we expected," he said. "That's why we came to sit in here rather than seeing the New Year in with the others in the bar. But don't worry, it's temporary."

"How do you know?"

"Because we had a visitor a few days ago – your old journalist friend, Keith Diamond. He explained it all. It seems that after you come back to the present, your two selves need a little time to merge back together."

"My two selves?"

"The one that's just arrived from forty years ago, and the one that's lived and breathed those four decades right here."

"Technically, it's thirty-nine years," she pointed out somewhat pedantically, without even knowing why. "So how long does all this take?"

"A couple of days, that's all. Right now, I guess you're going to need me to fill you in with all the details. Like the kids, for a start. I'm guessing you don't remember them."

"I don't even know how many we have."

"We have four – they're all grown up, all in their thirties, all married, and all out there in the bar celebrating. Oh, and then there are the grandchildren too."

"Oh my, this is a lot to take in. I feel proper old now. I didn't have kids in the other timeline, and never even countenanced the idea of grandchildren."

"We've built a whole new family dynasty," he replied. "You'll remember it all in time, but I guess I'd better give you the basic details now. Then, if you feel up to it, we can go back out to the bar."

"Do the others know about any of this? The children, I mean."

"No," he replied. "So you're just going to have to play along until your memory comes back. But hopefully, this will help."

He handed her a family photograph, showing the two of them with the four children, so he could talk her through who was who. It seemed bizarre, having to be introduced to her offspring this way, and she could only hope this amnesia would indeed prove temporary.

There was Ella, their eldest, born in the summer of 1984 after Jenna got pregnant on her trip to the past. She was now a teacher at the local school, which Alfie assured her was still thriving. Next was Ed, who had come along a couple of years later. He had taken over the surf shack, which was still going strong after Alfie and Jenna took over the running of the pub.

Then there was Arthur, keeping up the family's nautical heritage by running fishing trips from the harbour – something he had started alongside Ned, who had now sadly passed on. And finally, Olivia, who had just turned thirty, now ran the café that had once belonged to Shelly.

She was delighted to discover that David and Morwenna were still alive, and still together – having moved into one of the old fishermen's cottages when they had retired from the pub. Once Alfie told her this, and that they were out in the bar with the other regulars celebrating, she could wait no longer. What did it matter if she couldn't remember anything? It was New Year, and if she made a few mistakes, no one would recall them the next day after all the celebratory drinks.

All of them that was except David, who she later discovered had stayed true to his word and had not touched a drop of booze since 1983.

Although initially she was shocked by the elderly appearance of her parents, her father being over ninety by now, this was overcome by the sheer joy of finding them still alive. Meeting the children was strange, and she even made the mistake of calling Arthur by Ed's name, but that wasn't that big a deal. Parents and grandparents made that mistake all the time.

By the morning, her memories had still not returned, and she was most curious to see what had become of Pencarven. Dawn came late to the West Country at this time of year, and it was gone eight o'clock before it began to get light. Leaving Alfie sleeping, Jenna crept downstairs, wrapped up warm, and after a single cup of coffee, headed out for a walk around.

She was reminded of the day she had first received the bracelet, when she had walked down from her caravan for the last time, bemoaning the changes that had transformed the village almost beyond recognition. How much of that had she been able to undo? Not all of it, no doubt. Life had to move on, but it was her fervent hope that progress had been able to work in harmony with tradition to preserve what she held so dear.

Jenna stepped out of The Fisherman's Arms, pausing for a moment just beyond the threshold to take in the exterior view. She had already been encouraged by the interior of the bar, little changed since 1983, with none of the gaudy furnishings that had been plastered all over the walls when it had been turned into The Gilded Mermaid. Now, the sign above the door still bore its rightful name, the one it had always had, and the outside looked exactly as she hoped, unchanged by the passage of time.

She wandered to the end of the harbour, to the spot where she had first met Wendy. There, on that first day, she had seen graffiti on the wall, written as an act of defiance against the incomers to the village but the faded scrawling was no longer there. The harbour was much changed too. Gone were the sleek yachts of before, replaced now with the tourist boats from the same places where Jack and Ned had begun offering trips. There were even one or two fishing boats in the water, suggesting that Pencarven still retained a small element of the fishing industry, borne out by the nets and crates still stacked against the wall at the far end.

After looking around the harbour, she strolled back along the still-solid wall that she had been responsible for building, past the pub, and further uphill into the village, past the rows of old fishermen's cottages. Some of these had been turned into holiday lets. She knew this from the tell-tale key safes outside them and the stickers in the windows advertising local letting agencies.

That was an inevitable change and one that she was prepared to accept because it was the price of tourism, which they needed to survive, and it wasn't all the dwellings by any means. At least half the properties still looked lived in, and she was even greeted by name by a couple of locals as she strolled by, one of whom knocked on the front window and waved. Back in the old timeline, this cobbled lane she was walking up used to be almost deserted for most of the winter.

Further up, she stopped in front of St Piran's Church. All sign of the Michelin-starred restaurant was gone, including the grand signage that had promised 'an immersive dining experience'. The board outside the church advertised services as still taking place once a month on a Sunday, on a rota with three other villages. That was understandable because congregations were not what they had once been. Jenna was not a practising Christian herself, but she was glad to see the church still being used for its intended purpose.

The nearby church hall, where she had once attended that demoralising parish council meeting, had also been restored to its original function, having been converted into a luxury private dwelling in the other timeline. It too had a board outside, and she was pleased to see lists of regular activities, meetings, and events – including a Christmas fair that had taken place a few weeks before.

Up in the highest part of the town, Jenna could see there had been some new building. It wasn't of the type that Blake and his friends had created, but more practical housing. There was a new estate of some fifty or so homes, which, as far as Jenna could see, looked to be largely owner-occupied. There were plenty of cars parked outside – for the most part, family cars roughly five to fifteen years old. These were not the flash vehicles of wealthy second-homeowners, and the fact that they were all here in the middle of winter gave her further encouragement that the village was still home to many local people.

She walked back down to the seafront, past some of the larger, older buildings, many of which she could see were still operating as B&Bs. But what about the front itself? What would that be like?

The amusement arcade had returned, with the pretentious art gallery that had replaced it consigned to a reality that was no more. She had no idea who ran it. Trevor had been middle-aged by 1983, so he was likely long gone. As for the swanky tapas bar, it was now restored to a chip shop, though it looked as if it had gone upmarket a bit since she had last seen it. There was a full menu outside, not just average chippy fare, and she could see that the whole of the upstairs had been converted into a dine-in restaurant, with large glass windows offering stunning views across the bay.

Next, she reached Shelly's Café, which had been taken over by her daughter, though interestingly she noted it retained its old name. The overpriced coffee house that had replaced it had also been cast into the oblivion of the alternate timeline, and it had returned to its traditional style. Through the window, she could see that even the red-checked tablecloths had returned, and also the large blackboard behind the counter, which didn't offer pretentious lattes for extortionate sums, but instead a simple menu featuring cream teas and pasties at prices ordinary people could afford.

Passing the beach she saw that Alfie's shack, now run by their son, had expanded considerably from the simple structure it had once been. She was also delighted to see a row of traditional beach huts had sprung up, similar to those she had seen at other seaside places. Whose idea had that been? she wondered. Had it been hers? Among the many things Alfie had told her was that not only had she stayed on the district council for the entirety of the time since she had first been elected, but she was also now the local mayor.

Later she was to find out that many of the things she had seen today had been down to policies that she had implemented to curb second-home ownership and preserve local traditions – policies that had been adopted by many other places across Cornwall. It seemed that her influence might have been beneficial to the whole county.

She took the path back up to the caravan park, which was not only still there but also a thriving concern, having expanded considerably over time. With the facilities now on offer, it could rival any Haven or Parkdean site, but under local ownership, it had retained its individual character. It was now in the hands of Morgan's son, who had been only a small child back in 1983.

Wandering back down towards the village, she paused at the same spot where she had observed the girl, Mary, drifting out to sea on the day she had carried out her dramatic rescue. The view on this clear and cold day was as stunning as ever, framed by the rocks at either end of the bay in the timeless landscape. The ever-present gulls were circling overhead, oblivious to the changes she had brought about. She thought about the wider world beyond Cornwall, both at home and abroad. Was that as it had always been?

She didn't know and didn't particularly care. It was something she could find out later. All that mattered right now was that the village she loved was still here – Pencarven, as it was meant to be. The people who belonged here had stayed, the gentrification that had stripped away its soul was no more, and she could breathe easy, knowing that both her world and that of the generations still to come were once again secure.

She turned her gaze back towards the harbour, where The Fisherman's Arms stood proudly at the heart of it all, knowing that Alfie would be waiting for her. Then she continued her descent, a pang of hunger gnawing at her after her long walk. It was time for breakfast.

THE END…but look out for the next story, 1984: A Year in the Life of Nobby Clarke – released September 2025.

Also by Jason Ayres

A Year in the Life

Travel back in time and relive the 1980s in this stunning collection of humorous and nostalgic tales.

Each book in this anthology series follows a different character in a different setting, and all of them can be enjoyed standalone.

The Time Bubble Collection

The Time Bubble is a complete fifteen book series, following a rich cast of characters from youth to old age, their lives intertwining across decades, alternate realities, and the very fabric of time.

The Ronnie and Bernard Adventures

The Ronnie and Bernard Adventures are a pair of humorous novels with mild science fiction and horror elements set in the 1970s. The stories follow the fortunes of two actors from very different backgrounds.

Together they tackle mysteries, travel in time, and negotiate the rocky path of life as jobbing actors, from daytime soaps to panto.

Anyone who remembers the 1970s will love these nostalgic stories looking back at a time when life was simpler, and the world didn't take itself too seriously. Packed with period detail, humour, and references to the era, they are the perfect antidote to modern living.

1) The Crooked Line
2) The Haunted Theatre

Follow the Author

To ensure you never miss a release, or to be informed of special deals on Amazon, sign up to follow me on my author page which can be found here:

https://www.amazon.co.uk/stores/Jason-Ayres/author/B00CQO4XJC

For exclusive content from me, regular newsletters and occasional freebies and offers, sign up to my mailing list here:

https://www.jasonayres.co.uk/contact/ or email me directly: jason.ayres@btinternet.com

And of course, there is Facebook, X, and YouTube!

https://www.facebook.com/TheTimeBubble/

https://twitter.com/TheTimeBubble/

https://www.youtube.com/channel/UCg13jmfTUTFCqWWZrPmXqJQ

Finally, if you loved this book and have the time to leave a star rating or review on Amazon, it is always hugely appreciated!

Printed in Great Britain
by Amazon